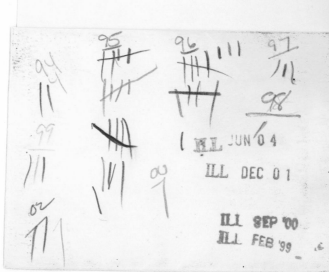

The Eye of God

THE EYE OF GOD

C. L. Grace

St. Martin's Press New York

Library of Congress Cataloging-in-Publication Data

Grace, C. L.
    The eye of God / C.L. Grace.
      p. cm.
    ISBN 0-312-10978-4
    1. Great Britian—History—Edward IV, 1461–1483—Fiction.
2. Women physicians—England—Canterbury—Fiction. 3. Canterbury (England)—Fiction. I. Title.
PR6054.O37E9   1994
823'.914—dc20   94-797
                                                 CIP

First Edition: July 1994

10 9 8 7 6 5 4 3 2 1

To George Witte, Senior Editor at St. Martin's Press, with grateful thanks and appreciation for all your help over the years.

Historical Information

In 1471, the bloody civil war for the crown of England between the Houses of York and Lancaster was brought to a brutal close by the Yorkist victories at Barnet in April 1471 and Tewkesbury, May 1471. The war had originated in the ineffective rule of the Lancastrian king, Henry VI. A pious, well-meaning man, Henry would have cheerfully given up the crown to his Yorkist cousins, but his interests were protected by his powerful and ambitious wife, Margaret of Anjou. For a time the struggle was intense, with casualties on both sides. The leaders of the Yorkist house, Richard, Duke of York, Lord Lieutenant of Ireland, together with his eldest son Edmund, were trapped at Wakefield and cruelly killed. The Yorkist challenge was now taken up by York's three younger sons: Edward; Richard, Duke of Gloucester; and George, Duke of Clarence. They were ably assisted by Richard Neville, Earl of Warwick. Edward proved himself to be an able general but he alienated Warwick and his brother George by marrying a beautiful widow, Elizabeth Woodville. Both Warwick and Clarence went over to the House of Lancaster, though Clarence later returned to his family allegiances. The Yorkist victories of 1471 resulted in Warwick's death, Margaret of Anjou's imprisonment, and Henry VI's murder in the Tower of London. It was an age which more than suited the couplet from Chaucer's "Pardoner's Tale":

"A secret thief, called Death, came stalking by Who hereabouts makes all the people die."

The Eye of God

Prologue

Easter Sunday, the Fourteenth of April, 1471

*R*ichard Neville, Earl of Warwick, strode out of his tent and peered through the fog-bound darkness. From all over the camp he could hear the sound of his men arming for battle. Warwick saw the thick fog rolling up from Deadman's Bottom near Wrotham Wood, blanketing the field of Barnet and making the small culverins he had brought no use at all. The fog made his armour clammy to the touch whilst, outside his pavilion, the Ragged Staff banners hung limply against their poles. A sign of things to come? Warwick touched the jewelled pendant hanging round his neck, stroking the sparkling sapphire. He looked down at it and muttered a prayer. Men called the jewel the Eye of God, but was God's eye on him today? In the distance, Edward of York with his bloodthirsty brothers Richard of Gloucester and George of Clarence were advancing up from Barnet to bring him to blows and utterly destroy him.

Warwick gulped and tried to steel himself against a fit of fear. If he won, the road to London would be open. He would re-instate the saintly Henry VI or, if the Yorkists had already killed him, perhaps put another on the throne? A trumpet sounded. Warwick, gripping his helm with its great black-and-yellow plume, strode into the darkness. Knights and squires of his household gathered round him. A page brought his horse whilst messengers from his captains awaited orders. Warwick signalled with a gauntleted hand and his armed retinue moved farther into the darkness. Away from the camp he mounted and inspected his troops already in battle formation: lines of armed men stretching away into the foggy darkness. Warwick's army was organised into three great phalanxes: his younger brother John Neville, the Marquis of Montagu, in the centre; the Duke of Exeter on the left; and the Earl of Oxford on the right.

A trumpet sounded, followed by shouts and jeers of derision as a group of horsemen broke from the darkness, galloping towards them. Warwick glimpsed the wooden cross the riders carried and the white sheet draped around it. He looked towards his men busily stringing arrows to their bows.

'At peace!' he roared. 'They are envoys and unarmed!'

He, Montagu, and Exeter rode towards the group of Yorkist horsemen clustered under their sign of peace. Warwick let his horse amble forward. How many were there? he wondered. Four, five? Or was it some trick? Perhaps, behind them, some skilful archers already had arrows notched to bow. Warwick reined in his great destrier and stood high in the stirrups.

'You are envoys?' he called.

'We come in peace,' the leader of the small group shouted back. 'We bear no arms but messages from His Grace the King.'

'I did not know you had King Henry with you!' Warwick taunted, his eyes searching the darkness behind the group of men.

'We come from the Lord's anointed, King Edward the Fourth, by God's grace, King of England, Ireland, Scotland and France!'

Warwick caught the faint Irish accent of the speaker and smiled to himself. He knew this man: Colum Murtagh, whom Edward of York's father had saved from a hanging. Now a marshal of the Yorkist household as well as Edward's principal scout and messenger, Murtagh was no assassin. Warwick dug in his spurs and his great war horse ambled forward, the Lancastrian generals behind him. He stopped within hand's reach of Murtagh, studying the Irishman's dark face, his raven-black hair damp under its chain-mail coif and brown protective hood.

'You are well, Irishman?'

'Aye, my lord.'

'And your message?'

'Honourable terms from His Grace, profitable to you, my lord earl, if you accept them.'

Warwick heard the angry murmurs of his companions. They understood the message. In former times, in a more golden age, Warwick and Edward of York had been closer than David and Jonathan, sworn brothers bound by amity and solemn oaths. Now all that was shattered but, even now, York still hoped he could win Warwick over.

'And my companions?' Warwick spoke up. 'These men who have been with me in my great cause? What does the King offer them?'

'He offers them nothing, my lord.'

Warwick forced a smile and nodded. He moved and the Irishman caught the brilliant glint of the sapphire on the golden pendant. Warwick caught his glance and fingered the pendant carefully.

'Gold and jewels, Irishman,' he murmured. 'Gold and jewels, I'd give them all for an honourable peace.'

'Then throw yourself on the King's mercy, my lord.'

Warwick gathered the reins of his horse into his hands and shook his head. 'I refuse!'

'Then, my lord,' the Irishman continued, raising his voice for all to hear, 'the King calls you traitors, rebels, and promises, if you're caught in the field, bloody death!'

'Is that all, Irishman?'

Murtagh turned his horse away. 'What more did you expect?'

Warwick urged his horse forward and the Irishman turned in alarm, his hand going to where his sword hilt should have been.

'Peace, peace, herald!' Warwick whispered. 'I bear you no ill will, Murtagh. You have your task and you performed it well.' He seized the Irishman's hand and pressed a gold piece into it. 'Take that!' he urged. 'And, if the battle goes against York, show it to one of my captains. Your life will be spared.'

The Irishman studied the gold coin carefully.

'If it goes badly for you,' he replied, 'as it will, my lord, I'll spend it on masses for the repose of your soul.'

Murtagh turned his horse and led the small Yorkist party back down the road towards Barnet.

Warwick watched them go. He turned and smiled cheerily at his generals. He hoped his genial reassurance would cure their sombre thoughts and anxious faces.

'They will come on fast,' he declared. 'My lords, it's best if you take your positions.'

He took off his gauntlets and shook the hands of his generals, watching each ride off until only he and his brother John remained.

'You must fight on foot,' his brother declared abruptly. 'The men are uneasy, they talk of treason and treachery. They say . . .' His words faltered.

'I know what they say,' Warwick continued evenly. 'How the great lords of the land will remain on their horses so, if a battle goes against them, they'll ride like the wind to the nearest port, leaving the peasants to their fate.'

Warwick heaved his armoured bulk out of the saddle, drew his great sword from the scabbard lashed to the saddle-horn. He threw the reins of his destrier at his brother.

'Give the order, John! All of us must fight on foot. Take mine and the other horses back to the lines!'

John rode off, Warwick's destrier galloping behind, its sharpened hooves stirring up a splatter of mud. Once more Warwick walked along the three great armoured phalanxes, then took up his command, surrounded by household knights, just behind Montagu's central division. He peered over their heads; the wall of fog still hung, shifting but thick. Warwick ordered silence; resting his hands on the great hilt of his sword he strained his ears, listening for any sound from the darkness beyond. He heard nothing, so he closed his eyes and muttered a prayer. A page ran up, telling him it was only eight o'clock in the morning, when suddenly Warwick heard, vague and muffled, the enemy marching towards him. Warwick ordered his war banners to be unfurled, but they hung limp and damp. He nodded at his trumpeters, lifted his hand and shouted.

'For God, King Henry and Saint George!'

The trumpets brayed brazenly into the darkness and the three battle phalanxes, archers and gunners, fired into the wall of fog. The Yorkist trumpets shrilled fiercely back; there were shouts and Warwick's heart lurched as, out of the fog, charged rank after rank of mailed men.

'Advance!' Warwick shouted.

Moresby, the captain of his guard, repeated the orders: the standard-bearers went forward and, with a crash which shattered the eerie darkness, the two armies clashed into a furious melee of twisting, whirling swords, spears and battle-axes. The air dinned with curses, prayers, cries of the dying, shrieks of horror and pain, as men fought in the misty darkness, drenching the soft earth ankle-deep in blood. Warwick wiped the sweat from his brow, peering into the darkness to glimpse his brother's banner. Beside it, the great blue-and-gold banner of York displayed a sun in splendour. Shouts and cries from the left made him whirl. Warwick watched in horror as a great white standard bearing a Red Boar Rampant appeared on the ridge, driving Exeter's men back towards him. York's brother, Richard of Gloucester, was trying to take them in the rear. Warwick rapped out orders, instructing the bulk of his reserve to go to Exeter's aid. The Red Boar Rampant disappeared. Warwick heaved a sigh of relief, grasped the Eye of God and prayed his patron saint, Archangel Michael, would come to his aid. He heard a shout from the melee in front of him and glimpsed more Yorkist banners around that of his brother. King Edward himself was leading in his reserve, hacking a path through to confront Montagu. Warwick moved his own small force forward. Within minutes he was part of that wall of steel, helmet on, visor down, hacking and hewing at anything which appeared through the slits of his helm. The Yorkists began to give. Warwick withdrew, drenched in sweat, his silver, gold-chased armour, the personal gift of Louis XI of France, now a rusty colour, spattered with blood and bits of bone. Warwick, his squires and pages around him, took off his helmet and stood gasping for air. He turned to the squire beside him and grasped the man by the shoulder.

'Brandon!' he shouted, 'Brandon, victory is ours!'

Suddenly, from the misty fog to Warwick's right, came screams and sudden movement. Bowmen were breaking away, loosing arrows at the horsemen appearing before them. Men were shouting, 'Treason! Treason!'

'In heaven's name!' Warwick screamed. 'Brandon, Montagu's men, they are attacking Oxford!'

Warwick ran across the battlefield, but the damage was done. Oxford, who had driven one party of Yorkists from the field, had now unexpectedly returned. Montagu's men, thinking they were the enemy, loosed a volley of arrows. Oxford's soldiers, sensing betrayal, cried 'Treason!' broke and fled. The shouts were now taken up by Montagu's troops. Panic rippled along the battle line, which began to break as men turned to flee. Messengers ran up, breathless, hot-eyed. Montagu was down! John Neville was dead! Warwick groaned but he had not time to listen. The trickle of fugitives was swelling. Men running away, throwing down their arms, ripping off their armour.

'*Aidez moi!*' the Earl shouted.

He pointed his sword to the battle line, urging the last of his household forward whilst he and a few squires stood beneath his banner, but to no avail. The now buckling battle lines shuddered and broke. Any semblance of order disappeared, even the household knights were shouting the day was lost. Warwick, grasping the Eye of God, stared round, he opened his mouth to shout but no words came out. An arrow whipped by his face as foot soldiers, wearing the livery of York, broke into view. Brandon, Moresby and the rest began to run. Warwick too, his breath coming in short, choking gasps. He was weighted down by steel, the prospect of death and defeat seemed to coil like serpents about him.

'*Tout est perdu!*' he whispered.

The horse line came into sight. Oh, thank God! Brandon was leading his horse forward but Warwick tripped, squelching in the mud, rose and lumbered forward. Behind him the Yorkist foot soldiers leapt and yelped like dogs. He reached the horse, grasped the bridle and found he hadn't the strength to mount.

'My lord.' Anxious-eyed, Moresby took the Earl's hand, gesturing at Brandon next to him to control their restless horses.

'My lord, you should flee.'

Warwick plucked the Eye of God from round his neck and thrust it into Brandon's hands.

'Take it!' he gasped. 'Go to the monks at Canterbury. My last gift. Ask them to pray for my soul!'

Moresby and Brandon were about to protest but Warwick shoved them away. The young men hurriedly mounted as a band of Yorkists reached Warwick. The Earl turned, struggling, but he was pushed to the ground, his visor clawed up. A foot soldier, sitting on his chest, thrust a knife into the Earl's throat. The Earl jerked once, twice, as his life and ambitions were snuffed out like candle-light. In the darkness, Brandon and the other horsemen rode away even as Colum Murtagh, the King's messenger, reached the group of soldiers now greedily stripping the rich armour from Warwick's body.

'He's dead!' one of them screamed. 'The enemy's dead! The great Warwick is cut short!' He peered up at Colum. 'You are too late for the riches. Rules of war! We got him! We killed him, his armour's ours!'

'I came to save his life,' Colum muttered, staring pityingly down at Warwick's white corpse, now naked except for a loincloth.

'What's the use of that?' another soldier shouted, now cavorting with Warwick's richly gilt helm on the end of his spear.

Colum shook his head. 'Nothing,' he said. 'But His Grace the King demands the pendant with its priceless sapphire.'

'What pendant?' the soldiers shouted. 'Before God, master, there is no cross or jewel!'

Colum insisted that they empty their wallets and purses. At last, convinced of their truthfulness if not their honesty, he turned his horse and returned to the King with the news that the Earl of Warwick was dead and the Eye of God had vanished.

The crossroads were bathed in the light of a hunter's moon and the chains of the gibbet glowed silver-like in the ghostly moonlight. The corpse dangling from the rotting rope hung motionless, as if listening for some sound from the desolate moorland which bounded the coastal road out of Canterbury. The woman waiting in the shadows found it difficult to keep still. She wetted her lips anxiously and peered into the darkness. The message was quite simple. She had to be here before midnight and yet she wished she could flee. She pushed her red hair back and felt the sweat coursing down her cheeks.

'Of course I could have refused,' she murmured to herself. She bit her lip. But what then? If I didn't come here, they would come for me, she thought. She heard a soft shuffling sound in the grass behind her. A twig cracked. She whirled round, her hand going to the dagger pushed into her belt. No one was there, only a silver-dappled fox trotted across the glade fringed by a line of bushes from the crossroads. The fox abruptly stopped, ears cocked, one foreleg slightly raised as it looked towards her. The animal's head turned, its eyes glinted a dullish red and the woman moaned in terror. Was it an animal? Or some malevolent ghost of the night? Some demon in the form of an animal? The fox looked at her once more, twitched its nose and then trotted on. The woman closed her eyes; she let out a deep sigh and turned back to look at the gibbet. She cut off her half-strangled cry of shock at the hooded, cowled figure now standing beside the scaffold. She would have crouched down and hid, but the shadow knew she was there. A gloved hand came up and beckoned her forward. She froze, her mouth going dry, her heart thudding like the beat of a drum.

'Come!' the voice ordered softly. 'Megan, come here!'

The woman rose to her feet. She just wished her legs would stop shaking. Her smock was drenched in a cold sweat, which the cold night air caught to deepen her chill.

'Will you not come?' The voice was sweet and low. 'You have no reason to be afraid.'

Megan stepped out from behind the bushes and walked slowly across to the stranger.

'Oh, come closer,' the voice repeated, a slight testiness there, like some benevolent father who was beginning to lose patience with a recalcitrant child.

Megan edged nearer. She tried to control the panic which threatened to reduce her to pitiful sobs or hysterical cries. She knew she must not do that, otherwise the stranger might suspect she was planning some attack or a secret ambush. However, if she turned and ran, the stranger would make sure that this would be her last night on earth. Megan licked her dry lips and walked head high, drawing so close she smelt the rottenness from the gibbet. She glimpsed the cadaverous skull and face of the hanged man, twisted to one side, so in the pale moonlight it looked as if he were grinning at her. The stranger had positioned himself well. The cowled cloak obscured every part of him whilst the mask across his face only revealed sharp white teeth and the glittering malice of his one good eye.

'I did come,' Megan murmured. 'I came as you said.'

'Of course you did.' The stranger's voice now had a gentle Gaelic lilt. His hand suddenly shot out and gripped her by the shoulder, squeezing hard like a metal vice. Megan closed her eyes and moaned in terror.

'Look around you, Megan!' He shook her. 'Look around!'

9

He loosened his grip and the woman did as she was told, staring round the tall, dark trees of Blean Wood.

'A strange place,' the man murmured. 'People say that here, magicians clothe themselves in long skins, the hides of animals with immense tails still attached. They are faceless and call upon Merderus, Queen of the Night, to come to their aid. Do you believe that? In Ireland we do.'

Despite the lilting accent of the stranger, if she told the truth, Megan was more terrified of him than any legion of hags flying through the dark watches of the night to attend Black Sabbaths or blasphemous Masses.

The man sighed. 'They say the war is finished,' he continued as if they were exchanging gossip. 'Did you know that, eh, girl?' He laughed abruptly. 'But of course you do. The Lancastrians are piled waist-deep and their blood soaks the hills of Barnet and Tewkesbury. King Edward the Fourth has come back to his own with his pretty doll-like queen and cruel brothers. And everyone has to go back home. No more killing time, just peace, until the next time.'

'What do you want?' Megan stammered.

'You know what we want,' the man replied. 'Edward the Fourth has settled his grievance with Lancaster. Now we must settle our grievances and you'll assist us, won't you, at the given time? When the message comes through, you will do what I say, won't you? We share the same blood, as did the traitor Colum Murtagh.'

Megan, white-faced, gazed back in round-eyed terror.

'Swear!' the stranger hissed. He forced her hand up against the slime-stained gibbet. 'Swear now to me, Padraig Fitzroy!'

Megan could stand the terror no longer.

'I swear!' she screamed. 'I swear! I swear! I swear!'

Megan pulled her hand loose and sank sobbing to her knees, her long hair flying out around her, but when she looked up, the stranger had gone. The crossroads were deserted, the silence broken only by the gibbet creaking in a cold, quickening south-westerly wind. Megan patted her red sweat-soaked hair and stared into the night. She was Irish-born and knew the horrors of the blood-feud: the Hounds of Ulster were in England and hunting her master. Colum Murtagh was their quarry and she was to be the bait.

Chapter 1

*S*how me the wound!'

The soldier pulled back the sleeve of his leather jerkin, then the dirty white linen of his shirt. The arm beneath was lean, brown and muscular except for the long suppurating gash just above the wrist. The woman leaned down and sniffed it gently. She noticed the green-yellow pus and caught a faint whiff of putrefaction. The scar was now an angry welt. The poison from the wound was creating a small circle of red which was seeping up the rest of the arm.

'Are you going to cure it or eat it?' the soldier gibed.

Kathryn Swinbrooke, leech, apothecary and physician, stared hard at the soldier.

'The wound's suppurating,' she said tartly. 'Who ever dressed it was an ignorant quack.'

'In which case, Mistress Swinbrooke, that was me!'

Kathryn half-smiled.

'Turn away,' she said. 'Thomasina,' she called to her plump, merry-faced nurse, 'pass me the knife.'

Thomasina was holding the blade of a long cutting knife over a candle flame. She didn't know why, but Kathryn always insisted on this, as had her father, poor physician Swinbrooke, who now lay under the cold slabs of Saint Mildred's Church in Canterbury.

Thomasina lapsed into a day-dream. She wished they were back there, in their house in Ottemelle Lane, where she could nag Agnes the scullery maid and listen to the chatter of young Wuf. Thomasina bit her lip. But oh no, she thought, thanks to that bloody Irishman, Colum Murtagh, she, her mistress and the Irish adventurer were now in the middle of London, preparing to go up-river for an audience with the King himself. Except Murtagh had still not finished dressing and Kathryn was now examining the wrist of this hard-faced captain of the guard who had come to escort them up the Thames to the Tower.

'Thomasina, are you asleep?'

Startled, Thomasina looked up, smiled her apologies and handed the ivory-handled, sharp knife to her mistress.

'You shouldn't do it,' Thomasina moaned. 'Your best taffeta dress.' She glared disapprovingly at the tawny-coloured material as if searching for any speck or mark.

'Thomasina, it's only a cut. I'll clean it, then we'll be gone.' Kathryn smiled at the soldier. 'This may hurt.'

The crop-headed soldier, his hard, unshaven face tense, just nodded, half-embarrassed by the kindness of this lady who smelt so sweet. As Kathryn began to cut slightly at the wound, the soldier studied the female physician. She is hardly buxom, he thought, her jet-black hair showed strands of grey and her face was slightly severe. Nevertheless, he secretly admired her creamy complexion, finely arched eyebrows and that small, straight nose, now sniffing at the pus beginning to seep from the small inflamed cut.

'How did it happen?' Kathryn looked up.

No, the soldier reflected, on second thoughts she was beautiful. Her lips were full and red, her eyes a serene sea-grey, honest and direct.

'How did it happen?' she repeated.

'I cut it,' the soldier mumbled, glancing away. 'On a piece of rusty chain mail.'

'If it ever happens again,' Kathryn said severely, though the soldier saw a glint of amusement in her eyes, 'wash it as I am going to do now.'

And before the soldier could object, Kathryn closed the lips of the wound together, forcing out blood and pus. She then poured a jug of hot water over it, making him wince. After that she rubbed some ointment round the wound, her fingers soft and gentle. Kathryn then took a roll of gauze-like bandage from a small basket held by the fearsome Thomasina, and bound it tightly round his wrist.

'There!' Kathryn inserted a small pin. 'That will keep the bandage secure.'

The soldier shuffled from one foot to the other. Kathryn smiled to herself at how a little gentleness could change some-one. When he had first entered the hostelry, the captain had looked fierce with his conical helmet cradled under his arm, boiled leather jacket, woollen hose, heavy boots and that great sword-belt strapped across one shoulder, with the naked sword hanging from a hook and two daggers strapped to his waist.

'I have come,' he had announced, 'to escort Master Murtagh, marshal of the King's household and the King's Special Commissioner in Canterbury, and Mistress Swinbrooke, physician of the same city, to His Grace the King at the Tower.'

Colum, who had scarcely finished breaking his fast, curtly told him he would have to wait. Whilst Murtagh had gone up to his chamber, Kathryn had noticed how the captain had been favoring his left arm, found the cause and immediately insisted on treating it.

'What do I owe you, Mistress?' he now asked.

Kathryn shook her head. 'A safe passage to the Tower and there will be no fee.'

The soldier coughed, muttered his thanks and went out into the cobbled yard. He yelled orders at his small escort of royal archers who were lounging there, ogling the slatterns and maids.

'I am ready.' Colum came downstairs. He blew a kiss at Thomasina, who just glared back, and made a mock bow at Kathryn.

'Quite the courtier,' Kathryn teased.

She stared at the Irishman. His black unruly hair was now carefully combed; his dark, swarthy face shaven. Although he had spent the night roistering with a friend at a Cheapside tavern, Colum's blue eyes were clear, and his face, which reminded Kathryn of a hunting falcon, was relaxed and smiling. Colum had dressed in his best: a white cambric shirt, a doublet of murrey fringed with lamb's-wool, which hung down mid-calf, and matching hose of motley colours. He, too, had strapped his great war-belt round his waist with its long sticking-dagger and broad-hilted sword.

'Should you wear them?' Kathryn asked. 'I thought you said that in the King's presence . . . ?'

'Oh, I will have to take it off,' Colum replied, flicking some dust from the quilted front of his doublet. 'But this is London, Kathryn, the streets are thronged with every rogue under the sun. But come, let's go!'

Colum strode out into the yard. The archers sprang to their feet, and with the captain leading three men before them, and three more trailing behind, they went through Budge Row, into the Walbrook, then down to the Steelyard near Dowgate where the royal barge would be waiting for them. Kathryn gripped Colum's arm; the day was fair and the crowds were out, shoving their way either up Cheapside or, like them, down to the river. Great houses, their plaster white as snow against beams of polished black, jutted out above them, almost blocking out the weak morning sun. Colum whispered to Kathryn to be careful. She lifted the hem of her skirts, stepping round puddles, wrinkling her nose at the open filled sewer which ran down the centre of the street. Yet the bustle of the streets excited her: pedlars and tinkers running up and down shouting their wares; merchants in their great beaver hats and quilted cloaks standing together in corners, sharing gossip about which ships were in and what commodities were available. A wedding party, making its way up to a church in Trinity, forced its way through: a group of giggling young men and women, their faces already flushed with drink. Beggars whined on the corners of alley-ways. A pardoner, garbed from head to toe in dirty white rags, tried to sell indulgences on scraps of tawdry parchment. Children baited dogs, housewives chattered in the shadows of doorways. Two friars, their faces hooded, walked behind a man, a forger who had been condemned to carry a huge boulder from one end of the city to the other.

Kathryn's head whirled from one sight to another. She gave up her attempt to avoid the dirt and rested more firmly on Colum's arm as the Irishman strode purposefully behind the archers, his free hand on his dagger. Colum carefully studied the crowds and tried to ignore Thomasina's stream of questions as the nurse huffed and puffed behind him. Colum was pleased that Kathryn so firmly held his arm. The physician had wanted to come to London to buy spices and Colum had been delighted; he wanted to show her off at court, as well as demonstrate to Kathryn how closely he was trusted by the great Yorkist war-lords waiting for him at the Tower. Nevertheless, Colum was uneasy. Born in the wild, green glens of Ireland, he was used to stables, horses, open fields, and he disliked the narrow city lanes, the mass of unwashed bodies and the foot-pads who seemed to cluster like rats around a dunghill. He turned sideways; yes, there was someone following him, a small, bent man with straggling grey hair, furtive eyes and a long, pointed nose. Colum glared at the man; he knew a foist when he saw one. The rogue was apparently stalking either Colum's party or those who stopped to watch this well-dressed couple being escorted through the streets by a small company of royal archers. However, the fellow posed no real threat, so Colum glanced away. He was not frightened of any London footpad, but the Hounds of Ulster were a different matter.

They'd condemned Colum as a traitor and had sworn to take his head, and what better place than some crowded London street, where a crossbow bolt could be loosed or a knife quickly slipped between a man's ribs?

'Colum, what do you think the King wants with you?'

The Irishman pulled a face. 'God knows, Mistress Kathryn. The letter was sent by his brother, Richard of Gloucester. I am to meet the King on the twenty-fifth of July, the feast of Saint James the Apostle, in the King's own chapel at the Tower. More than that, God knows!'

Kathryn pressed his arm. 'Are you nervous, Colum?'

'In the midst of life we are in death,' he quipped.

Now Kathryn pulled a face. Sometimes she regretted ever buying a copy of Chaucer's work. The Irishman, an avid reader, was forever regaling her and Thomasina with extracts from Geoffrey Chaucer's *Canterbury Tales*.

'From what story is that?' she teased.

Colum held up a finger like a reproving schoolmaster.

'No, most learned of physicians, not from Master Chaucer but from God's own story, the Bible.' He grinned. 'Though yes, as Chaucer's Pardoner says, "I search here for Death, all pale and withered is its face." '

Kathryn's smile faded. 'Here!' she hissed. 'Here in London? Surrounded by royal archers?'

'Oh, yes,' Colum whispered back. 'My comrades, the self-proclaimed Hounds of Ulster, are no respecters of persons. I am more at risk here than I would be on a deserted road.'

Further conversation was impossible. They had reached the riverside and went down the slippery steps into the waiting royal barge. It was broad and large, with comfortable seats for Kathryn, Colum and Thomasina under a leather awning. The archers clambered in. The captain rapped out orders, the four oarsmen pulled away from the steps and into midstream. Despite the tidal change, the barge seemed to skim above the water as it passed under the arches of London Bridge where the river frothed and roared like water in a cauldron. Kathryn, a little frightened by the speed and surge of the current, looked away. She closed her eyes in disgust at the huge poles stuck out over the bridge which bore the rotting heads of traitors. Colum, following her glance, tried to divert her by pointing out the different sights: the white stones of the palaces, the lofty spires of different churches, and the various ships—galleys from Venice; huge, fat-bottomed cogs from the Baltic; and the great two-masted warships of the King.

At last they reached the Tower. Despite the sun, the fortress was grim and sombre. They left the barge and walked along the shingle path towards the Lion Gate, heavily guarded by men-at-arms wearing the royal livery, the Red Boar of Gloucester or the Golden Bull of Clarence. Warrants were inspected and they were led up the narrow winding trackways. Kathryn peered apprehensively around. Wasn't it here, she thought, just recently, when the Yorkist war-lords returned in glory after their victories at Barnet and Tewkesbury, that old King Henry, who some said was a saint and others a mad man, had been stabbed to death? They turned a corner and walked across the green towards the great white keep, passing soldiers sitting on the grass cleaning their hauberks with old rags and small dishes of dry sand. At the foot of the steps leading up to the keep, their escort took their leave. Once again the captain repeated his thanks, and before Colum could ask Kathryn what the fellow meant, a chamberlain appeared dressed in blue, red and gold, and pompously led them into the keep. They went up a further flight of stairs and into the chapel of Saint John. Two knights bannerets, their features hidden by heavy conical helmets with broad nose-guards, stood on guard at the chapel door, their swords drawn. Colum took off his belt, handed it to one of them and with Kathryn walked inside.

Kathryn immediately caught her breath at the sheer white dazzling beauty of the place. The columns were painted in brilliant colours. The floor was of polished stone, cloths of gold hung from the walls, but her attention was caught by the group at the far end seated before the altar. Whilst the chamberlain went forward, Colum lowered his head and whispered to Kathryn.

'His Grace the King and his wife, the Lady Elizabeth. Behind them are His Grace's brothers; the russet-haired one is Richard of Gloucester, the other George of Clarence. The King can be trusted, but watch the rest!'

Kathryn gazed down the chapel. The air smelt fragrant with incense and the candles on the altar were still smoking whilst a tonsured monk, dressed in alb and stole, cleared away the precious vessels after a late-morning Mass. Kathryn stared down at these figures talking in a huddle: the King resplendent in dark-blue satin, a silver chaplet round his golden hair. A giant of a man well over six feet, Edward was the greatest warrior of his age, and if scandal could be believed, dangerous with the ladies. His wife Elizabeth Woodville looked like a snow queen with her beautiful silver-white hair and a face that would have been strikingly lovely if it hadn't been for her expression of disdain. The two princes were, as Colum had described, resolute warriors but dangerous. Richard of Gloucester, with his russet hair, white, pinched face and green eyes, reminded Kathryn of a cat her father had once owned. Gloucester turned away and whispered something to Clarence, who looked up. A handsome man, Kathryn thought—too handsome, almost woman-like with his golden curls and petulant mouth. The chamberlain waited until he caught the King's eye, then sank to one knee and whispered, moving his head to indicate Colum and Kathryn. Edward drew himself up, straightened his crown and winked mischievously at Kathryn, gesturing with his hand for them to approach.

They did; Colum and Kathryn sank to one knee. The King made them stay there. He watched over his shoulder until both chamberlain and chaplain had left and indicated to Gloucester to ensure all doors were secure. Kathryn drew in her breath. She wished Thomasina had been allowed entrance but Colum had been most insistent: only those specifically invited entered the King's presence, and Thomasina had not been named.

'On your feet, Colum.'

The King's voice was rich and mellow. He threw off his ermine-lined cloak, rose and came down proffering a large hand.

'Mistress Swinbrooke, you are most welcome.'

Kathryn stared into the broad, tawny, handsome face. Edward looked every inch the king, with his slightly hooked nose, neatly clipped golden moustache and beard; his dark-blue eyes were both friendly and teasing. Kathryn recalled Colum's words—how Edward could make even the poorest subject in his kingdom feel at ease.

'Mistress Kathryn, you are most welcome,' the King repeated. Kathryn blushed and stammered her thanks.

The King covered her hand with his.

'You are right, Colum.' He let Kathryn's hand go and turned to clap the Irishman on the shoulder. 'A beautiful, wise woman, a rare treasure.'

Edward grinned mischievously at his queen, who forced a smile before glaring hot-eyed at Kathryn. Gloucester came round the side of the throne, followed by Clarence. They shook Colum's hand and then courteously kissed hers. Sharp daggers in velvet sheaths, Kathryn thought. Gloucester seemed friendly enough with his lopsided smile, but Kathryn took an immediate dislike to Clarence, with his arrogant sneering looks and foppish ways. She was sure he was mocking her, so Kathryn deliberately let her own fixed smile fade. Over Clarence's shoulder she caught Edward's eye; he, too, was glaring sullenly at his brother.

'Clarence is treacherous,' Colum had declared on his way to London. 'He fought with Warwick and the Lancastrians. He only changed sides before Barnet. One day, brother George will move too slowly and the King will have his head.'

Kathryn quickly glanced at these four powerful people who held the kingdom in their hands. She tried to hide her unease as she realised how silent the chapel had become. The King

leaned forward, tapping one soft, bejewelled buskin on the floor as he pointed at Colum.

'Well, Irishman, how are my stables at Kingsmead?'

'The manor is being rebuilt, Your Grace, the paddocks prepared, and the stables, at least, are ready for your horses.'

The King drummed his fingers on the arm of his chair. 'And Canterbury itself?'

'Most loyal, Your Grace.'

Edward grimaced and his eyes slid away. 'And the rebel, Nicholas Faunte?'

Colum shifted uneasily. He was not only the Master of the King's stable at Kingsmead but Special Commissioner to Canterbury. The city had supported Warwick and the Lancastrians in the recent civil war under their mayor, Nicholas Faunte, now a fugitive traitor. Colum knew his royal master. Once Edward believed a man should die, be he prince or pauper, that man would go to the block; Edward had not forgotten how Faunte's support of Lancaster had almost cost him control of the important routes to Dover.

'So you have not captured him yet?' Clarence spoke up, coming round the side of the throne, thumbs pushed into the beautiful embroidered belt round his waist.

'I have not captured him,' Colum replied, his eyes not leaving the King, 'because I have been involved in other duties, my lord. As His Grace knows, treason is a weed with very deep roots.'

Clarence caught the hidden taunt and flushed. Gloucester bowed his head to hide his smirk but the King continued to stare at Colum.

'Faunte will be captured,' Edward replied slowly. 'Master Murtagh has other matters on his mind.' He darted a glance at Kathryn. 'And you, Mistress Swinbrooke, you have taken this Irishman into your house?'

'I gave him lodgings, Your Grace,' Kathryn replied hotly. 'I am an honourable widow. My father was a physician of Canterbury.'

'And your late husband?'

Kathryn's embarrassment deepened. She lowered her head.

'Your husband,' the King insisted, leaning forward. 'Alexander Wyville, a spicer by trade who, I believe, joined Master Faunte's forces.'

'There are many who followed Lancaster.' Colum spoke up sharply. 'Your Grace, it is no crime of Mistress Swinbrooke!'

'We did not say it was,' the Queen intervened, her voice soft and cooing like a dove.

'My husband,' Kathryn said defiantly, 'followed his heart.'

'But is he dead?' Clarence asked.

Kathryn shrugged. 'To me he is, my lord. But only God knows whether he lives or dies.' Kathryn threw all caution to the winds. She could hardly believe she had been summoned here to be interrogated about her private life. 'Alexander Wyville may be with Faunte,' she added. 'He may be in France. He may be in heaven or hell. He may even, Your Grace, be in your household or your city. After all, there are many who supported Lancaster, as Master Murtagh has just said, who now sleep serenely between silken sheets.'

Colum moved his elbow slightly to give Kathryn a warning nudge. The King glared down at her, then suddenly clapped his hands and threw himself back, laughing over his shoulder at his brother Richard.

'I have won my wager!' he roared, clapping his hands. He smiled at Kathryn. 'When we saw you at the back of the church, I accepted my brother's wager. I said that no woman who was wise would keep a still tongue in her head.'

'I am always prepared to tell the truth,' Kathryn snapped back, angry that her presence had been the cause of a wager.

Edward's grin widened. Even the Queen relaxed slightly. Richard bit his lip, wagging a finger at Colum. Only Clarence stared sullenly at the Irishman. Edward clapped his hands again.

'Enough! Enough! Master Murtagh, you are well?'

'Yes, Your Grace.'

'Then let us get on with this business.'

The King took his circlet off his head and turned sideways in his chair, crossing his great legs as he played with a diamond ring on his finger.

'Master Murtagh, you remember Barnet?'

'Aye, Your Grace, a bloody fight.'

'No, no.' The King waved his hand. 'When you took my defiance to Warwick before the battle began? You said the Earl was wearing a gold pendant containing a beautiful sapphire?'

'Yes, Your Grace. I saw it as clearly then as I see you now.'

'And after the battle,' Edward continued, 'when you returned to see if Warwick had been spared?'

'The pendant was gone.'

'Are you sure of that?' Clarence purred like a cat, one hand on the back of the King's throne-like chair.

Colum caught the hidden accusation, his lip curled in contempt.

'Remove your hand from my chair, brother,' Edward said softly. 'If the pendant was there, Colum would have had it.'

Rebuked, Clarence stepped back. Kathryn wondered why such a pendant was so valuable. Clarence's interest was obvious. The Queen was sitting forward, hands clenched in her lap, listening intently. Gloucester stood legs apart, one shoulder slightly raised, eyes narrowed, his body taut and tense.

'I want that pendant,' Edward continued. 'And you, Master Murtagh, shall find it. You owe it to me and my father.'

Edward gazed steadily at Colum, silently reminding the Irishman of how the King's father, Richard of York, when he was Lord Lieutenant of Ireland, had captured Colum and other rebels. He had shown mercy to Murtagh because he was only a boy. He had taken him into his own household to train as a squire, developing Colum's special gift for working with horses.

'God rest your father's soul,' Colum said.

'Aye, God rest him,' Edward replied, staring down the nave as if trying to summon up his father's ghost. 'You know how he died, Colum, trapped in the wild, snowy wastes outside Wakefield. The Lancastrians took him and my elder brother Edmund, he who should be sitting on this throne now. They cut their heads off and festooned them with paper crowns. They put them on spikes above Micklegate Bar in York, his own city, so the commoners might laugh and the crows could fill their bellies!' Edward raised one clenched fist to his mouth; he bit his whitened knuckle, then blinked as if dismissing the ghosts. 'Aye, they have all gone,' Edward whispered. 'And those who did it have gone into the darkness as well. Despatched just as violently as they did my father. Do you remember it, Colum?'

'Aye, Your Grace, how can I forget? I, too, was captured at the same battle. My life was spared only because I was a commoner.'

'Enough! Enough!' Edward straightened in his chair. 'Colum, my father brought from Ireland a beautiful pendant of solid gold and, in the centre, a sapphire which shines so brilliantly they call it the Eye of God. My father always kept it about his person. He rarely wore it, for it made every man's hand itch and could turn the most honest fellow into a rogue. Now, as you know, my father's great friend and ally in those days was Richard Neville, Earl of Warwick. Golden days, Colum, before Warwick turned sour.' The King grinned bleakly. 'As they say, "Lilies that do fester smell rank and worse than weeds." Now, before the fight at Wakefield'—Edward wetted his lips—'my father and the Earl of Warwick swore the most solemn oaths to each other. My father gave the pendant to Warwick as a gift; a pledge of friendship. In his turn, Warwick swore that if he ever turned against the House of York, the rightful heirs of the crown, the pendant would be returned to my father or his descendants.'

'Now it's gone,' Gloucester said and leaned forward, his hard, green eyes scarcely containing his fury. 'At first His Grace and I thought it may have been taken in battle, filched by some petty soldier, some camp thief.' Gloucester shook his head.

'But we have searched high and low. Sent special surveyors and spies into the markets. Even alerted envoys at foreign courts, but the Eye of God has not been seen.'

He looked at his brother, who nodded at him to continue.

'We questioned this person and that. We know Warwick wore the pendant in battle even as his troops broke and fled. However, by the time he had been cut down, the Eye of God was gone. To make a long story short, Master Murtagh'— Gloucester spread his hands—'the solution is quite simple. Warwick must have given the pendant to someone else.' Gloucester stopped and stared up at the hammer-beamed roof.

Kathryn studied Gloucester carefully. The Prince was small in stature but exuded a strength, a fiery determination not even the King possessed. Gloucester's eyes were red-rimmed and he kept toying with a ring on his finger or the hilt of his small dagger. A hasty, excitable man, Kathryn concluded, much given to fretting and impatience, but still a dangerous one with his sharp, shrewd face and darting green eyes. She thought the Prince was slightly misshapen, even a little hunchbacked, but this was the way Gloucester moved, with short, sharp gestures followed by long periods of silence, as he stood—almost—still as a statue. His head came up and he caught Kathryn's glance.

'The House of York,' he whispered, 'the King and myself want the Eye of God returned.' He tapped his boot on the marble floor. 'Brandon has it,' he declared.

Colum looked quizzically at him.

'Brandon,' the King repeated, getting to his feet and stretching until every muscle in his body cracked. He padded softly down the steps, his fingers tapping the stiffened brocade over his stomach. 'Brandon was one of Warwick's principal squires. He fled Barnet after the battle but was later captured just outside Canterbury. Like others of Warwick's army, he was thrown into the nearest gaol, which happened to be Canterbury Castle. Now'—the King began to walk up and down, reminding Kathryn of a schoolmaster delivering an important lesson—'at first Brandon was dismissed as one among many prisoners. In normal circumstances, he would have kicked his heels for months and then been released. However, my brother Gloucester discovered that Brandon was probably the last man to see Warwick alive. If he didn't have the pendant, he would at least know where it was.' The King laughed drily. 'Now Fortune has given her fickle wheel another twist. We made enquiries at Canterbury Castle, only to find Brandon is dead from gaol fever, gone into the darkness, taking the secret of the Eye of God with him.' The King stared at his younger brother. 'But we don't believe that, do we, Richard?'

Gloucester shook his head, his eyes never leaving those of his brother. The King came over and tapped Colum on the chest.

'Now you can see why we need you, Colum. You must go to Canterbury Castle and find out the circumstances surrounding Brandon's rather mysterious death.'

'Mysterious, sire?'

'Yes: why should a sturdy young man of robust health die so quickly?'

'You suspect someone at the castle, Your Grace?'

'Oh, no, not necessarily, but Brandon may have chattered. He must have revealed something of the whereabouts of the Eye of God.'

Colum glanced at Kathryn.

'Oh, I know what you are thinking,' the King continued. 'Brandon may have had it on his person when he was taken.'

'Who did capture him, Your Grace?'

'Robard Fletcher, deputy constable of the castle, a dyed-in-the-wool King's man, a soldier of the old school. He has been before our King's Bench and has sworn an oath on our sacred relics that Brandon carried nothing.'

'And the Constable, William Webster?' Colum asked.

'He knows nothing, as does our mutual friend, the master-at-arms, Simon Gabele.'

Colum's eyes fell away and the King laughed softly.

26

'Oh, yes, Colum, your old friend Simon with his raven-haired beauty of a daughter, Margotta.'

The King walked back to his chair, sat down and stared up at the ceiling.

'I want that pendant back,' he muttered. 'It belongs to the House of York.' His eyes swivelled to Kathryn. 'Mistress Swinbrooke, you have questions?'

Kathryn wanted to ask about Margotta but she thought that this was hardly the time or place.

'Your Grace,' she said softly, 'I think you know my question.'

The King leaned forward. 'Yes, let me guess. Why should His Grace the King, his queen, princes of the blood require the services of Mistress Kathryn Swinbrooke, physician, leech; widow, perhaps, of Alexander Wyville, a Lancastrian?' The King paused. 'Well, let me answer, my pretty, and so spare your blushes.' Edward's voice became hard as he ticked the points off on thick, stubby fingers. 'First, Bourchier, Archbishop of Canterbury, and that ubiquitous little clerk of his, Simon Luberon, swear you are honest, as does my commissioner here, Colum Murtagh. Secondly, you did the Crown and the Church good service in trapping that poisoner who was killing the pilgrims to Becket's tomb. Thirdly, we need information about Brandon's death. You can use your skills on our behalf.' The King spread his hands. 'What more can I say? Bring back the Eye of God, Colum. Place it in my hands and I will never forget you.'

The King turned and whispered to his queen. Colum took that as a signal of dismissal. He and Kathryn bowed and walked down the small nave of the church to the door. Kathryn would always remember the scene as some royal tableau. Edward in his silks, bluff and hearty, yet his blue eyes cold and menacing. The icy snow queen, Elizabeth. Gloucester, as taut as a greyhound in the slips. And Clarence, why did he look so subdued? Kathryn pressed Colum's hand.

'Did you tell them,' she teased softly, 'I was beautiful and wise?'

Colum blushed.

'And did you believe all the rest?' she whispered.

'If I did,' he replied, 'pigs might fly!'

'In which case,' she retorted softly, 'we'll find pork in the trees round Canterbury!'

Chapter 2

They left the chapel and collected a garrulous Thomasina. She had spent the entire time they had been with the King giving the guards the rough edge of her tongue. Behind the broad nose-guards of their helmets both men were grinning broadly.

'Goodbye, sweet Thomasina!' one of them called.

At the top of the steps, Thomasina turned.

' "Sweet Thomasina"!' she mimicked: 'I'd take both of you lads together and crush the life out of you!'

And with the soldiers' laughter ringing in her ears, Thomasina followed her mistress and Colum down and out onto Tower Green. She now turned her attention on Kathryn with a furious spate of questions.

'What did the King look like, Mistress? Was he as tall as they say? Was he handsome? Did he have strong legs? Men good in bed always have strong legs. And the Queen? Was she so beautiful? And what did they say? Is the Irishman in trouble?' Thomasina concluded hopefully.

Colum and Kathryn just walked on.

'And why wasn't I admitted?' Thomasina demanded. 'Why

wouldn't the King see a good Englishwoman when he shows such favour to ragged-arsed Irishmen?'

Colum stopped and turned, his face grave.

'As Chaucer's clerk would say, "Oh flower of wifely patience," hold your tongue!'

'If I'd held yours I'd need a basket,' Thomasina snapped back. 'My father said, "Never trust an Irishman: tongues like daggers and the Devil's own liars!"'

Colum grinned. ' "She was a worthy woman all her life," ' he quoted again from Chaucer. ' "And husbands at the church door she had good five." '

'Three!' Thomasina shouted back, puffing herself up beside Kathryn, who was still lost in her own thoughts, trying to ignore the usual banter between Colum and her maid.

Kathryn was about to intervene when she heard her and Colum's names being called. They turned to see Gloucester, a feathered cap upon his head, hurrying across the grass towards them.

'Not so hasty, Irishman!' Gloucester doffed his hat and caught his breath. 'His Grace my brother is well pleased with you.' His green, cunning eyes studied Colum and Kathryn. 'Did you believe all that?' he whispered.

'The King spoke the truth,' Kathryn answered.

'But . . . ?' Gloucester added.

'The truth can be as long as a piece of string,' Kathryn replied. 'There is more, my lord?'

'Yes,' Gloucester sighed. 'However, once the Eye of God is back with us, then it is our concern. But come, I'll tell you a little more.'

He beckoned with his hand and, hurrying ahead, led them across the Tower grounds through a postern gate and into the narrow alley-ways of Petty Wales. Kathryn looked at Colum but the Irishman shook his head, raising a finger silently to his lips and indicating backwards with his head. Kathryn turned. She nearly screamed at the four hooded figures, cowls pulled well over their heads, who padded like ghosts behind them.

'Gloucester's dogs,' Colum whispered. 'Where he goes, they follow. He trusts no man.'

They went through Poor Jewry, where the houses were shabby, their paint flaking, and the streets were piled with dirt, across Mark Lane and down past Dunstan-in-the-East where Gloucester stopped before a large four-storied timbered house. Its timbers and plaster were painted a gleaming black, the windows tinted so people could look out but not stare in. The huge front door was of pure oak reinforced with iron bands and metal studs. Gloucester paused, one hand on the metal clapper shaped in the form of a gauntlet.

'Have you ever been here before?' he asked Colum.

The Irishman shook his head.

'Then welcome to the House of Secrets.' Gloucester grasped the gauntleted hand and rapped three times.

A small grille high in the door opened.

'By what name?' a low voice asked.

'By the Sun in Splendour,' Gloucester replied.

Bolts were thrust back and the door swung open. They entered a dark passageway where the light was so poor, candles fixed to the wall glowed eerily in the gloom. The passageway smelt sweet, the floor was polished, the walls covered with dark wooden panelling. Kathryn shivered; soldiers dressed like monks stood on guard in small recesses along the passageway. She wouldn't have seen them if it hadn't been for the candlelight glinting on their drawn swords. Gloucester walked on, the shadowy figure who had let them in trailing like a ghost behind. They crossed a small entrance hall. Purple-gold cloths draped the walls and candles flickered, shedding pools of light up the high, sweeping staircase which disappeared into the darkness above them.

'What is this place?' Kathryn whispered. Her words echoed like a bell through that sombre place.

Colum's hand fell to his dagger. Thomasina, usually so garrulous, peered about her like a frightened girl. Gloucester must have heard Kathryn's words. He came back, his sallow features even more sinister in the dancing candle-light.

'This is the House of Secrets,' he whispered. 'Here, the King's clerks work in different chanceries. Each chamber is a chancery. One chancery for the Papacy, another for the Low Countries, the Empire, France, the kingdoms of Castille and Aragon, Burgundy. The clerks collect information, sift the gossip of courts and merchants. We have enemies, Mistress Kathryn, both at home and abroad, and they must be rooted out!' His eyes became fanatical. 'Francis of Brittany keeps Henry Tudor, the Earl of Oxford and other Lancastrian malcontents happy at his court. Others, close to our king, play a double game. It is my duty, Mistress, to root out the weeds without disturbing the flowers. But come.'

He led them up the great staircase onto the second gallery and knocked gently on a door. A cheery-faced clerk, a quill stuck behind his ear, opened it, bowed and ushered them in.

Kathryn glanced round. The chamber was a hive of activity. Against the whitewashed walls stood high desks and stools, each occupied by a clerk busily scribbling, their quills squeaking against newly scrubbed parchment. On each desk were fastened two huge candles in iron clasps, whilst the large table down the centre of the room was covered with scrolls of vellum.

'This is the chancery for England,' Gloucester declared. 'Or at least those shires south of the Trent.' He pushed a small stool over. 'I do you a favour, Mistress. Please sit.'

With Thomasina and Colum standing behind her, Kathryn gingerly sat down whilst Gloucester rested against the table beside her, his face now smiling, as solicitously and as caring as an elder brother. He touched her lightly on the cheek. His fingers were as cold as ice, but Kathryn remained impassive.

'You are the widow of Alexander Wyville,' Gloucester began. 'A young man who lived in the parish of Saint Mildred. An apothecary by trade, who linked his fortunes to the House of Lancaster. He probably left Canterbury in the spring of 1471 with the rebel mayor, Nicholas Faunte. Am I correct?'

Kathryn nodded.

'Am I correct?' he repeated.

'We do not know,' she confessed slowly. 'Alexander'—she paused—'Alexander in his cups could become wild.' Kathryn lowered her head and picked at a thread in the hem of her cloak. 'There is a rumour,' she continued flatly, 'that he may have committed suicide by throwing himself into the river Stour. His cloak was found on the bank but . . .' Kathryn's voice trailed off.

'But you don't know whether he's alive or dead?' Gloucester continued.

Kathryn nodded, aware of the clerks around her busily scribbling. She daren't tell anyone the real truth. How Alexander was a drunken wife-beater. How her father, on his deathbed, had confessed that he was so sickened by his degenerate son-in-law, he had tried to poison him. Kathryn had been left to face the uncertainties of whether Alexander had fled, been poisoned or truly committed suicide. Yet no corpse had been found and Kathryn had heard nothing of Alexander's whereabouts.

'Mistress Swinbrooke is right.' Colum spoke softly. 'Wyville may be dead or in hiding.'

'Is it true, Mistress,' Gloucester asked, ignoring Colum's intervention, 'is it true, Mistress, that someone accused you of murdering him and sent letters blackmailing you over the matter?'

Kathryn froze. Such letters had been sent, but then, just as mysteriously, stopped, so she had let the matter rest. Sometimes Kathryn wondered if Colum or Thomasina knew more than they'd told her. She looked over her shoulder, but her nurse was stony-faced. Thomasina had recovered from her shock of entering the House of Secrets; she was now staring protectively at her mistress, vowing, on one of those rare occasions in her life, to keep a still tongue in her head, even though she knew the full truth. Alexander Wyville had been a degenerate hiding beneath the veneer of courtly etiquette and good manners. A drunken wife-beater, Wyville had vomited the poison physician Swinbrooke had given him and fled to his former paramour, the plump, lecherous Widow Gumple, who provided him with fresh clothes and some silver to leave Canterbury. Oh, Thomasina knew the truth, but she just wanted this powerful, sinister prince to leave her mistress alone.

Gloucester got to his feet. 'Mistress, I don't mean to pry but to help. The King is pleased by your services and one of the reasons I brought you here'—he smiled thinly—'is to give you further news of your long-lost husband.'

Kathryn went cold, her stomach lurched.

'Where?' she gasped.

Gloucester clicked his fingers. 'Walter!' he called to the clerk who had let them in. 'The memorandum on Alexander Wyville?'

The merry-faced clerk smiled and, finger to his lips, looked at the rolls of parchment stacked on shelves which stretched from floor to ceiling.

'Ah!' He plucked a small scroll out, undid the red cord and handed it to Gloucester. 'This is the news, my lord, of all the traitors who followed Faunte.'

Gloucester ordered the clerk to bring a candle and unrolled the parchment.

'A few entries,' he murmured. 'According to this, Alexander Wyville was at Leamington when Warwick mustered his troops. He was with the traitor when they passed through Hertfordshire towards Barnet, but he has not been seen since.'

Kathryn's heart skipped a beat. She didn't know whether to be happy or sad but took cold comfort from the evidence her father had not murdered Alexander.

'My lord,' she murmured. 'Accept my thanks. If you ever have further news?'

Gloucester gave that strange shrug. He sat back on the table, the parchment on his knees.

'Thank your good friend, Master Murtagh. He asked me to search it out.'

Kathryn bit her lip. The Irishman should stay out of her business though, deep in her heart, Kathryn knew Colum meant well.

'If we have further news,' Gloucester continued lightly, 'we shall send it to you. But if Wyville is alive and returns, what then, Mistress?' He held up a hand. 'If I may be so bold as to ask?'

'I shall give you the same answer as I have given others.' Kathryn answered bluntly. 'When I married Alexander Wyville, I thought he was one man; he proved himself to be another. Father Cuthbert, warden of the Poor Priests' Hospital in Canterbury and my confessor, has said that if Alexander returns I should apply to the Church courts for an annullment.' She drew her breath in. 'He says, my lord, that if I had known what Alexander was really like I would not have married him. I will swear before the courts how that is the truth!'

'So,' Gloucester intervened. 'You'd ask for a ruling from Holy Mother Church that your marriage should not have taken place and the bond be annulled?'

Kathryn nodded and plucked at the loose thread in her cloak.

'These are matters of the heart and conscience,' she murmured. 'My lord, I have said enough.'

'True, true.' Gloucester got to his feet briskly. 'But who knows, perhaps your husband met his death at Barnet. Four thousand of the common soldiers were slain there and lie buried in a mass grave. Perhaps it's best if he did die there.'

Kathryn caught the menace in his voice and quietly vowed to have close speech with the Irishman. She wanted no sinister lord to act as an assassin on her behalf.

'There are other matters.' Gloucester clapped Murtagh on the shoulder and smiled dazzlingly at Thomasina. 'You, Mistress, don't look so stern. I mean to help your lady.'

And before Thomasina could think of a suitable reply,

Gloucester had led them out into the passageway, down a gallery and into another chamber very similar to the one they had left. As soon as they were inside, Gloucester gripped Colum by the arm.

'We know so little about Brandon,' he murmured, 'or those from Warwick's retinue who fled from Barnet.' He gnawed his lip. 'They're probably across the seas, though we found the corpse of one of them, the captain of Warwick's guard, Reginald Moresby, in a ditch near Rochester. He was still wearing the Bear and Ragged Staff livery. We only recognised him by a signet ring.' Gloucester pulled a face. 'His features were unrecognisable.'

'Who killed him?' Colum asked.

Gloucester shrugged.

'Probably footpads, outlaws.' He sighed. 'If we'd only discovered Brandon's whereabouts earlier, but the war, the chaos . . .' His voice trailed off and he stared down the chamber.

'Moresby may have had the pendant?' Kathryn remarked.

'We doubt that. If he had, outlaws would soon try and sell it, yet there's not even been a whisper of the pendant's whereabouts.'

'Of course,' Colum spoke up, 'with Moresby dead and the others fled, Brandon is our only link to what really happened to the Eye of God.'

'Even though he died,' Gloucester added wryly, 'in rather mysterious circumstances. Now you must discover the truth.' He smiled bleakly. 'Whatever that may be.'

Gloucester walked over and had words with the clerk. He then came back, this time ignoring both Kathryn and Thomasina. He stood in that lopsided fashion before Colum, fingering a piece of parchment, his lower lip caught between his fine white teeth.

'The Eye of God should concern you in more ways than one, Master Murtagh. You and Brandon may have been the last to see it. Now—I tell you this in confidence—my father took the pendant from Saint Patrick's Cathedral in Dublin when he was

Lord Lieutenant there.' Gloucester caught the Irishman's swiftly intaken breath. 'Oh, yes, there was much debate about whether he took it or was given it. As you may know, Irishman, that pendant has a long and tangled history.' Gloucester stroked his chin with one bejewelled finger. 'Legend has it that the pendant was fashioned out of gold once owned by the Druids whilst the Eye of God comes from the crown of the ancient kings of Ireland.' Gloucester shrugged. 'To put it succinctly, Master Murtagh, some of your compatriots in Ireland want the Eye of God back! Those same men who intend to take your head!'

'The Hounds of Ulster!' Colum exclaimed.

'The same.' Gloucester looked down at the scrap of parchment. 'And so I give you two pieces of information. First, merchants in Bristol talk of an Irishman, with long red hair and a black patch over his eye, asking questions about a golden pendant of one of the leading silversmiths in the city. Secondly, two weeks later, the same Irishman is in London. He not only makes similar enquiries amongst the goldsmiths of Cheapside but also frequents the taverns used by clerks of the chancery. He asked them whether they knew the whereabouts of his old comrade-in-arms, Colum Murtagh.'

Colum paled and stared bleakly at Gloucester.

'You know the man?' Kathryn asked anxiously.

'Padraig Fitzroy,' Colum replied slowly. 'Once, a lifetime ago, we were roaring boys running through the dark woods and green glens outside the Pale of Dublin. Young puppies of the Hounds of Ulster.'

Gloucester threw the scrap of parchment down on the table.

'I have done what I promised,' he said. 'I can do no more.'

He led them out onto the gallery, down the stairs past the silent guards and into the street, where he abruptly left them. Colum, Kathryn and Thomasina stood for a while lost in their own thoughts, ignoring the clamour and noise of the London tradesmen. Colum shook himself from his reverie and grasped Kathryn's arm.

'Do you remember the "Pardoner's Tale?" ' he abruptly asked.

'Oh, no!' Kathryn groaned in exasperation. 'Colum, we both love *The Canterbury Tales,* but not now!'

Colum smiled weakly. 'No, when Gloucester was talking, I remembered those three revellers who went looking for Death and found it in a pot of gold. Only this time it's a golden pendant, a beautiful, brilliant sapphire, and there's more than three prepared to kill for it!'

'Sombre thoughts on an empty stomach,' Thomasina grumbled, 'only deepen melancholy.'

'Did Chaucer say that?' Colum asked.

'No, he bloody well didn't, but it's still true!'

Colum laughingly apologised. They walked along the street and down an alley-way towards the gold-painted sign of a spacious tavern. Inside, the taproom was thronged by traders, tinkers, pedlars, all snatching something to eat before the day's trade resumed. They were busily catcalling three one-legged men who performed a strange dance in return for pennies tossed at them by the customers. Kathryn looked pityingly at the beggars and the small boy who helped the dance with a reedy tune on a flute whilst, beside him, an old woman beat lack-lustrely on a small drum.

'London's a cruel place,' she observed.

'And noisy,' Colum replied.

He grabbed a scullion by the shoulder, found the landlord and hired a small chamber above-stairs with a table and stools. A servant brought up a jug of watered wine and a beef pie, the meat still fresh and not too heavily disguised with herbs and spices. For a while all three ate silently, till Colum pushed away his trencher of iron-hard bread.

'A strange man, Gloucester,' he began. 'He and his House of Secrets.' He wiped his mouth on the back of his hand and stared at Kathryn, who was sipping carefully from the pewter cup. 'Once,' Colum continued, 'during the war, when Edward of York had to flee to the Low Countries, we were staying in the port of Dordrecht, where there was a house with a hall of mirrors. It was owned by a glass-maker who had fashioned long mirrors for the amusement of some wealthy nobleman. Apparently this nobleman fell on hard times, so the glass-maker seized the mirrors. He installed them in his own hall and charged visitors to go in and look. I visited the place, being bored with nothing to do; the hall was small but every wall was covered by those mirrors. Each gave a distorted view of what you saw.'

Thomasina clicked angrily with her tongue.

'What are you saying, Irishman? Why do you have to speak in parables?'

'Hush, Thomasina!' Kathryn interrupted. 'Colum speaks the truth. Everything we learnt this morning was like that hall of mirrors, distorted, twisted. Am I right, Colum?'

The Irishman glared angrily at Thomasina.

'Let's reflect on what was shown to us,' he said, pushing the cups aside and leaning his elbows on the table. 'First, our noble king's family. Edward's infatuated with his queen but she hates his two brothers, particularly Clarence, who has already tried to betray the House of York. Secondly, this sapphire, the Eye of God, why is it so precious to the King? And why now? Thirdly, did Brandon have it? And, if so, where is it now? Fourthly, Gloucester's visit to the House of Secrets; we know your husband left Canterbury hale and hearty, but did he die at Barnet with the rest?' Colum smiled at Kathryn. 'At least we can exorcise two ghosts: that your father may have murdered Wyville or that Alexander committed suicide.' Colum stared down at the table-top. 'Perhaps someone else in Canterbury already knew the truth, that's why those blackmail letters stopped. Don't you agree, Thomasina?'

The nurse stared stonily back. She had vowed to tell no one how she had discovered that Widow Gumple had been the perpetrator. Or that she, Thomasina, had threatened that pompous bitch with the most dire warnings if any further letters were sent.

Colum shrugged off Thomasina's silence.

'Finally, we have the Hounds of Ulster, who want not only my head but the Eye of God.'

'Were you a traitor to them?' Kathryn asked.

Colum rolled the wine-cup between his hands.

'Never! When I was captured, I was, oh, fifteen, sixteen summers old. I was sentenced to die and was on the gallow steps when York pardoned me.' He put the cup down. 'The rest, apart from one other, were hanged, including Fitzroy's brother. Once my former comrades heard what had happened, they put the cart before the horse. I became the traitor responsible for the capture and execution of all those men.' He smiled bitterly. 'And there's the rub. It looks that way. I can't protest my innocence, and if I did, they wouldn't believe me. Only one other person knows the truth, John Tuam. He was also pardoned, being two years younger than I am.'

'And where is he now?'

'A Dominican lay brother in Blackfriars here in London. Before I leave the city, I'll send him a warning. A simple message, "Fitzroy is hunting us." At least he will be warned.'

A short while later they left the tavern. Colum stopped at a parchment-seller's where he wrote a short note and paid the apprentice a penny to take it to Brother John Tuam at the monastery of Blackfriars. After that they went down to Queenshithe where Kathryn became engaged in sharp but successful negotiations with various spice merchants over the purchase of saffron, mint, angelica seeds, calamine, powdered cloves, basil and thyme. Once she was satisfied, Kathryn visited a journeyman's yard and entered into an indenture, drawn up by a tired-looking clerk, regarding the hiring of carts to bring the same spices to her house in Ottemelle Lane, Canterbury. By the time she had finished, darkness was beginning to fall. Colum, the thought of Fitzroy's face still clear in his mind, insisted that they return to the tavern and begin preparations for an early return to Canterbury the following morning.

*   *   *

In the monastery at Blackfriars, Brother John Tuam had received Colum's note. He studied it carefully, threw it in a brazier and went to pray in the monastery church. The note had been a sharp reminder from his past. He had left the violence, the clash of swords, the sudden ambush. Like Colum, he had stood in the courtyard of Dublin Castle with the hangman's noose about his neck whilst his comrades, one after another, had been forced up the ladder, then turned off to dangle and jerk like broken dolls. Only he and Colum had been spared. Murtagh had entered the service of York but John believed his pardon was a sign from God. He had entered the Dominican order in Dublin. Four years later, at his own request, he had been sent to the Blackfriars Monastery in London. John stared up at the huge cross and the carved, writhing figure of the crucified Christ.

'I had forgotten the past,' he murmured. 'But oh, sweet Lord, the past has not forgotten me. I am no traitor, no Judas. I have no man's blood on my hands!'

He was still praying intensely when the master almoner tapped him on the shoulder.

'Brother John, Brother John, is there anything wrong?'

Tuam raised his face and stared at the old friar.

'No, Father, just remembering past misdeeds,' he joked.

The almoner patted him gently on the shoulder.

'The past does not concern God,' the almoner remarked. 'But the present does. John, we have guests.'

Tuam smiled and rose. He genuflected towards the glowing sanctuary lamp and followered Father Almoner through the cloisters into a large open yard before the main gate. The place was now thronged by the beggars, the pitiful and pathetic wrecks of London life: the cripples, the maimed, those incapable of fending for themselves. Every dawn and dusk they thronged into Blackfriars for a loaf of bread, some dried meat and a cup of ale. On long trestle tables the brothers already had the food ready, and the dirty, huddled beggars massed, mouths salivating at the sweet, savoury smells. John seized a basket and moved amongst them. He tried to smile at the disfigured faces, one man with his eye plucked out, another with his nose slit from top to bottom. One woman had an ear missing, another, both legs cut off beneath the knee. Hands grimy, caked in dirt, thrust forward.

'May Christ bless you, my brother. May Christ bless you, my sister.'

John repeated the phrase he always used at the distribution of bread. He reached the back of the crowd. A man lay huddled there. John glimpsed red hair as he pulled the threadbare blanket back. He shook the man, pushing a small loaf of bread under his nose.

'Christ have mercy on you, brother.'

Suddenly the man turned, his face full, fresh and strong. He seized John's hand in an iron grip and, before Tuam could pull away, stuck the long dagger straight into his chest.

'May Christ have mercy on you, Judas!' Padraig Fitzroy hissed.

And even before Tuam slumped to the ground, the assassin had fled like a shadow out through the open gate.

Chapter 3

*K*athryn and Colum sat before the table in the stark upper chamber of Canterbury Castle waiting for the others to take their seats. Outside the arrow-slit windows the sky began to darken. Kathryn and Colum had returned to the city earlier the same day and immediately Colum had demanded an audience with the Constable and the principal members of his household. Now they trooped in casting long dark shadows against the dimly lit walls. Sir William Webster, his rubicund face looking worried, was constantly dabbing his balding pate, forehead and shaking jowls with a grimy rag. Fletcher, his deputy, thin and gaunt, had an ashen face and tired eyes under a mop of greasy hair. His leather jacket was worn and the white shirt underneath none too clean. Gabele, the master-at-arms, was a typical soldier, hair closely cropped, his tanned face lean and lined. He stood with his great thick military coat wrapped close about him. Father Peter, the chaplain, looked grey-faced and fussy. Beside him was the waspish, vinegar-faced clerk Fitz-Steven, with bulbous eyes and a slack mouth, the oil on his thick black hair making him look even more distasteful. The introductions were quickly made. Kathryn caught a flicker of contempt from the priest and the clerk. She stared stonily back, being used to such silent insults.

'Why is the good doctor here?' Fitz-Steven rudely interrupted Colum's opening courtesies.

'I am here, Master Clerk,' Kathryn replied, 'because His Grace the King demands it.' She chose to ignore Colum's warning glance. 'He is most concerned at the death of a prisoner, the squire Brandon. When did he die?' she continued remorselessly.

Webster's little, darting eyes became more agitated. He wetted his thick lips, obviously frightened that the King saw Brandon's death as his responsibility.

'When did he die?' Colum repeated.

'A month ago, on Midsummer's Eve,' the Constable stuttered. 'But it was·not our fault. He was well housed and fed. He died of a fever.'

'Who tended him?' Kathryn asked.

'I did.' The priest spoke up. He smiled thinly at Kathryn. 'He had a fever. There was little we could do. He died just before dusk on Midsummer's Eve. He was placed in a coffin and lies buried in the small graveyard behind the castle outhouses.'

'Did he say,' Kathryn continued, 'anything about a pendant or a sapphire called the Eye of God?'

All looked confused and shook their heads.

'How was he captured?' Colum asked.

'On the road north of Canterbury,' Fletcher squeaked, straining his scrawny neck so his Adam's apple bobbed like a cork on water. 'I captured him. We had heard of the King's victory at Barnet. His clerks had already sent out warrants ordering us to arrest Nicholas Faunte and other malcontents. I took some mounted men-at-arms and scouted the main road. We found Brandon's horse standing in a field, beside it the squire was sleeping as peacefully as a babe.' Fletcher nodded meaningfully. 'It was obvious he was a rebel. His horse was exhausted, Brandon himself still wore a mail hauberk and he was covered from head to toe in mud and dirt.'

'What date was this?' Kathryn asked.

Fletcher drummed his fingers on the table-top.

'It was a Sunday; yes, Sunday, April twenty-eight.'

Two weeks after Barnet, Kathryn thought. She looked at the assembled men, a motley group with their mixture of disdain and fear. Kathryn reflected on what she had learnt: Brandon had been captured on April 28, 1471, and six days later, the last of the Lancastrians had been defeated at Tewkesbury. The kingdom had been plunged into confusion. By the time the Yorkists realised that their search for the Eye of God was futile and began to suspect Brandon, he'd died in a castle cell on June 23.

'And he was brought direct to the castle?' Colum asked.

'Oh, yes,' Webster replied. 'I interrogated him here in this very chamber, he made no pretence at hiding who he was. Rather proud that he had been the personal squire of Richard Neville, the dead Earl of Warwick. So I clapped him in a dungeon and wrote to the Chancellor in London. However, the civil war was continuing, what with Queen Margaret's landing in the West Country, the bloody fight at Tewkesbury Field and the general lawlessness, so no reply was heard until about two weeks ago. Richard, Duke of Gloucester, sent one of his squires to interrogate Brandon, but by then the fellow was dead.'

'How was Brandon in himself?' Kathryn asked.

'I was his gaoler,' Gabele said gruffly, ignoring Kathryn but staring at his old comrade Murtagh. 'We moved him from the castle pit, that's the lowest dungeon, and into a more comfortable cell just beneath the keep. He was a soldier, fairly cheerful, talkative but said nothing amiss. He seemed rather relieved that the war was ended. He was sad at the Earl's death but hopeful that the King, in his fresh batch of pardons, would order his release.'

'In the six weeks he was here, did Brandon ever talk about the Eye of God?' Kathryn asked.

Gabele shook his head. 'What is this diamond?'

'It belonged to his dead master, the Earl of Warwick.'

'No. No.' Gabele straightened up on his stool. 'But he did talk of Warwick, especially his death.'

'Repeat what he said,' Colum ordered.

'Well, he described the last moments at Barnet. How the battle line buckled. The confusion over Oxford's arrival and Warwick's men fleeing into the darkness. He said he went back to the horse lines. He took the Earl's horse and shouted at him to come. But Warwick was weighted down by his armour, the field was muddy and York's soldiers were beginning to appear. Warwick told them to flee. He ordered him to do so and Brandon obeyed. He rode off into the darkness, the howls of triumph from the enemy soldiers ringing in his ears. He realised his master had been killed. Brandon still felt ashamed, but what was there he could have done?'

Colum nodded sympathetically.

'What else?' Kathryn asked sharply, resentful at the knowing looks passed between Colum and Gabele.

'What do you mean?' Gabele shifted his hands slightly.

'Well,' Kathryn began, then leaned her hands on the table. She momentarily wondered if Thomasina was scrubbing the medicine table at the house in Ottemelle Lane. Kathryn expected a long troop of patients the following morning. She rubbed her eyes. She felt tired and silently vowed she would write down everything she learnt at this meeting.

'What I mean,' she continued, 'is that Brandon fled from Barnet Field early in the hours of Sunday, the fourteenth of April. He was captured two weeks later. Didn't he say where he had been and what he had done?'

'Oh, yes,' Webster replied. 'Brandon had been fearful of looters and the usual depredations which take place after every battle. Master Murtagh, you are a soldier. You know what happens. Some take prisoners, others think it's easier to slit a man's throat.'

'What had Brandon been doing?' Kathryn interrupted coldly.

'He had been hiding out in the countryside, buying food

from the occasional farm, trying to conceal himself from the King's soldiers.'

'Did you ask him why he was coming to Canterbury?'

Webster blinked. He glanced pointedly at this rather cold, formidable young woman who refused to be deflected from her questions.

The Constable looked at Colum, who nodded imperceptibly. Kathryn caught the glance.

'Please answer my question,' she insisted.

'I asked him that,' Webster replied tactfully. 'To put it bluntly, Mistress Swinbrooke, Brandon said he was tired, cold and hungry. He intended to reach Canterbury and take sanctuary at Christchurch Priory.'

Colum was about to take over the questioning but Kathryn put her hand on his arm.

'Sir William, when Brandon was arrested and brought here, you knew he was a fugitive from the battle.'

Webster nodded.

'And you must have interrogated him at length. Did you keep a record?'

'Yes, yes, we did,' Fitz-Steven the clerk interrupted, now slightly over-awed by Kathryn and eager to please.

'Sir William, shall I fetch it?'

Webster agreed and they all sat in silence until Fitz-Steven breathlessly reappeared, a piece of parchment in one hand, a candle in the other. The clerk sat down on his stool.

' "Robert Brandon," ' he began to read, ' "Fugitive from the battle of Barnet, squire to the late dead traitor called Richard Neville, Earl of Warwick, captured by Fletcher, deputy constable, in the Potter's Field just north of Canterbury. He had little on his person except a belt, dagger, wallet and a slightly dented sword." ' Fitz-Steven drew in his breath. ' "He made a full confession of his treason and threw himself upon the mercy of the King." ' Fitz-Steven raised his head, his finger running along the small, cramped writing. ' "Since Barnet, Brandon had separated from his companions and had been hiding in the countryside north of the city. He had decided not to visit the place of his birth where he had kith and kin, the parish of Saint James the Less at Maidstone." ' Fitz-Steven tossed the parchment down on the table and shrugged. 'That is all, Mistress.'

'So he said nothing about his companions?' Colum asked.

Webster shook his head. 'No, Brandon claimed that after the battle, everyone made their own escape, though Reginald Moresby, captain of Warwick's bodyguard, did try and impose some order.'

'He's dead,' Kathryn intervened. 'Moresby's corpse was found, badly disfigured, in a ditch outside Rochester.'

Webster shrugged. 'What does it matter? Brandon would keep quiet about his friends. Apart from him and Moresby, the rest of Warwick's retinue probably reached a port and crossed to foreign parts.'

'Did Brandon form any special friendships during his six weeks' captivity?'

'Not really.' Gabele shook his head. 'My daughter Margotta visited him a few times. I spoke to him about the war but nothing untoward. There was another prisoner in the next cell and there's a small gap in the dividing wall. I suspect Brandon and he often whispered together.'

'Who was this?' Colum asked.

'A murderer, Nicholas Sparrow,' Webster replied. 'He'd been involved in a brawl in a tavern in Westgate and stabbed a man in the throat. We were holding him here for the next Assize.'

'And where is Sparrow now?'

Webster's head drooped. The rest of his household looked equally discomfited.

'Well?' Colum repeated. 'The murderer, Nicholas Sparrow, where is he?'

'He escaped,' Webster rasped. 'For God's sake, Master Murtagh, it was easy. Both he and Brandon, as is the custom, were allowed an hour on the green in front of the keep.' Webster chewed his lip. 'Now we have few soldiers here. Some joined Faunte, others went south to meet the King whilst, after the war, the remaining garrison were used to patrol the roads and river crossings. For God's sake, that was how we caught Brandon in the first place!'

Kathryn remembered the castle as she had entered it. The great forbidding keep of flint and mortar, the darkening, rain-sogged green and, beyond that, the archways and high walls of the inner and outer baileys.

'How on earth did he escape?' she asked. 'Surely he may have known something about Brandon?'

'All we know,' Gabele replied defiantly, 'is that Brandon went out for his hour of fresh air, then he was taken back. Sparrow followed. It was early in the evening. The sun was beginning to set. Sparrow was alone on the green, but we thought there was no danger, because he was chained and manacled at both wrist and ankle. Somehow or other he inveigled the turnkey to let him go over to a wall to relieve himself, there's a small recess there. Sparrow apparently wrapped the chain round the turnkey's neck, took the keys, released his manacles, changed clothes with the dead man and walked through the castle gates into Winchepe.'

'Some time elapsed,' Webster continued the sorry tale, 'before it was released that Sparrow was missing. Everyone thought he had been taken back to his cell. Only when food and drink were brought was the mistake discovered.' Webster sighed wearily. 'A report has been drafted to the Sheriff. Proclamations were issued for Sparrow's arrest but now he could be in Wales, Scotland, or even across the Narrow Seas.'

Kathryn glanced at Colum. She wondered if he shared her suspicions. Had Sparrow managed to wriggle into Brandon's confidence? Had he escaped after making some pact about the Eye of God?

'How long after this did Brandon fall ill?'

'Oh, about five days,' Peter the chaplain said. 'At first I thought it was nothing serious, but then the fever became hot, disturbing the humours of the body. I tried what remedies I knew, but he died. I gave him the last rites. The body was anointed. I sang a Mass in the castle chapel and poor Brandon was buried with the rest of the forgotten prisoners in the old graveyard.'

'And there's been no sign of Sparrow?' Colum asked abruptly.

Webster shook his head. 'None whatsoever.'

Somewhere high on the castle walls, a sentry called to a comrade; a bell began to toll, the sign for the garrison to assemble for evening prayer before supper in the hall. The men round the table grew restless. Webster pointedly looked at the flame of the hour-candle edging its way down to the next red hour ring.

'If there are no more questions?' he murmured.

'Are you certain,' Colum asked, getting to his feet, 'of your allegiance to the King? Are you all sure that Brandon made no mention to the pendant or the Eye of God?'

All brusquely agreed. Colum stretched and glanced at Webster.

'And Brandon said nothing else?'

The Constable shook his head, but Kathryn wondered why Webster still looked so nervous and agitated.

'And, Father—' Colum stared at the priest. 'You anointed him and placed the lid over the coffin?'

'Yes, I have said.'

'Tell me, Father,' Kathryn spoke up. 'I know you can't break the seal of confession, but you must have shriven Brandon?'

The priest nodded his head in agreement.

'So,' Kathryn continued, 'he may have made some reference, when talking to you, about the whereabouts of the pendant?'

The priest just stared fixedly back. Kathryn realised he would not even discuss the matter.

'Very well,' she changed tack. 'Who nursed him?'

'My daughter,' Gabele snapped. 'Sometimes Father Peter did. Why do you ask?'

'Well . . .' Kathryn's eyes rounded in mock innocence. 'Master Gabele, you are a soldier, well acquainted with camp fever. Such men often babble in their delirium.'

'Brandon didn't,' Gabele retorted. 'And it wasn't that sort of fever. He just grew listless, hot and clammy.' Gabele turned to the Constable. 'Sir William, we have other matters to attend to. Master Murtagh, are there any more questions?'

'No, but perhaps we can visit the cells where Brandon and Sparrow were kept. Oh, and the prisoner's belongings?'

'Kept in a sealed bag in the castle store-room.'

'We'll see them,' Colum demanded. 'Who else was in the castle when all this happened?'

The Constable shrugged. 'Just the small garrison, servants, scullions.'

'No, I mean, did anyone else approach the prisoner?'

'As I have said,' Gabele answered, 'my daughter, Margotta. Oh, yes, and the Righteous Man.'

'The Righteous Man?' Colum queried.

'Well, he calls himself that. He's a pardoner with a host of relics and indulgences from all over Christendom. A strange character.'

'I gave him lodgings,' Webster interrupted. 'He said the inns and taverns in Canterbury were too expensive.' Webster waved his fingers in the air. 'God knows, there's enough room here.'

Kathryn could only agree. Canterbury was like a magnet to relic-sellers, religious quacks, counterfeit-men, all the human fleas who battened on people's superstitions. In summer every hostelry in Canterbury was packed with pilgrims; the Constable, like private householders, would always be prepared to sell the space of a bed.

'We should see him,' Kathryn insisted. 'Indeed, anyone who spoke to the prisoner.'

The Constable agreed and the meeting broke up. Colum and Kathryn watched the different members of the household leave the room. Most of them were grumbling, throwing dark glances, especially at Kathryn, insulted at being interrogated by a woman. Fletcher, Fitz-Steven, Webster and Gabele gathered at the door, talking in murmurs.

'You are a hard woman.' Colum spoke out of the corner of his mouth. 'Your questions were most insistent.'

'I'm a busy woman!' Kathryn snapped. 'Why can't people answer a question put to them?'

Colum leaned across and stared into her face.

'What do you think?' he asked.

'Someone's lying. Three things strike me as wrong. First, Brandon's death: he was a sturdy young man in a comfortable cell. Why did he succumb to gaol fever with such strange symptoms? Most cases suffer high fever and become delirious.'

'And secondly?' Colum asked.

'I find it strange that Brandon made no mention of the Eye of God. Finally, Sparrow's escape. The fellow was well named,' Kathryn wryly concluded. 'He literally flew over the castle walls!'

Colum tapped his fingers on his dagger hilt.

'Such escapes are common,' he replied. 'There's even a bill before the next Parliament listing the complaints from the worthy burgesses about how prisoners can walk from gaols or clinks with effortless ease. As for the gaol fever . . .'

Colum was about to continue when Gabele came over. He totally ignored Kathryn as he clasped Murtagh's hand.

'It was good to meet again, Irishman. I'm pleased fortune has favoured you.' Gabele turned and smiled dazzlingly at Kathryn. 'Mistress Swinbrooke, I apologise for my sharp retorts, but as this bog-trotter here will explain, my manners are more of the camp than the court.'

Kathryn, surprised, accepted the rather nicely turned apology.

'I had not intended to be so insistent,' she stammered.

Gabele held a hand up. 'Enough. Come, I'll show you what you want to see.'

He led them out of the chamber and onto the bottom floor of the keep. He unlocked an iron-studded door and, taking a pitch torch from the wall, led them down to the cells. There were six in all, three on either side of the dank, dimly lit passageway. The one Gabele opened was large and airy, with a grille high in the wall to allow in some light and fresh air. The walls were lime-washed and the room had a table, a battered stool and a simple crucifix on the wall. The rushes on the floor were surprisingly clean. Gabele pointed to the metal holders for candles as well as the oil-lamp on the table.

'This is where Brandon was kept,' he explained.

Then the master-at-arms lay on the bed, drew his dagger, chipped away at the wall and loosened a brick.

'Apparently the same can be done in the other cell.'

'Was that Sparrow's work or Brandon's?' Colum asked.

Gabele shook his head. 'Oh, no, some long-forgotten prisoner.' He slid the brick back and got to his feet. 'We should hire a mason to have it put right.' He grinned. 'But, there again, the Constable's a kind man. Very few people escape from Canterbury Castle and it's a mercy for the prisoners to talk to one another.'

'Who is allowed down here?' Kathryn asked.

'Well, myself, indeed, and any of those you met in the chamber above. Mistress Swinbrooke, we are not cruel men. Father Peter would come down to give the sacraments, Webster and Fletcher to see that all was well. Margotta would bring food or just talk to them. Of course, when there are prisoners here, a soldier always stands guard in the passageway.'

He led them out back upstairs and into the large sombre hall of the castle. At the far end the Constable and his household were eating supper. A fire had been lit but the chimney-stack was poor because some of the smoke came back, mingling with the smell of freshly baked bread and cooked fish. Fitz-Steven the clerk rose and came down the hall. He held a leather bag, sealed at the top with a piece of string and a blob of wax. Resentful at being disturbed at his meal, he thrust the sack at Gabele.

'Brandon's belongings! Itemized and sealed, now the property of the Crown, whatever value it may find in them.'

And, spinning on his heel, Fitz-Steven stamped back to the high table.

Gabele winked at Kathryn, Colum drew his dagger, cut the cord at the neck of the sack and sifted the pathetic belongings out onto the bench. A pair of hose, a boiled leather jacket, a very soiled linen shirt, a war-belt with purses and sheaths for dagger and sword. Gabele tapped one of these.

'They were good quality. We now have them in the armoury.'

In the wallet were some coins, a set of dice and a piece of rolled-up parchment. Colum handed this to Kathryn, who went under the torchlight and opened it.

'It's nothing,' Gabele called out. 'Just a prayer.'

'Levate oculos ad montes. "Raise your eyes to the hills," ' Kathryn translated.

'What's that?' Colum asked.

'Raise your eyes to the hills,' Kathryn repeated, 'From where my Saviour cometh. It's from one of the psalms. Apparently a favourite prayer with prisoners.'

Kathryn paused, remembering the flickering lights in Brandon's cell and Gabele removing the brick from the wall.

'Brandon had scrawled the same words in his cell,' Kathryn murmured.

'Yes, just above the bed,' the master-at-arms replied. 'Don't forget, Mistress, Brandon hoped for a pardon and a quick release. Every soldier has a favourite prayer.' He grinned at Colum. 'Do you remember yours, Irishman?'

Colum, who was sifting amongst the dead man's possessions, now looked sheepish.

'What was it?' Kathryn, intrigued, came over.

'Why not tell her, Irishman?' Gabele teased.

Murtagh threw down the sword-belt, looked at Kathryn and closed his eyes.

'Oh, God, treat me today as I would treat you if I were God and you were Murtagh.'

Kathryn smiled and clapped her hands. 'I never knew you were a theologian, Colum.'

Any further banter ended as the group on the dais at the far end of the hall finished their meal. Webster came down accompanied by two others. The first, a raven-haired woman, dressed in a brown smock with a white collar and cuff-bands, walked purposefully towards Kathryn and Colum. She was small and fresh-faced, with large dark eyes and a smiling mouth. As Webster mumbled his excuses and left, she kissed Gabele on the cheek, then, crowing with delight, seized Colum's hand.

'Irishman, you have come back to marry me!'

Colum laughed with embarrassment. He seized the woman by the shoulder and kissed her lightly on each cheek.

'Margotta, you are as pretty as ever.' He turned and made the introductions. 'Mistress Kathryn Swinbrooke, Margotta Gabele, a veritable minx.'

Kathryn smiled in acknowledgement, quietly cursing her small pang of jealousy. She was relieved by the distraction caused by Margotta's companion, one of the most garish individuals Kathryn had ever met. A tall, well-built man, he had a smooth, youngish face framed by hair dyed a dirty yellow, which hung down to his shoulders. He was dressed quite fantastically in battered black leather from head to toe. He carried no sword or dagger but a huge belt with little pouches on, whilst round his neck was a thick string with what looked like fragments of animal bone. As he stepped forward into the light, he pushed his hair back like a woman and Kathryn glimpsed his cheap ear-rings glittering in the light. He stretched out one black gloved hand towards the ceiling.

'I am the Lord's servant,' he announced in a hollow, sepulchral voice. 'The Righteous Man!'

For once in her life Kathryn saw Colum totally surprised. He just stared at this man with his dyed hair, black-garbed like a crow.

'Master Murtagh, Mistress Swinbrooke, may I introduce the Righteous Man,' Gabele declared stoically. 'A pilgrim from Avignon, Rome, Jerusalem, Compostella.'

'Aye,' the Righteous Man interrupted. 'And more! I have seen the Great Cham of Tatary! The Golden Hordes of Kublai Khan and the icy pastures of the Indus Kush!'

Kathryn bit her lip in an effort not to laugh, for the pardoner had all the tricks of his trade. His strange garb, the ear-catching voice and the exotic tales. Yet, of all such rogues, the Righteous Man seemed the most skilled. He sketched a blessing in the air before her and then clasped Colum's unresisting hand.

'Brother in Christ,' he intoned. 'We are well met. You wish to have words with me? About the man Brandon, a prisoner in Christ, whose soul is now before God. Let us pray he suffers the fires of Purgatory rather than those of Hell. For, as the Good Book says, "It is indeed a terrible thing for any mortal soul to fall into the hands of the living God." '

Kathryn stole a look at Margotta. She was now staring at the floor, shoulders shaking with laughter, whether at Colum's look of surprised bemusement or the Righteous Man's antics, Kathryn did not know.

'Quite so. Quite so.' Colum recovered his poise and pointed to the bench, pushing aside Brandon's possessions.

'Do sit down.'

The pardoner held a hand up. 'No, sir, I always stand when I have speech with a brother. As the Good Book says, "The just man stands upright, his face ever turned towards the Lord." '

'What is your real name?' Colum snapped, getting tired of the man's antics.

'What's in a name?' the pardoner replied. He pointed to the rushes on the floor. 'Grass is still grass whatever you call it. And we are like the grasses of the field, here today, gone tomorrow. I have no name, I have no past. I just stand in righteousness before the Lord.'

Colum kicked at the rushes. 'I am the King's Commissioner in Canterbury,' he whispered menacingly. 'You, sir, are a subject of the King. You are present in this castle. You spoke to the King's prisoner, Brandon. I have every right to ask you who you are and whence you came.'

The pardoner's head went back like that of an angry bird and he peered at Colum.

'My name is the Righteous Man,' he repeated. However, seeing the Irishman's growing annoyance, he unclasped his wallet, plucked out a handful of greasy parchments and thrust them at Murtagh.

'These are letters, licenses of passage.'

Colum handed them to Kathryn, who studied them quickly.

'He's right,' she declared. 'These are signed by port bailiffs, town reeves, sheriffs, declaring the person who calls himself the Righteous Man to be a pardoner with full licence to go about his business. Some of them are sealed, so they can't be forgeries.'

She handed them back to the pardoner, who smiled his thanks.

'So, what are you doing in Canterbury?' Colum asked.

The pardoner tapped his wallet. 'I have indulgences and bulls from Rome. Letters of absolution as well as relics, verified by all of those holy men and women who have shown us the path of righteousness.' He pointed to the small white bones hanging round his neck. 'You can have, sir, at a reasonable price, the knuckle-bone of one of the seven thousand virgins of Cologne. And here, sir'—he pointed to another—'is part of the skull of the good thief, the rib of the blessed Samaritan!'

'Shut up!' Colum roared.

Kathryn looked warningly at the pardoner. The fellow gulped and smiled thinly at this irascible Irishman.

'I asked you a question!' Colum repeated.

'Then I will answer. I am in Canterbury to do business amongst the pilgrims. You can check, and you very well might, sir, but I have presented my letters at the Guildhall and at the cathedral. I also sought a bed and clean lodgings at the Chequers, the Tabard, the Sun in Splendour, and even the Poor

Priests' Hospital. However, like the good Lord, I found no room at the inn. So I came to the castle and, for a price, I have a clean bed, breakfast in the hall, and the last meal of the day.'

'Good,' Colum breathed. 'Now, Master Brandon?'

The pardoner spread his hands dramatically. 'Sir, he was a prisoner. I wondered if he was interested in one of my relics or, if matters grew worse, in a papal bull or letter of indulgence.'

'And was he?'

'Oh, no, sir. He had his heart set on freedom.'

'How many times did you meet him?'

'Just once, sir.'

'And Sparrow, the other prisoner?'

'Oh, a veritable limb of Satan. Brandon was courteous but his companion was a fiend from hell. He cast me from his cell and mocked me as a rogue.'

The look of outraged innocence on the pardoner's face was too much for Colum. He turned to Margotta, who was still trying to stifle her laughter.

'And you, Margotta?' he asked.

The girl smiled prettily whilst her eyes flirted with Colum.

'Well, Brandon was handsome, he was kind, he was courteous.'

'Yes, yes,' Colum said testily. 'And what else?'

'He was also lonely, rather pathetic. He talked of his early days at Maidstone and the death of Warwick.'

'Did he talk of anything else?'

'Such as?'

'A golden pendant with a beautiful sapphire called the Eye of God?'

'For Lord's sake, Colum, no. What would a poor squire have to do with that?'

Kathryn saw the gleam of profit in the pardoner's eyes.

'A golden pendant and a beautiful sapphire,' the Righteous Man muttered. 'Did Brandon have something like that?'

'He may have,' Kathryn answered.

The pardoner whistled softly under his breath. 'Now I see your interest.' He smiled.

'Mistress Gabele,' Kathryn continued, 'did you speak to Sparrow?'

'Of course not! He was a caitiff and a knave!'

Colum sighed. 'Well, in which case thank you for coming.'

Margotta smiled at him and kissed him gently on the cheek. 'It's good to see you again, Colum,' she whispered.

Then both she and the pardoner sauntered away.

Kathryn waited until they were out of earshot.

'Quite the troubadour, Irishman. What is it, a girl in every town?'

Colum winked at her. 'Aye, and in every camp. I fought with Gabele from the Welsh march to the Scottish border. Margotta has always been a minx.' He looked away, troubled. 'She has an ability to make men talk, yet it's strange that she nor anyone else in this castle heard Brandon mention the Eye of God.'

'What happens if Moresby, not Brandon, had the sapphire?' Kathryn asked. 'Perhaps the outlaws who killed him still have it.'

Colum kicked moodily at the rushes. 'No, Warwick would have given it to a body squire.' He glanced at Kathryn. 'I served as marshal of the royal household with the spurious honour of questioning many a thief. An outlaw would try and sell that immediately, before another took it from him.' Colum bit the quick of his thumb. 'I wonder how Moresby did die?' he murmured. 'Was it outlaws or someone else? I suspect only Brandon could answer that. But come, we are, for the moment, finished here.'

He and Kathryn collected their cloaks, made their farewells and walked through the inner and outer baileys and out, by a postern gate, into Winchepe. They hurried along the darkening alley-ways and up into Wistraet. At the small gate which guarded that street, a man slipped out of the shadows. Colum's hand fell to his sword.

'Peace, Master!'

Holbech, Colum's burly lieutenant from Kingsmead, stepped into the poor light from the sconce torch fixed above the gate.

The burly northerner bowed at Kathryn. 'Mistress, good evening. I have been to your house in Ottemelle Lane. Thomasina gave me the rough edge of her tongue and said you and Murtagh were at the castle, so I waited here.'

'What is the matter?' Colum asked.

'A messenger, Master, from His Grace the Duke of Gloucester. Your friend, John Tuam, a Dominican at Blackfriars, was mysteriously stabbed to death. The Prince's messenger said you would know what this would mean.'

'Oh, my God!' Colum breathed.

He walked a little farther on and leaned against the wall of the alehouse. He stared at the slivers of light coming through the narrow windows, half-listening to the sounds of drunken revelry.

'Poor John!' he whispered. He remembered a wild boy running along the green side of a hill, shouting and leaping like a young deer. Colum stared down the darkened alley-way. 'Gone!' he whispered. 'Oh, Christ, have mercy on his soul!'

Kathryn came up beside him.

'They are here, aren't they?' she asked and felt a surge of fear, for despite his abrupt ways and hot temper, she had grown close to this enigmatic Irishman, with his changeable moods and sardonic smile.

'Colum, you are in danger!'

He took her hand and pressed it gently.

'I have always been in danger, Kathryn, but yes, the dogs are closer now!'

Kathryn withdrew her hand and walked a little farther on.

'Woman!' Colum called softly. 'You're not afeared for me, not you, Kathryn Swinbrooke?'

'I'm not your woman, Colum,' Kathryn replied, not daring to turn and show her face. 'No matter what you told your masters in London.'

'Then what are you?'

Kathryn let that question hang for a while, as she had ever since she'd met this Irishman.

'What are you then?' Colum repeated insistently. 'Am I like Wuf, an orphan taken into your care?'

Kathryn grinned over her shoulder. 'I'm now Wuf's mother,' she teased. 'But to you, Irishman? For the moment be satisfied I'm your guardian angel!'

Chapter 4

*Y*ou will let me in! You have no right to obstruct me!'

Kathryn Swinbrooke stood in Jewry Lane in the parish of Saint Mary Redman, spots of fury high on her cheeks. She glared at the two corpse-collectors who stood truculently in front of the door of the small house on which the red plague cross was garishly daubed. The corpse-collectors, brothers with the ugly, pitted faces of bull mastiffs, stood just as obstinately, thumbs tucked in their belts, and shook their heads.

'You know the rules, Mistress.' One of them spoke up. 'Once plague strikes a house, all doors and windows are to be locked and the red cross painted on the door. The inmates are not allowed to leave and no one is permitted to enter.'

Kathryn advanced threateningly on them.

'I am a physician,' she insisted. 'In that house live sisters, two old ladies, Mistress Maude and Mistress Eleanor Venables. True, their servant may have died of the plague and she has been buried, but the two ladies are hale and hearty. I demand the right to speak to them!'

'We have been appointed by the parish,' the uglier of the two said pompously, 'to enforce civic regulations. The old ladies will die and their corpses will be removed to the burial pits outside the city walls.' He unhooked his thumb from his belt.

Thomasina and the young boy, Wuf, standing behind Kathryn, moved together. Wuf sped forward and kicked the man heartily in the shins. The fellow screeched in pain. His brother tried to seize Wuf but the young boy hid behind Kathryn's skirts. Thomasina advanced on both of them like a man-of-war, her great cloak billowing, and brandished Kathryn's baskets of ointments and unguents as she would a battle-axe.

'You filthy, thieving poltroons!' she roared, her broad face becoming even redder, her small dark eyes ablaze with fury. 'Don't you touch my mistress!'

The corpse-collectors moved back behind the shelter of their grease-stained handcart.

'She's a personal friend of Richard, Duke of Gloucester. A physician in the service of the city of Canterbury and,' Thomasina added, 'the good friend of the King's own commissioner, Lord Colum Murtagh.'

Kathryn bit her lip to hide her smile at Thomasina's swift elevation of the Irishman. Thomasina glared at the small crowd assembling in the narrow street.

'Are you,' she roared, 'going to allow two caitiffs to stop an act of mercy?'

Thomasina took one step forward, jabbing her finger at the corpse-collectors.

'You're bloody thieves!' she bellowed. 'I know what you are up to. You remove the dead and anything valuable in the house. These two old ladies have fair good stock and you know that.'

Her words were greeted with a murmur of approval from the small crowd.

'Yes, but you could spread the plague!' one of the corpse-collectors countered and his words won even greater approval from the bystanders.

Kathryn looked up as a small shutter was opened, then quickly shut. She looked in desperation at the red cross daubed on the door. If she lost this argument and walked away, Maude and Eleanor would think she had deserted them. They might not die of the plague, but they would weaken from hunger and sheer desperation.

'I am going into that house!' she declared.

One of the corpse-collectors moved to block her way.

'That's enough! That's enough!'

A small, bald-headed, cheery-faced man walked out of the crowd towards the two corpse-collectors. He was dressed in a long green coat lined with squirrel fur. His portly face, puffed-out chest and slight waddle gave him all the dignity of an outraged sparrow. However, Simon Luberon, clerk to His Grace the Archbishop of Canterbury, and a member of the city council, knew his rights. He turned and winked quickly at Kathryn.

'Who are you, you little bugger?' one of the rogues snarled.

Simon Luberon soon put the man right. The corpse-collector, a hang-dog expression on his face, muttered an apology.

'I am a city official,' Luberon proclaimed for all to hear. 'And you, sir, could lose your post because of such contumacious language!'

'We are only doing our duty,' the other one muttered.

Luberon, who carefully avoided Kathryn's eyes, glared in outrage.

'Your duty! I ask you solemnly, sir.' Luberon raised one quivering finger. 'Does anyone in this house suffer from the plague?'

'Someone did.'

'That wasn't my question,' Luberon remonstrated. 'According to City Regulation Number 738, as well as the Codex Medicus, not to mention Clause 4 of the Act of Parliament passed in the third year of the reign of good King Henry the Fourth, a house where someone has died of the plague is to be cordoned off. However, healthy people remaining inside may have the services of a physician.'

The two corpse-collectors, now completely dumbfounded

by Luberon's profuse, if very inaccurate quotation of the law, decided to call it a day. They walked off with their handcart grumbling that the old bitches would soon be dead anyway.

The crowd dispersed. Kathryn took the little man's hand and stared into his light-blue, childlike eyes.

'Simon, you were magnificent,' she whispered.

The little man squirmed with embarrassment.

'It was nothing.' He stared up at her. 'I met Master Murtagh on his way to Kingsmead this morning. He said that you have been to London and are now back in Canterbury on the King's business.'

Kathryn nodded. Luberon looked expectantly at her.

'If there is anything you can do to help, Simon, be sure we will ask you.'

Luberon smiled.

'More importantly,' Kathryn continued, 'my application for a licence to trade as a spicer?'

Luberon spread his hands. 'You know, Mistress, in these present troubles the King has suspended the city council, so the Guild of Spicers has not met. There are some who will oppose your application.'

'Why? Because I'm a woman?'

'No, Kathryn, because you are successful.' Luberon grinned. 'If you weren't, they would be only too willing to see you make a fool of yourself.' He patted her reassuringly on the wrist. 'I will do what I can. Have you heard the news?'

Kathryn shook her head.

Rawnose the beggar had tried to catch her attention as she left Ottemelle Lane but she had swept by before the garrulous man could delay her any further. Luberon looked around dramatically.

'The rebel Faunte has been seen again, lurking on the outskirts of Blean Wood. They say he is not alone.'

Kathryn bit her lip. She'd confided in Luberon about her husband, Alexander. The industrious little clerk had promised to do all he could in discovering any information. They both knew there was a rare chance that Alexander might be with the fugitive mayor and other traitors hiding in the forests to the north of Canterbury. Again Luberon patted her on the wrist, said he would keep her informed, and hurried on.

'What that man doesn't know isn't worth knowing,' Thomasina murmured.

'He means well,' Kathryn replied, rapping on the door daubed with the red cross.

She stared down at the angelic-faced Wuf, patting him gently on his blond cropped head.

'Wuf, you were very brave, but kicking the corpse-collector could have been dangerous.'

The orphan's grin just widened as he gazed in admiration at this taciturn but kindly woman who had provided him with a home, hearth and bed.

'Promise me you won't do it again,' Kathryn admonished.

The boy solemnly promised and, when Kathryn turned to knock again, stuck his tongue out at a glaring Thomasina.

Another fracas could have occurred but the door opened. Two old ladies stood huddled together, their lined old faces and tired eyes full of anxiety.

'Oh, we heard you, Mistress,' Eleanor said. 'They are dreadful men.'

'Have no fear,' Kathryn replied, walking into the house. 'All will be well.'

The two sisters led Kathryn and her companions into the small solar. Kathryn looked around approvingly. The rushes on the floor were clean and fresh. The walls had been scrubbed with a mixture of water and lime whilst the fire in the hearth provided warmth without making the room swelter.

'We have done everything you said,' Maude said. 'We have seen no rats. We kill the flies, not that there's many left now. We pour our refuse away and drink only fresh water from the well, though the butt needs refilling.'

'Thomasina will see to that,' Kathryn assured her. 'We'll

come back later today. More importantly, you are only eating soft, fresh bread?'

The two old ladies nodded solemnly.

Kathryn sent Thomasina to check the scullery, kitchen and garderobes whilst she sat the two women down. Wuf stood beside her, owl-eyed, sucking his thumb, staring curiously at these aged ones. Kathryn had explained to him and Thomasina again and again how this house posed no danger; Kathryn now repeated this for the benefit of the two old ladies.

'You see,' she began, 'your servant, Miriam, may not have died of the plague. In many ways the plague has the same symptoms as what my father taught me was pellagra.'

'You mean Saint Anthony's disease?' Maude stammered.

'That's right,' Kathryn said. 'As in the plague, the skin reddens, dries and cracks. Sometimes there are pustules, boils and tumours, a high fever, blood in the urine, and the stools are either infected or there is diarrhoea.'

'Miriam had all of those,' Maude confirmed.

'And we had something similar,' Eleanor added. 'But now it's gone.'

'Yes,' Kathryn replied soothingly. 'You must be very careful about what bread you eat or anything made from corn or maize. Rye bread in particular. If you eat any food where the maize or rye is infected, these symptoms will re-occur. It is important, therefore, that you eat good bread and flush these evil humours from the body with fresh spring water. You will recover. You must keep your hands and nails clean and the same for this room. Change the rushes every two days.'

The two old women nodded.

'Burn the old.'

'Oh, we do that,' Eleanor spoke up. 'We have fresh sheaves of rushes in the garden.'

'And the medicine, Mistress?' Maude asked.

'Yes, yes.' Kathryn lifted the basket Thomasina had carried and brought out four fresh loaves, a linen cloth with strips of dried meat, a small flask of wine and a small jar of herbal drink she had prepared. Kathryn pointed to the latter. 'Take one spoonful, each of you, every evening before you retire.'

'Why? Will it make us strong?'

'Of course,' Kathryn said, not adding that the potion also contained a slight opiate to calm their nervous agitation.

Thomasina returned, declaring the water butt was now fine and all was well in the kitchen and scullery. Kathryn reassured the old ladies once more, took the few coins they offered and walked back into Jewry Lane. Only at the corner did she stop and stamp her foot.

'In God's name!' she muttered to Thomasina. 'If anyone has a fever, pustules, or the bloody flux, everyone shouts plague! I often think that as many people die of fright of the pestilence as by its infection.'

'Why the water?' Wuf asked, jumping from foot to foot. 'What's so special about that, Mistress Kathryn?"

Kathryn tapped him on the cheek with one finger.

'God be my witness, lad, I don't really know, but a very famous doctor from Salerno . . .'

'Where's that?'

'In Italy. And, before you ask, Wuf, Italy is near the Middle Sea, half-way to Jerusalem.'

The boy's mouth opened again. Kathryn pressed her finger gently against his lips.

'This doctor,' she continued, 'discovered how stale or brackish water spread infection. He wrote a famous treatise and my father studied it. Now, when we came to Canterbury, my father, God rest him, noticed how the monks of Christchurch Priory suffered from very little illness. He put it down to two things.'

'Diet and water,' Thomasina interrupted triumphantly.

'Yes,' Kathryn continued. 'The monks eat fresh meat, fresh fruit, and their water is brought in by elm-wood pipes from untainted springs and wells.'

'Priests always live longer,' Wuf said. 'When I followed the camp, the soldiers were always saying that if they had their lives to live again, they would be priests and so live longer.'

Kathryn grinned. 'Perhaps they are right but I have noticed the same in some of my patients. Do you remember Mollyns the baker?'

'Yes, he smells.'

'But he rarely suffers from infection. I asked him about his diet. He eats plenty of apples and only drinks water from a spring near his mill.' Kathryn looked over her shoulder down Jewry Lane. 'I just hope those two old ladies will be fine. Those corpse-collectors, they——'

'They are bloody evil!' Thomasina broke in.

'Ah well.'

Kathryn walked out of Jewry Lane past Saint Mary's Hospital for Poor Priests and down towards Ottemelle Lane. On either side of her were narrow winding streets leading up to Burgate or down to the castle. Kathryn walked gingerly, for the ditch or gutter down the centre was now filled with decaying rubbish, which the early-morning rains had flushed out across the cobbles. At the same time she kept a wary eye, for most of the houses on Stour Street were two or three storeys high, and it was still early enough for maids and scullions to throw slops out of the window in the malicious hope of hitting someone. Farther down, the small market was now busy: farmers selling butter, eggs, corn, wool, vegetables or plucked fowls heaped high on their small handcarts. Pedlars moved about with silk ribbons, laces, buttons and buckles on their trays.

Beyond the market were the proper shops: chandlers, tanners, mercers, tailors, glaziers and others. Kathryn stopped to study the beautiful leather gloves displayed on one stall. Wuf wandered off smacking his lips, to watch the apprentices, dressed in canvas and leather jerkins, kneading the dough in the bakers' shops. Kathryn caught him up and bought him a gingerbread man. The boy bit into the sweet pastry and Kathryn was about to walk on when suddenly a group of beggars forced their way through the throng. Their ragged leader, boldly swinging a staff, paced across to the old stone cross and stood on the high step whilst his disciples thronged about him.

He then launched into a passionate appeal about how they had fought for good King Edward but now they were cast out with only the clothes on their backs.

'Oh, the poor man,' Wuf murmured between mouthfuls of gingerbread.

'Nonsense!' Thomasina hissed. 'He's a counterfeit crank.'

'A what?'

'He's a cunning man. A trickster. I wager he's never held a sword in his life.'

Suddenly, one of the counterfeit man's followers, a ragged beggar, sprung to his feet groaning and yelling, before falling to the ground in a writhing fit. A crowd immediately gathered round him. Kathryn saw the counterfeit crank swiftly cut one spectator's purse whilst the rest of his group fanned out to nip a wallet or foist a pocket.

'Stop that!' Kathryn strode towards them.

The counterfeit crank and the others melted away. Kathryn forced her way through the crowd and knelt by the writhing beggar. His arms and legs twitched in a peculiar manner, his eyes rolled in his head and his mouth was covered in a thick white foam.

'He's having a fit!' a bystander shouted.

'He's as healthy as you or I!' Kathryn replied.

She suddenly slapped the beggar on the face. The twitching and moaning stopped, the man's jaw fell open in surprise. Kathryn dug into his mouth. The beggar tried to resist but Kathryn pinched his nostrils as she dragged out a small white object. She held it up for the crowd to see.

'A piece of soap!' she declared. 'The man's a counterfeit and his companions are pickpockets.'

Kathryn threw the soap to the ground. Market bailiffs seized the still surprised beggar whilst the crowd took count of their losses. Kathryn walked on, turning the corner into Ottemelle Lane. She almost bumped into Widow Gumple, the portly arrogant matron who dominated the parish council of Saint Mildred's. During the last few weeks, Gumple had become very deferential towards Kathryn; the widow's white, doughy face quickly creased into a submissive smile.

'I am sorry,' she gasped. 'I am sorry, Mistress.'

'Good morrow, Widow. Are you well?'

'Yes, yes,' the woman whispered; her face became red and flustered, she hitched up the hem of her dress and scurried on by.

Kathryn watched her go.

'In God's name!' she breathed. 'What is wrong with the woman?'

Thomasina hid her smile. She would keep her secret and Widow Gumple would keep her place and not send malicious, anonymous letters about the whereabouts of Alexander Wyville. Kathryn raised her eyebrows, then jumped in surprise as a young man, his blond hair crimped, his fat face sweaty, darted out of a doorway.

'Mistress Swinbrooke, good morning.'

Kathryn glared despairingly at Goldere the clerk. Her would-be suitor looked even more ridiculous in his tight-fitting brown jerkin, stretched yellow hose with stuffed codpiece and long-toed shoes.

'Goldere, are you well?'

The man's watery eyes blinked and his hand went towards his codpiece. 'I have a slight ailment, Mistress. A scratching . . .'

Kathryn sighed in desperation, the same Goldere with the same complaint. She stepped inside and passed on.

'See your physician!' she murmured.

Goldere would have harassed her further, but as he turned to run alongside Kathryn, Thomasina gave him a shove which sent him flying across the lane. Before he could recover his wits, Kathryn, Thomasina and Wuf had disappeared through the door of their house.

The clerk just scratched his head. Suddenly Wuf's face peered round the door and, with one hand extended, made an obscene gesture. He would have repeated it if Kathryn had not seized him by the scruff of the neck and pulled him indoors.

'Stop that!' Kathryn hissed. 'Goldere's more to be pitied than to be reviled.'

Wuf struggled free and fled, crowing with laughter, out into the garden, knocking aside the housemaid Agnes as she came in all a-fluster to say visitors had arrived. Kathryn handed Agnes her cloak and went to stand in the quiet, deserted front room with its huge boarded-up windows. Kathryn looked at the empty counters, the shelves and cupboards raised against the wall. Empty and dusty, she thought, just like her dreams from her early days when she had been courted by Alexander Wyville, a personable apothecary. They had planned to open this as a shop and sell herbs, not only home-grown, but also rare and exotic ones imported from abroad. Kathryn flailed her hands gently against her skirts; within a year it had all turned into a nightmare. Alexander proved to be two men; the sober apothecary and the drunken, violent husband. The rift between them became a chasm which could not be crossed.

'If only . . .' she murmured.

'Mistress.'

Kathryn started. Thomasina stood in the doorway.

'Kathryn,' she repeated. 'Your patients, I've put them in the garden. You have someone special who wishes to see you.'

'Who?'

'The physician Roger Chaddedon.'

Kathryn did not know whether to be pleased or dismayed. She followed Thomasina back to the large, spacious kitchen. Chaddedon rose as she entered, pushing back the chair at the head of the table, his smooth, saturnine face bright with pleasure at seeing Kathryn. She noticed how his black hair was neatly combed and he was wearing a costly blue gown lined with ermine whilst the belt round his waist was of expensive shiny leather.

'Kathryn.' He gripped her by the hands. 'You received my letter?'

'I did,' Kathryn stammered.

Chaddedon shrugged. 'You are embarrassed?'

'I find it strange,' Kathryn declared, half-listening to the conversation from the garden where Wuf was entertaining her patients.

'Oh, for God's sake!' Kathryn continued, annoyed by Chaddedon's look of puzzlement. 'Look at our situation, Roger! You are a member of a collegium, a group of powerful physicians in Queningate. How can I respond to your invitation when I am responsible for sending the father-in-law of one of those physicians to the scaffold as a poisoner?'

'That does not concern me,' Chaddedon stated flatly.

'But it concerns me, Roger. I have my patients, my work. My husband's gone . . .'

'And the Irishman,' Chaddedon added.

'Yes, Roger, there's the Irishman.'

'He lives here?'

'No, he lodges here because the manor at Kingsmead is not fit for human habitation. Roger,' she insisted quietly, 'that is my business.'

The physician's glance fell away. 'You should be careful,' he muttered.

'Don't worry about that,' Thomasina declared, returning to the kitchen from the garden. 'Whilst I am around, Mistress Swinbrooke is safe from the King himself!'

Chaddedon, realising the meeting threatened to turn sour, smiled and picked up a small package resting against the leg of the table. He handed this to Kathryn.

'You said you were interested in this. John Ardene's *Herbarium!*'

Kathryn rested her fingers lightly on it. She knew Chaddedon would be waiting for her to return it.

'Thank you,' she replied lightly. 'I'll study it carefully and make sure it's safely returned.'

Chaddedon picked up his cloak. 'Don't say I have to wait until then to see you again.'

Kathryn just smiled. She accompanied Chaddedon down the passageway to the door, then closed it behind her, embarrassed at their awkward leave-taking.

'He's a good man,' Thomasina called from the kitchen. 'He's a widower, a fine physician.'

'Oh, shut up, Thomasina!' Kathryn muttered and rubbed the side of her face. She liked Chaddedon, but . . .

'But what?' she whispered to the empty passageway.

She thought of the Irishman and realised what was amiss: Chaddedon was safe, secure and established, a member of a powerful fraternity. Colum, however, was different; he frightened her a little but his presence would ensure her life would never be the same again.

'You shouldn't be so ungrateful.' Thomasina appeared at the head of the passageway.

'Thomasina!' Kathryn warned.

'Nothing,' Thomasina replied in a mock sweet-girlish voice. 'I suppose Chaddedon's right, there's always the Irishman.'

Kathryn just swept by her into the kitchen, trying to ignore Wuf's wild screeches from the garden.

'Who's out there?'

'Rawnose with Henry the sack-maker.'

'What's wrong with him?'

'He put a dirty needle straight through his finger.'

'And who else?'

'Edith, Fulke the tanner's daughter,' Thomasina replied. 'Nothing serious. Aches and pains.'

'Then let us prepare bandages, a bowl of hot water, a lighted candle, baskets of salves and herbs.' Kathryn took out the book Chaddedon had brought. 'Who knows, Thomasina, we may even discover something here to silence Rawnose's chatter!'

Chapter 5

*K*athryn dealt quickly with her stream of patients; Henry the sack-maker had a slight gash which she cauterised, then cleaned the wound with wine and smeared a salve made from dried primrose onto it. Fulke the tanner's daughter, Edith, came in clutching her dress, her face white as snow. In alarm she proclaimed her belly was draining blood. Kathryn, fearing some internal injury, examined her carefully. She then fought to keep her face straight—the only problem was that Edith had begun to menstruate. She sat the girl on a stool and carefully told her what this meant: how important it was to wash regularly and, during the menstruation, use linen cloths which Kathryn would provide.

Edith, however, remained dissatisfied.

'I feel pain,' she murmured, her dark eyes full of concern. 'I feel pain in my stomach and back!'

Kathryn gave her a small potion, a flask of rose-water containing crushed angelica.

'This will relieve the pain,' she assured her.

The girl seemed happy and trotted away.

Clem the cobbler came next, complaining of a cough.

'It's worse in the evening,' he moaned.

Kathryn listened to him carefully. She remembered when her father had taken her to the man's dusty workshop.

'What you must do, Clem,' she declared, 'is clean your shop more regularly, allow the air to circulate.'

'Is that all?' he exclaimed.

Kathryn pushed a small pot which Thomasina had prepared towards him.

Immediately the cobbler's face grew longer. 'What's that? How much does it cost?'

'Clem! Clem!' Kathryn shook her finger at him. 'Now, you are a trader and so am I. You are one of the best cobblers in Canterbury. I know, I am wearing a pair of your shoes. All I am going to charge you is two shillings.'

The cobbler's face lightened.

'Skinflint!' Thomasina muttered.

This stung the cobbler. 'Forget the money!' he said airily. 'I will make you a pair of boots, Mistress, a set of buskins and a fine pair of leather sandals for the boy.'

'Agreed.' Kathryn smiled and shook the cobbler's hand.

'What about me?' Thomasina said.

'I haven't got enough leather to go round your ankles,' Clem retorted. He moved quickly to avoid Thomasina's jab, grabbing the jar off the table. 'What is this?'

'A mixture of wood-sage, rue, cumin and pepper. You must boil them together,' Kathryn replied, 'with honey. Every morning and evening fill your horn spoon to the full and take the mixture. In a week you should be better. If not, come back.'

Others followed and finally Rawnose, the most garrulous man in Canterbury; his poor, twisted face, with his cut nose and scar where his ear had been, all agog with the news. Kathryn breathed a prayer for patience.

'Well, Rawnose, what's wrong?'

'Faunte's been seen in Blean Wood,' Rawnose said. 'And you have heard of the murder of the priest at Rye? Three of his parishioners, moved by most malignant spirits, joined in a cruel plot against this priest. The good man was preparing to go to church and celebrate Mass when these emissaries of Satan, goaded by pricks and mad hatred, came to the sacristy door and invited him into the graveyard. They put a cord round his neck and—'

'Rawnose!' Kathryn shouted.

The beggar blinked. 'Ghosts have been seen,' he continued, changing the subject dramatically, 'a ghastly green light outside Saint Gregory's Priory, five foot high and a yard across.'

'Rawnose!' Thomasina said warningly.

'A tailor in Chatham played dice with the Devil. They met in the graveyard—'

'Shut up, Rawnose!' Thomasina roared.

'Oh, and an Irishman has been asking about you, Mistress.'

'Don't be silly. Why should Colum speak to you about me?'

'Oh, no, Mistress, another one. Red-haired, with a patch over his eye,' Rawnose announced, now thoroughly enjoying Kathryn's attention. 'Tall and broad he was.'

Kathryn crouched before the beggar. 'Rawnose, what did he say?'

'Oh, he asked about you and Master Murtagh. Where the Irishman lives, what he did.'

'And you told him what you knew?'

'Oh, of course, Mistress, he gave me sixpence.'

Kathryn rose and went to stand at the kitchen door. She clutched her throat, trying to control the shivers of fear. The Hounds of Ulster were in Canterbury and hunting Colum.

'Oh!' Rawnose shouted, delighted to have such an attentive audience. 'Spectres have also been seen outside Canterbury. Disembodied voices round the gallows at the crossroads and a witch with red hair.'

'Hush!' Kathryn replied, coming back to the table. 'Now, Rawnose, what is wrong with you?'

'A slight fever and a cold in the head.'

Kathryn sighed and asked Thomasina for yarrow, some

camomile and thyme, a little honey and a spoonful of mustard. She put these into a small pot to boil over the fire, mixing in a little water, and told Rawnose to come back for the potion. She gracefully refused the penny he thrust at her, then led him, still chattering like a squirrel, out of the house. She came back into the kitchen where Thomasina was now bending over the fire.

'The Irishman's in danger, isn't he, Mistress?'

'Yes, yes, he is, Thomasina, but let me think.'

Kathryn washed her hands in a bowl of rose-water, dried them on a napkin and went into her small chancery, or writing-chamber. She sat at her father's desk staring at the blank wall, her thoughts all a-jumble, the panic seething within her.

'For God's sake, woman!' she muttered. 'Take a hold of yourself.'

She picked up a roll of vellum, smoothed it out and tried to calm herself. She sharpened a quill and nibbled at the feathered tip.

'I'll write down everything,' she whispered to herself and closed her eyes, recalling all she and Colum had learnt. Rawnose's news still alarmed her, but if she wrote and kept busy she might contain the problem, at least until Colum returned from Kingsmead.

Primo—[She wrote in a large, bold hand, then sat and watched the blue-green ink dry quickly on the parchment.] On 14th April 1471, Richard Neville, Earl of Warwick, was killed at Barnet. When Colum saw him, the Earl was wearing the gold pendant with the Eye of God sapphire. After the battle, however, when Neville was dead, both pendant and sapphire had disappeared.

Secundo—The pendant is of Celtic origin, probably taken from the cathedral in Dublin by the present King's father, Richard, Duke of York, and given to Neville as a pledge of friendship.

Tertio—Neville probably gave the pendant to Brandon, his squire, who was captured north of Canterbury on 28th April, but no sign of the sapphire was found on him. Where had Brandon been between the Battle of Barnet and the day he was captured? What had happened to his companions? How had Moresby, captain of Neville's guard, been killed? Why didn't Brandon say anything to his gaolers at Canterbury Castle? Did he talk to Sparrow? How did Brandon die? Did the escape of the murderer, Sparrow, have anything to do with the Eye of God?

Quarto—Where is the Eye of God? Did Brandon have it on his person, or did he hide it somewhere? Are the Hounds of Ulster seeking its return as well as Colum's death?

Kathryn's writing was interrupted by the arrival of other patients. She returned to the kitchen, ignoring Thomasina's chatter as she briskly dispensed horehound for a sore throat, a potion of sage for raw gums, applied poultices and salves to cuts and wounds. She then returned to her chancery and continued writing.

Quinto—The pendant and the Eye of God are undoubtedly valuable. But why is the King so insistent on their return?

Kathryn recalled the meeting with the King at the Tower and the macabre stillness of the House of Secrets.

Sexto—Does someone in Canterbury Castle know about the Eye of God? Webster seemed apprehensive, and that strange pardoner, the Righteous Man, did he have a role to play?

Septimo—My own problems? Alexander Wyville had definitely escaped from Canterbury, but is he still alive?

Octavo—Colum Murtagh. What do I really think of him?

Kathryn gripped her quill, erased the last question and went back to study the previous ones.

Thomasina brought in a jug of ale and a platter with bread and cheese on it. Kathryn thanked her, then ate and drank absent-mindedly. She let her mind float, trying to grasp the certainties whilst ignoring the questions she couldn't answer. She reached one firm conclusion. Brandon's death was mysterious, too much of a coincidence. A young, lusty squire, well looked after, dying suddenly of gaol fever! Her mind whirled with the possibilities. Had Brandon been murdered? Had he really died? And this strange escape of Sparrow the murderer . . . Kathryn tapped the quill against her face, enjoying the feel of the smooth, soft downy feathers. She jumped at the loud rapping on the door, quickly rolled up the piece of parchment, replaced the quill in its holder and closed the ink-horn. Raised voices came from the kitchen, interspersed with Thomasina's sharp replies. Kathryn rose, smoothed the front of her dress and went back along the passageway. In the kitchen Gabele and Fletcher stood with hang-dog expressions on their faces.

'What is it?' she asked, going over to close the door to the garden.

'Sir William Webster, Mistress,' Fletcher replied. 'He's dead of a broken neck. He fell from the tower of the keep.'

'When was this?'

'Early this morning, Mistress, just as dawn broke,' Gabele explained. 'A guard saw him taking his usual morning walk on the tower. Sir William liked to watch the sun rise, said he could think more clearly.'

'Was he alone?'

'As always, yes. Sir William insisted on that. The sentries on the parapet-walk below always saw him there, come rain or shine.'

'And what happened?'

'As I have said, one minute he was there, the next the guard

heard a scream and turned to glimpse Sir William's body falling.'

'Hell's teeth!' Fletcher breathed. 'What a mess. Sir William's
face is almost unrecognisable.'

'How could it happen?' Kathryn asked, remembering the
mighty crenellated wall at the top of the tower. 'I mean, Sir
William could hardly slip, and he was too level-headed to step
between the crenellations.'

Fletcher looked down at the floor.

'It may have been suicide, Mistress,' Gabele spoke up.

'Suicide? Why?'

'Sir William was much aggrieved by Sparrow's escape and
Brandon's death. Even more so since he discovered Brandon
held a secret the King would dearly love to possess.'

Kathryn turned her back on them and stared at the small
sack of onions hanging from the rafters next to a flitch of
bacon. Suicide? she thought. Oh, no! This is murder! Too many
deaths at Canterbury Castle, too many secrets, too many unex-
plained coincidences. She turned round.

'Master Gabele, how was Sir William yesterday?'

'A little withdrawn, rather anxious, but he kept himself busy
with the duties of the castle.'

'And you are sure he was by himself on the tower?'

Gabele wetted his lips. 'Yes, Mistress Swinbrooke, we are.
The entrance to the top of the tower was through a trapdoor.
Sir William always bolted that behind him.'

'And you haven't been up there yet?'

'No, we thought it best if Master Murtagh ordered the trapdoor
to be opened. I know what you are thinking, Mistress—Sir
William's death may be due to foul play rather than any accident
or death wish, and the tower will reveal this.' He held up a hand
to still her questions. 'Sir William was always cautious. The top of
the tower is of pure stone, smooth and even, like a frozen pond.
Webster covered it with at least two inches of fine sand.' He
coughed. 'I've put a guard on the stairway to it.'

Kathryn nodded. She was about to question the men further

when the door to the garden was thrown open and Wuf rushed in.

'I have a slug!' he said. 'Look, Thomasina!'

He ran across to where the nurse was standing quietly by the hearth, one eye on the bubbling pot, the other on Kathryn's two visitors. Thomasina stroked the boy's head gently as she fought back the tears. The lad's abrupt entrance was a clear reflection of the past. Could things happen twice? Thomasina wondered. A lifetime ago, in the first of her three marriages, her own child, Thomas, rushed in holding a snail to show her. Two weeks later he was dead with the sweating sickness. Thomasina chewed her lip and crouched by the boy, totally ignoring her mistress and the two visitors. I must be getting old, she thought, my mind slips. She silently cursed the tears pricking at her eyes.

'Come on, Wuf!' she said.

And grasping the little boy's hand, Thomasina bustled into the garden to see if they could find more slugs.

The two men, startled by her abrupt departure as well as by Kathryn's terse questions, shuffled their feet.

'Mistress,' Gabele spoke up, 'I have told you what we know. Webster's body has already been coffined. We thought it best to seek out Master Murtagh.'

'He's at Kingsmead.' Kathryn went across and took a cloak from the peg on the wall. 'I'll take you there,' she continued. 'Murtagh would insist on that.'

Kathryn went into the garden and quickly told Thomasina where she was going. The nurse, sitting on a small wooden bench watching Wuf, just nodded and averted her face lest Kathryn see the tears brimming in her eyes.

'Thomasina, are you all right?'

'Yes, it's nothing, Mistress.' Thomasina forced a smile and pointed at Wuf. 'Just a sunbeam from the past.'

Kathryn, accompanied by Gabele and Fletcher, entered Kingsmead. They rode along the muddy track winding between the great paddocks and meadows up to the cluster of manor buildings behind a clump of trees. Even as they approached, Kathryn could hear the hammering and sawing of the carpenters and builders, whilst the fields they passed already bore signs of Colum's arrival. New fences had been erected, hedgerows pruned, ditches dug and gates rehung. As they came through the line of trees, Kathryn stopped and looked at the old manorhouse, still uninhabitable, though its rebuilding was under way. Masons and stone-cutters were busy on the walls. The roofs had been stripped; carpenters were replacing beams and joists whilst a tiler and his apprentice were busy removing stacks of red tiles from a cart and laying them carefully on wooden slats. The place was as busy as a beehive in summer. Soldiers, those whom Holbech had hired, were practising archery on a meadow in front of the house. Farther down, around their tents and bothies, the soldiers' womenfolk tended the cooking fires, whilst grubby-faced children ran shrieking about, chasing noisy dogs and adding to the tumult. Kathryn and her party dismounted. A groom, recognising Kathryn, ran up to hold the reins. Serjeant Holbech appeared, his woman, the Irish red-haired Megan, clinging like a leech to his arm. The burly soldier strode up and bowed.

'Mistress, is there anything wrong?' His guttural voice betrayed a Yorkshire burr. He dismissed Fletcher with a flicker of his eyes but studied Gabele carefully. 'You are?' He pointed a thickset finger.

'Simon Gabele, master-at-arms at Canterbury Castle.'

Holbech grinned and extended a hand. 'Holbech's the name. I fought with you at Towton.'

'A bloody fight, Master Holbech.'

'Aye, and some good men died. Mistress Swinbrooke'— Holbech turned back to Kathryn—'Master Murtagh's in the stables.'

Kathryn had been studying the wild-haired woman, who just as coolly stared back. Kathryn was fascinated by Megan. She had never seen such rich, beautiful hair, so thick its tresses fell down to the girl's waist; it framed a face of remarkable contrast—alabaster skin and green, somewhat slanted eyes. Kathryn secretly admired Megan's fierce pride and wild ways, even though she remembered Colum's grumbles.

'Megan's a bloody nuisance!' he had once declared. 'She loves one man to distraction, then, if someone else catches her eye, drops him like a hot cinder and runs in pursuit.'

'I wonder if she's caught Colum?' Kathryn primly thought as Holbech led them round to the stables.

'Do you like my ring, Mistress?' Megan leaned across, one hand extended, showing the mother-of-pearl ring in its silver clasp on a white, slender finger.

'Beautiful,' Kathryn murmured. 'It becomes you, Megan.'

'I earned it,' the girl declared, flouncing her red hair and squeezing Holbech's arm. 'Didn't I?'

The serjeant-at-arms could only gulp in embarrassment and began calling Murtagh's name even before they entered the cobbled yard. Colum emerged from the stable leading a horse, a beautiful strawberry roan. Apparently the animal was in great distress, for it raised its right foreleg and could only hobble forward.

'Kathryn.'

Colum tossed the reins at Holbech, his smile fading as he noticed Gabele and Fletcher.

'What's wrong?'

Gabele informed him in terse, succinct phrases. Colum nodded and asked the same questions Kathryn had raised. He was about to continue when he noticed how Megan, leaning on Holbech's arm, was listening intently.

'Holbech,' he said softly, 'keep an eye on the workmen. I think one of the carpenters is bloody drunk.'

He waited until both were out of earshot.

'So, Sir Webster's dead.' Colum played with the horse's reins, then turned and stroked the horse, gently whispering endearments. 'I suppose I had better come. But'—he smoothed the horse's flanks—'Pulcher here is in terrible pain.'

Kathryn looked at the horse's gentle, liquid eyes.

'What's wrong?' she asked.

'I don't know. He was shoed yesterday and something has gone wrong.'

'Let me have a look.'

Colum, whispering in Gaelic to the horse, gently raised its sore leg. Kathryn crouched down and saw the swelling just above the hoof. She looked more closely at the shoe.

'One nail has been driven in too close,' Colum explained. 'It's scarring the flesh, but why should it cause such pain?'

'I don't think it is,' Kathryn replied. 'The hoof was probably inflamed before shoeing, the nail's made it worse.'

'I'll have the shoes removed.' Colum angrily gnawed at his lip; such leg injuries could cripple a horse. 'What then?' he demanded.

'Make a poultice prepared from the juice of fresh moss, wrap it round the hoof and change it twice a day.'

'You are sure it'll heal?' Colum asked.

Kathryn grinned and got to her feet. 'If it doesn't, I'll let you quote Chaucer to me all the day long.'

Colum stared at the offending horseshoe. 'The blacksmith should have seen that,' he murmured. He walked to the entrance of the yard, his face white with fury. 'Holbech!' he roared. 'Holbech, where the hell are you?'

His master-of-arms came running round, Megan in tow, her red hair flying behind her like a veil.

'Get that bloody blacksmith!' Colum shouted. 'Give him a boot up the arse! He's not to drink any wine for a month. He's made poor Pulcher lame. He's to have all these shoes off and apply moss poultices twice a day. If the horse is not well within the week, I'll hang the bastard!'

Colum went over and washed himself at the well. He saddled a horse and, joined by Kathryn and her two companions, galloped out of Kingsmead. Gabele and Fletcher rode behind, slightly fearful of Colum's hot temper. For a while, Kathryn allowed Colum his head as he swore in English, then in Gaelic, about what he would do to the blacksmith.

They cut across country past the smoke and stench of the tanneries in North Lane and crossed Saint Dunstan's Street. As they passed Westgate, they saw the spires of Holy Cross Church jutting into the sky before turning left through London Gate and into Canterbury. Colum was still morose, only half-listening to Kathryn's speculations about Webster's death. At last, just before they turned into Castle Row, Kathryn reined in. She glanced around at the crowds jostling about the stalls and booths of the small market, leaned across and gripped Colum's hand.

'Irishman, I have other news.'

Colum was still only half-listening.

'Irishman,' Kathryn insisted, 'the Hounds of Ulster are in Canterbury; Fitzroy's been asking about you.'

Colum's hand fell to the hilt of his sword, which hung from his saddle-horn.

'How do you know?'

Kathryn repeated what Rawnose had told her.

'Padraig Fitzroy,' Colum replied. 'So, at last the bastard's come.'

'Do you fear him?'

'Yes and no. In a green field, face-to-face with sword and buckler, I could take Fitzroy's head.'

Colum looked round. He studied the hooded beggars, the cowled monks, the merchants in their beaver hats, the rich and the powerful jostling with the pickpockets and rogues of the city. So many people, Colum thought—everywhere, at the doors of taverns or corners of streets—pilgrims, all strangers to the city, dressed in strange garb and makeshift garments, milled about.

'Fitzroy won't meet me in a field,' he murmured. 'He's an assassin, he could be in that crowd watching us now. No, when he strikes it will be like a thief in the night, suddenly and unexpectedly.' Colum felt a shiver between his shoulder-blades. He urged his horse forward. 'Kathryn,' he warned. 'I'll be blunt. Don't unlock your door to any stranger. Fitzroy is no respecter of persons.'

86

Chapter 6

Once inside the castle, Gabele and Fletcher took them through a warren of corridors up a flight of stairs and into the small chapel. A polished wooden coffin, ringed by purple candles, lay on trestles before the simple stone altar. Kathryn detected the stench of corruption, of putrefaction like that of a death house. Gabele removed the lid of the coffin.

'I didn't nail it down.' He glanced quickly at Kathryn. 'I thought you may wish to look.'

Kathryn did, then turned away. Webster's corpse had not been prepared for burial. Still dressed in the clothes he had died in, the top part of his body looked misshapen, his battered head almost pushed down between his shoulders. Kathryn swallowed and went back to study the body more closely, remembering her father's words.

'Don't be frightened of a corpse, Kathryn. It's only the shell from which the spirit has now gone. Be gentle and remember there is nothing to fear.'

She told Gabele to remove the lid completely and, grasping Webster's head between her hands, turned it round.

'One side of the face is battered.' She spoke clearly and

matter-of-factly. 'The fall was a great one, the neck and shoulder bones are broken.' She pointed to the left side of his face. 'This is how he hit the ground.' She glanced up but all three men had turned away. 'Oh, for heaven's sake!' she breathed, 'you have all seen corpses in your life!'

Colum walked across.

'Please,' she said, 'turn the corpse over.'

Colum did so and Kathryn carefully examined the shattered head. She was about to withdraw her hand but felt again, just behind the right ear, and stood back.

'Strange,' she muttered.

'What is?' Gabele asked.

'Well,' Kathryn said, 'Sir William fell from the wall.' She used her hand to demonstrate. 'The body would spin and turn like a stone. Now, Sir William, when he hit the ground, fell on his left side. Hence the damage to that side of his face and head. He didn't hit any of the brickwork in his fall, so the right side of his head and face is relatively undamaged.'

'So?' Colum asked.

'Why is there a lump behind his right ear?' Kathryn replied. 'To answer you bluntly, before he fell from the tower, Sir William was struck on the back of the head.'

'Does that mean,' Fletcher asked, 'somebody else was on top of the tower with Sir William?'

'Apparently so.'

'But that's impossible,' Gabele asserted. 'Sir William locked the trapdoor behind him whilst the guards on the parapet-walk below only saw Sir William.'

'Someone,' Colum said, 'could have been waiting on the tower for Sir William?'

'Impossible!' Gabele replied. 'There's no place to hide up there. Moreover, Sir William was walking around for some time before he fell. Surely he would have noticed and raised the alarm.'

'It's useless to speculate,' Kathryn interrupted. 'Master Gabele, you say the top of the tower is still padlocked?'

'Yes.'

'Then it's time we went up there, isn't it?'

Gabele sent for the guards, three country lads who had been on sentry duty on the parapet below the tower keep. They all agreed that they had seen Sir William.

'Oh, aye,' one of them, a gap-toothed lad, said. 'He always went there, God rest him, wearing his beaver hat, his military cloak wrapped about him. I waved at him and he waved back.'

'Did you see anyone else there?' Kathryn asked.

'Don't forget, Mistress, we were on the parapet-walk looking up, some sixty feet! Still, we didn't see anyone else. The only thing we did glimpse were the flames from the brazier Sir William always lit to keep himself warm.'

'And you saw that this morning?'

'Oh, aye.'

'And how did Sir William seem?'

'As I said,' the gap-toothed fellow replied, 'I waved at him. He waved and shouted some greeting back. I was too far away to hear exactly.'

'And you noticed nothing untoward?'

'No,' they all chorused.

'And you saw Sir William's fall?'

'Well, Mistress, we were walking about,' one of them replied. 'We look out over the walls towards the town. We had been there for hours. Suddenly I hear a cry. I turn and catch a blur of colour. I hear a thump, and when I look down, Sir William's body lies flat on the bailey-yard.'

'You heard a scream?' Colum persisted.

'That's what I said.'

Colum shook his head, nonplussed. 'Master Gabele—' He placed a coin on the table. 'A drink for these three veterans, but only after we have forced the trapdoor.'

Gabele, Fletcher, the three eager soldiers in front, took Kathryn and Colum along more corridors and up the gloomy spiral staircase to the top of the tower. The steps were narrow, the climb steep, and they all had to stop to catch their breath before continuing. At last the stone staircase ended at a great wooden trapdoor to the roof above. Looking to her right, Kathryn saw a large window embrasure the size of a man, its great shutters held firmly closed by a thick wooden bar.

'That's just under the tower,' she remarked.

'Yes, Mistress.'

'And what's it for?'

'A small sally-port,' Colum explained. 'If the castle is ever attacked, the besiegers would bring ladders or siege towers against the keep. The defenders would open those doors and be able to knock ladders off or set the siege towers ablaze.'

'Couldn't besiegers break in there?' Kathryn asked.

Gabele smiled. 'No, it would be reinforced and two good bowmen could defend that sally-port until the Second Coming.'

Kathryn stared at the wooden shutters.

'What's the matter?' Fletcher gibed. 'Surely you don't think Sir William was thrown out of there, do you?' He caught the angry look in Kathryn's eyes and blushed. 'I mean, Mistress, he was on the tower, with the trapdoor bolted!'

Colum decided to end the deputy constable's embarrassment by ordering the soldiers to use the huge log they had brought from the bailey. Sweating and cursing, they began to hammer at the trapdoor. At last they broke through, the wood snapping, the trapdoor shuddering. Colum ordered them back. He pushed the trapdoor open and stepped out. Kathryn followed, gasping as the wind caught her breath and whipped her hair. She noticed the bolts and clasps, both on the inside and outside of the trapdoor, were now free. She walked gingerly towards the battlements, peered over and turned away, feeling rather dizzy at the awesome drop. Gabele popped his head through but Colum told him to stay as he examined the top of the tower. In a far corner the charcoal brazier only held a pile of white dust. Colum knelt and carefully examined the footprints in the fine layer of sand which covered the surface of the tower.

'Hell's teeth!' he whispered. 'Kathryn, come here!'

She did, making her way carefully. Colum pointed to the footprints. 'Webster's!' Colum explained. 'The same imprint everywhere. There's no sign of any other person being here on the tower top with Webster.' He stared around, wiping the sand from his hands. 'Mistress, are you sure Webster was knocked on the back of the head? For if he was, then it's a real mystery. Here is a man who climbs to the top of the tower and bolts the trapdoor behind him. He stays here for some while, the sentries vouch for that. The sand shows no one was hiding here; moreover, there's no place of concealment. So how did the murderer come through a locked trapdoor, walk across sand without leaving his imprint, seize the Constable without a struggle, knock him on the head and toss him over the battlements, all undetected by the guards? Then'—Colum sighed—'leave the tower, somehow managing to bolt it from the inside?'

Kathryn shook her head angrily and walked back to the battlements. She looked over. Directly beneath her was the bailey-yard, bounded by a defensive wall, guards were patrolling its parapet-walk. Kathryn shook her head again and came back.

'I have seen enough,' she muttered.

Those on the stairs below withdrew to allow Colum and Kathryn back into the tower, then everyone went downstairs. The guards were dismissed and Gabele sent for Peter the chaplain and Fitz-Steven the clerk. They all met in the large sombre hall, sitting uncomfortably on benches just below the dais. Colum began the proceedings.

'Now here's a mystery,' he declared.

He paused as Margotta entered the hall. She grinned girlishly at him and sat beside Gabele, her father.

Kathryn held her hand up. 'Master Murtagh. Someone's missing. Where's our friend the Righteous Man, the pardoner?'

'He's gone into the city,' Peter the chaplain explained. 'The pilgrim season is at its height and the man is probably looking for a lucrative profit.'

'Was he in the castle when Webster was killed?' Kathryn asked.

'Oh, yes.' Fitz-Steven the clerk spoke up. 'He departed just before you arrived. Why, what is all this? I thought Sir William either fell or committed suicide.'

'That is what we thought,' Fletcher muttered. 'But Mistress Swinbrooke here believes Sir William may have been knocked on the head and pushed.'

'Nonsense!' Fitz-Steven pompously declared. 'Who would kill Sir William, and why? What proof do you have of this?' He stared disdainfully at Kathryn. 'Sir William was a lonely, rather quiet man. He had no enemies.'

'I can't answer your questions, Master Clerk,' Kathryn replied. 'If I did, I would solve every mystery under the sun. Nor did I say Sir William had enemies. Perhaps he suspected something was wrong.'

'Such as?'

'The truth behind Sparrow's escape. Or Brandon's death. Or even the whereabouts of the Eye of God.'

'Fiddlesticks!' the chaplain retorted.

'Fiddlesticks, aye. One stick in particular,' Kathryn said hotly, 'hit Sir William on the right side of the head behind the ear. And I have one question for all of you. Did any of you go to join Sir William on the tower?'

Fitz-Steven got to his feet. 'I don't have to answer these questions from a mere woman.'

'In which case your mother and I have a lot in common!' Kathryn snapped.

Fitz-Steven pushed his face close to hers.

'I have heard of you, Swinbrooke,' he hissed, a malicious smile on his dirty, sweaty face. 'Oh, yes, you with your airs and graces, your knowledge of physic, your appointment to the council or what's left of it.'

'Have you heard of me?' Colum asked, rising and grasping

Fitz-Steven by the shoulder. 'Believe me, sir, I am famed neither for my good looks or my patience, and the latter you are sorely trying. I am the King's Commissioner in this matter, and, if you are not careful I will educate you briefly in courtesy towards a lady.'

Kathryn raised her hand as Fitz-Steven opened his mouth to add insult to protest.

'Please, sir, I beg you, sit down.' She forced a smile. 'My questions are well-meaning.'

The clerk slumped back on the bench. 'Then, to answer you, Mistress, I went nowhere near the tower, nor did I notice anything untoward in Webster's manner.' He coughed. 'A little subdued, perhaps, anxious that he may have betrayed the King's trust, but nothing else.'

The rest chorused his answer.

'Are you sure?' Colum asked.

'No, that's not strictly true,' Peter the chaplain said. 'If he was concerned about anything, sir, then it wasn't Brandon's death, he saw that as an act of God.' The priest chewed his lip. 'He was more interested in Sparrow's escape. Last evening, just before dusk, he asked me to come out onto the green before the keep. He played a strange mummery, asking me to pretend to be Sparrow whilst he was the poor turnkey who was killed.'

'Why did he do that?'

'I don't know. He made me go to the middle of the green.'

'Ah, yes,' Gabele interrupted. 'I wondered what you were doing there.'

'Well, I did as he asked. Sir William pretended to be the turnkey who was killed. We tried to reconstruct the circum-stances of Sparrow's escape. I went into an enclave, Sir William followed, then, quite abruptly, he shook his head and walked away. That was all.'

'He was very quiet last night,' Margotta spoke up. 'At table he just toyed with his food and retired early. He muttered some-thing about you, Colum. He said he had to see you.'

'Is there anything else?' Kathryn quietly asked.

They all shook their heads. Colum declared that he was finished. He refused Gabele's offer of refreshment and said they would find their own way out of the castle. Colum, however, waited until the rest had left the hall.

'Kathryn, are you sure Webster was struck on the head before he fell?'

'I am certain. And do you know something, Colum? I don't think the guards heard Webster scream, that was someone else. I strongly suspect the poor constable was knocked unconscious before being sent spinning into eternity. He was murdered because of what he knew and it's something to do with Sparrow's escape.'

They left the hall, pausing for a while on the small green, then walked over to the shadowy recess in the bailey wall where Sparrow and the hapless turnkey had their grim encounter. Colum shook his head.

'God knows what Webster was hoping to find. Perhaps, in time, it will come to us.'

They collected their horses and rode back into the city. Kathryn asked if Colum would accompany her, for she had calls to make at the Poor Priests' Hospital. The Irishman agreed so they turned down Bullock Lane and into Steward Street. The sunshine had brought the crowds out. Pilgrims were making their way up from the hostelries to pay their respects to Becket's shrine in the great cathedral. The streets were so raucous and thronged they had to dismount and lead their horses. As they passed Crocchere's Lane, Kathryn heard her name called and groaned to see her kinsman Joscelyn, with his waspish-faced wife, bustling through the crowds towards her.

'Good morrow, Kathryn. And you, Master Murtagh.' Joscelyn's narrow face was lit by a false smile.

Sanctimonious prig, Kathryn thought; she studied her kinsman's prim face and tried to ignore the look of righteous disdain on that of his wife. Joscelyn was her father's cousin, a spicer by trade and, despite his show of bonhomie, hardly Kathryn's friend. For a while they exchanged pleasantries. Joscelyn's wife kept looking at Colum and sniffing disdainfully until the Irishman frightened her by staring back with the grimmest look he could muster.

'I am busy.' Kathryn smiled, gathering her horse's reins. 'I have business at the hospital.'

'Yes, yes, sweet Cousin, but how does your application for a licence proceed?'

'It goes before the Guild, but I am already buying stock. A London merchant, Richard of Swinforfield, has promised to send cloves, mace, saffron, sugar, cinnamon, ginger—oh yes, and some coriander, aniseed and buckwheat whilst'—Kathryn hid her smile, 'I have also placed orders for cinnamon cassia, calamus and aloes to be imported from abroad.'

'And you'll sell those from your shop?' Joscelyn's false bonhomie had been replaced by genuine anxiety.

'Of course! Now the war is ended there is a great demand, particularly for rue, to keep floor rushes sweet and free of infection.' Kathryn shrugged, now enjoying herself. 'As you know, Joscelyn, I also need them for my medicines. Have you ever read Theophrastus?'

Joscelyn bleakly shook his head.

'According to him,' Kathryn answered, 'Such spices are an aid to medicine. Or, as Hippocrates more pointedly put it, "Let food be your medicine and medicine your food." '

'Yes, yes, quite.' Joscelyn stepped back, one hand fluttering in the air. 'In which case, Cousin, I hope your application is successful.'

And grasping his sullen wife's arm, he disappeared into the crowd, leaving Kathryn shaking with laughter.

'He doesn't like you,' Colum commented. 'And you don't like him. So why the merriment?'

Kathryn wiped the tears from her eyes. 'Oh, Colum, can't you see? If Cousin Joscelyn had his way, I'd be married to some boring merchant and know my true place. Instead, I practise as a physician and now intend to sell spices in rivalry to him. Joscelyn does not like that. What old Chaucer wrote about the physician is true of Cousin Joscelyn.' She smiled wryly. 'And perhaps of me. How does it go? "For gold in physick is a cordial, therefore he loved gold especial." '

'I don't think so,' Colum muttered.

'You don't think what? And don't mutter!'

'I don't think you love money.' Colum carefully removed a loose thread from Kathryn's dress. 'And if you did, what hope for the rest? As the poet says, "If gold rusts what shall iron do?" '

Teasing and bantering, they walked farther up Steward Street. Kathryn stopped at the Poor Priests' Hospital opposite Hawks Lane. Whilst Colum held the horses, she went in to see Father Cuthbert, the keeper. However, the old priest was absent, so they continued through the jostling crowds into Hethenman Lane, then up onto the High Street.

'Where are you going now?' Colum asked.

'If you were a pardoner,' she answered, 'where would you go?'

Colum just smiled and nodded.

They were just past the Guildhall, pushing their way through the crowds clustered around the Checker of Hope, the greatest tavern in Canterbury and the centre of the pilgrim trade, when a red-faced, perspiring Luberon caught up with them. At first neither of them could make sense of what he was saying. Luberon gabbled out his words and tried to catch his breath at the same time. Colum told him to calm down.

'Fine, fine,' Luberon gasped; the clerk took a deep breath and lowered his voice. 'You've got to come!' he said. 'A corpse has been dragged from the river!'

Kathryn closed her eyes and groaned.

'Oh, yes,' Luberon insisted. 'Master Murtagh, you are the King's Commissioner and coroner in these matters, and Mistress Swinbrooke, you are his physician.'

Chapter 7

Luberon took them back up the High Street, explaining how the corpse had been taken to the death house in the parish of All Saints, a low, ramshackle shed at the far end of an over-grown graveyard. As they reached this, Luberon stopped, his hand on the latch.

'I thought you might wish to see it,' he explained. 'First, someone has to make a ruling on the corpse, that's city regulations. Secondly, and more strangely, no one has reported anyone missing, yet this corpse is someone who was well fed, strong and vigorous. Thirdly'—he smiled at Colum—'I wondered if it was related to the present tumults following the war.'

Still chattering, he led them into the darkness which smelt strongly of fish and stale water. Luberon lit a torch and lifted the lid of the makeshift coffin. Kathryn tried not to look where the head should have been. This gave her an eerie, macabre feeling; she felt slightly dizzy and steadied herself by gripping the table on which the coffin lay.

'It's been in the water for some time,' Colum observed.

Kathryn stared at the puffy blue flesh soaked by the river.

The corpse also bore marks of where it had been nibbled by fish; the blood round the severed neck was dry and caked.

'Where was it found?' Kathryn asked.

'Bobbing beneath one of the arches of the old city wall where it spans the river. Two boys playing there saw it caught in a clump of reeds. The bailiffs were alerted and the body brought here. Strangers who die in Canterbury, if the corpse remains unclaimed, are always buried in All Saints.'

Colum grabbed the torch and pushed it even lower. Bits of pitch fell off and sizzled on the river-soaked corpse.

'Kathryn, what do you think?'

Kathryn, now feeling slightly stronger, managed to overcome her nausea.

'A young man,' she replied, 'well-built and strong.'

'Do you think it could be connected with events in the castle?'

'You mean Sparrow?'

'Yes. After all, he was a stranger to Canterbury, his death would go unnoticed,' Colum said.

'If that was the case,' Kathryn asked, 'why should someone murder him by severing his head? Believe me, this is a murder!' She waved her fingers at the neck of the corpse. 'The wound is old. This man lost his head by an axe or sword blow, not in the river.' She smiled thinly at Luberon. 'Master Clerk, I think we've seen enough.'

Luberon lowered the lid and Kathryn gratefully walked out into the fresh air.

'What is this business at the castle?' Luberon came after them. 'I have heard of Webster's fall.'

Kathryn gazed at Colum, who nodded.

'He is the city clerk,' the Irishman commented, patting the small, fat man on the shoulder. 'And if we don't tell Master Luberon, he'll die of curiosity.'

They left All Saints and entered a tavern on Best Lane where Kathryn, swearing Luberon to silence, briefly described the events at the castle.

'So,' Luberon breathed, 'you have a prisoner who dies unexpectedly. Another who escapes just as surprisingly and a constable who is knocked on the back of the head and thrown off the tower?' He sipped his wine. 'As far as I can see, you have very little evidence to work on, Mistress Kathryn. Brandon is dead and gone. Webster's death is a complete mystery. I know the tower keep at Canterbury Castle and Webster's preference for walking there all alone. And as for this headless corpse'— Luberon pulled a face—'why should Sparrow escape, be recaptured so easily, bearing in mind he was a violent man, and then decapitated?'

'If it was Sparrow.' Kathryn ran her finger round the rim of her own cup and gazed at a group of hawkers busily dicing in the corner. 'The corpse we've just looked at was well-fed, not like that of a prisoner kept in reduced circumstances in Canterbury Castle. Secondly, Master Luberon, you can help here: prisoners are manacled at wrist and ankle. Yes?'

'True, Mistress, and there is a tight chain between the wrist and leg irons.'

'Well,' Kathryn replied, 'the corpse we looked at bore no trace of wrist gyves or ankle clasps. Accordingly, Master Clerk, you should record that the corpse belonged to a stranger and arrange for the remains to be given a decent burial.'

'If you find the head,' Colum remarked drily, draining his cup, 'do let us know.'

'No, wait!' Luberon indicated for Colum to sit. 'This Brandon, he may have been carrying a precious pendant and was captured to the north-west of the city?'

'So we were told. Why?'

'Well think, Master Murtagh. The Earl of Warwick knew he was going to die, he also knew that the pendant was sacred. Now . . .' Luberon rubbed his chin. 'If it was you, Master Murtagh, or Mistress Swinbrooke, what would you have done with such a pendant when you are only a few minutes away from death?'

Kathryn grinned, leaned over and kissed Luberon on the brow. The clerk turned puce-red with embarrassment.

'Of course, most subtle of clerks, I'd give it to a church or shrine. And the greatest shrine in England is that of Saint Thomas of Canterbury!'

Colum tapped the table-top with his hand.

'Brandon may have been captured . . . not coming to Canterbury but going away? But surely the monks at Christchurch would tell the King of such a gift?'

'Not necessarily,' Luberon retorted. 'Our clever monks would keep the pendant and only reveal it after it had been in their possession for a number of years.' Luberon finished his wine and jumped to his feet. 'You have business in Canterbury?' he asked.

'We are looking for a pardoner.'

'A man with dyed-yellow hair dressed in black who calls himself the Righteous Man?'

Kathryn nodded.

'He's at the Bullstake in the Buttermarket. Look,' Luberon continued, peering at the hour-candle on its iron spigot, 'you see your pardoner and I'll meet you, within the hour, by the Black Prince's tomb in the cathedral. Let me make enquiries. If our good monks own such a relic'—he tapped the side of his nose—'they'll tell me.'

Luberon bustled out. Colum and Kathryn followed, going down Best Lane back into the High Street. The thoroughfare was thronged with jostling pilgrims, traders, hawkers and pedlars. They went up the Mercery towards the Buttermarket. Outside the Sun Inn in Burgate a large crowd had gathered round a mountebank dressed garishly in green, red and scarlet. The man was sitting on an ordinary-looking horse; he was promising anyone who could ride the animal would win a silver piece. However, if he fell off, then he, Saladin, once keeper of the Imperial stables at Cologne, would receive sixpence. The crowd laughed and jeered as hands went up to accept the wager. Kathryn looked at the gentle cob, with its plump haunches, soft mouth and liquid brown eyes.

'It looks quiet enough,' she whispered.

Colum shook his head and grinned. 'I know this fellow,' he said. 'Just watch, Kathryn.'

Saladin had now dismounted, the little silver bells sewn to his quilted tunic ringing merrily with every move he made. A young merchant, his face glowing with arrogance, mounted the horse and gently urged it forward. The crowd's jeers grew. The horse plodded away like some tired hack, then, as the merchant dropped the reins and rode hands extended, the mountebank shouted, 'Flectamus Genua. Let us bend the knee!'

Immediately the horse went down on all fours, the merchant rolled off and the crowd's jeers faded away.

'Levate et vade!' the mountebank shouted. 'Rise and come!'

Up the horse got, turned and trotted back to its master, who rewarded it with a sugared apple. The young merchant, his finery covered in mud and dirt, clambered to his feet, seething with rage. However, the crowd's fickle mood had swung behind the mountebank and the young man was jeered until he churlishly agreed to pay the wager.

Colum took Kathryn's elbow and moved her on.

'I have seen him play that trick in many a town,' he declared. 'And even when people see it, they still think they can't be duped.'

Kathryn looked over her shoulder when the crowd roared its approval as another hapless victim took the mountebank's wager. Eventually they were through the jostling throng and crossed the Buttermarket where Kathryn glimpsed the Righteous Man. He was standing on the top step of the market cross and, in a reedy voice, kept inviting people to listen to what he had to say.

'Friends, brothers in Christ.' The Righteous Man's bright eyes surveyed the crowd. 'I have travelled by sea and land, enduring many hardships in the work of Christ, to bring you this!' He held up a scroll of parchment with a blob of purple wax on the end. 'Sealed by the Holy Father himself in Rome. This bull, this papal letter, will absolve you from all sin or, if you are freshly shriven, release you from thousands of years in Purgatory! What is more—' The pardoner held up bulging saddle-bags. 'I have here relics guaranteed by the Archbishop of Bordeaux, the Bishop of Claremont, and Cardinal Humbert of Saint Priscilla-Without-the-Walls, holy objects: wood from Saint Peter's bark, a mallet once used by the saintly Joseph, a piece of the Virgin's veil and part of the rod Aaron used when he confronted the magicians of Pharaoh!'

Kathryn and Colum, standing at the back of the crowd, could hardly believe either the pardoner's farrago of nonsense or the stupid incredulity of his audience. Many people were already digging into their purses, stretching out their hands in a bid to buy.

'By the light!' Kathryn said. 'He's a rogue and a charlatan.'

'This pardoner,' Colum chanted, ' "Had hair as yellow as wax and it hung lank as does a strand of flax. His wallet," ' Colum continued, quoting Chaucer, ' "Was stuffed full of pardons brought from Rome." Strange,' he mused.

'What is?'

'Such similarities between this charlatan and Chaucer's Pardoner.'

At last the Righteous Man's tawdry display was finished. The crowd dispersed and he picked up his bags and walked directly towards Kathryn and Colum. Kathryn knew he had seen them during his sermon. Close up, the pardoner looked even more ghastly than he had in the castle, his hair still daubed with a crude yellow dye, his face so pasty Kathryn suspected he rubbed powder into it.

'A moment of your time, Master Pardoner, and not about your relics.'

The Righteous Man smiled. 'I wondered when you'd come. I have heard the news. Webster's dead and his soul's gone and no, Master Murtagh, I know nothing about it or why it should happen.'

'Shrewdly said,' Colum replied. 'How long do you intend to stay in Canterbury, Master Pardoner?'

'How long is a piece of string?' the fellow retorted and, picking up his bags, made to move off.

'Master Pardoner, where you go and where you stay is your concern,' Colum declared. 'But if you leave Canterbury without my permission, I'll declare you a wolf's-head.'

The pardoner simply sketched a benediction in the air and walked away, shrugging off Colum's warning.

'We'd best go,' Kathryn urged. 'Luberon will be waiting for us.'

Colum stared at the pardoner's retreating back. 'Two things are strange,' he muttered. 'First, why is our pardoner so much like Chaucer's? And secondly, God be my witness, why did he come to Canterbury Castle?'

'Are you sure he is not one of the Hounds of Ulster?' Kathryn replied. 'If the assassin strikes, Colum, he'll either do so in secrecy or by pretending to be someone he's not.'

'No, no. Let's deal with Luberon.'

They walked past the Sun inn, through Christchurch Gate and into the south door of the great cathedral. The nave was thronged with pilgrims quietly chatting as they waited to be admitted into the shrine. Colum and Kathryn pushed their way through and down one of the transepts, to the Black Prince's tomb where Luberon was standing.

'I've been waiting here for some time,' he said testily.

Kathryn made their apologies.

'Not that I object,' Luberon confessed. 'Master Murtagh, have you ever seen such beauty?'

'Every time I come here, Master Clerk, I stand in wonder.'

Colum glanced up at the great windows with their wonderful paintings; the colours were so bright they turned the sunlight into brilliant rainbows which caught the heart and dazzled the eye. Colum then gazed at the marble tomb of the Black

Prince; the effigy of the knight, hands joined, the stonework decorated with the prince's motto "Ich Dien" and the brilliant colours of his livery.

'You asked our question?' Colum said abruptly.

'Yes, I did,' Luberon replied. 'No squire or any from the late Earl of Warwick's party ever came to Canterbury. No mention was made of any gold pendant or a brilliant sapphire known as the Eye of God.' Luberon shrugged. 'I am sorry, I could not learn more.'

Colum stamped his feet impatiently. 'So what was Brandon doing so close to Canterbury when he was captured? If he had been coming to the cathedral, he would have been carrying the pendant.'

'The Prior did say one thing,' Luberon continued. 'When I explained to him about Brandon's capture, he said that three years ago Warwick and his party came here on a pilgrimage. The monks entertained the Earl and his squires in their refectory. Brandon was there. He remembered him as a subtle, cunning man who claimed he was born and raised in Maidstone.'

'Strange.' Colum stared at Kathryn. 'Here we have a high-ranking squire, a man who knew the locality well, of cunning mind and subtle wit, yet he allowed himself to be so easily captured. There is only one thing to do,' Colum concluded defiantly. 'Brandon's body must be exhumed. Perhaps his corpse can tell us something.'

They left Luberon in the cathedral and walked back through the enclosure.

'Will you do that?' Kathryn asked. 'Exhume Brandon's body? What will it prove? Who will recognize it?'

Colum watched the pilgrims stream out of the great door of the cathedral.

'I just wish,' Colum replied, 'there was someone who knew him well, who might recognise him. Perhaps someone who fought with him at Barnet.' Colum smiled sourly. 'And there's the difficulty. Who's going to be foolish enough to proclaim that they were on the losing side in the recent rebellion against the King?'

'But you think,' Kathryn said, 'that Brandon may not have died?'

'Possibly. Perhaps it was Sparrow who died. Whatever'— Colum toyed with the hilt of his dagger—'Brandon's body must be exhumed.'

They left the enclosure and collected their horses from the Sun tavern. Colum left for Kingsmead and Kathryn watched him ride off. I wish I could talk openly to him, she thought. More importantly, I wish he'd talk to me, just say what he thought.

She watched the Irishman ride up Sun Street. She could tell from his posture that he was not relaxed: his head was turning, his eyes searching the crowd for a possible assassin.

'Oh, God!' Kathryn prayed. 'Please, not that way.'

She took a deep breath and smiled as a young urchin ran up to help her into the saddle. She gave the lad a coin and rode absent-mindedly through the crowd, down the Mercery into Hethenman Lane. She stopped to ensure that the two old sisters, Maude and Eleanor, were well. She had to knock insistently before a sickly, pallid-faced Eleanor opened the door.

'What's the matter?' Kathryn exclaimed, sweeping into the house. She put her arm round the old lady, who led her into the solar where her sister was crouched on a chair, holding her stomach. The room smelt stale and fetid.

'We've been sick,' Eleanor whispered, clutching her stomach. 'That and the flux.' She started to cry. 'I feel dirty.'

Kathryn made her sit down. 'You've only eaten what I told you to?'

The old woman nodded.

'Are you sure?'

Again the nods. Kathryn held the back of her hand against Maude's face; her skin felt slightly hot, her lips were dry, slightly cracked at the corners, her eyes dull. Kathryn hid her exasperation. It doesn't make sense, she thought. Pellagra is a simple disease. Remove the cause and the symptoms disappear. So why have they returned?'

Kathryn did her best to comfort the old ladies. 'I'll come back,' she promised. 'I'll bring some honey, boiled with salt and fat in a little wax.'

Kathryn hurried out of the house and towards Ottemelle Lane. Thomasina was waiting indoors to greet her with the usual litany of crimes Wuf had committed, but Kathryn brushed this aside.

'Eleanor and Maude have a slight fever,' she announced. 'But God knows the cause!'

Agnes brought her some watered wine and two oaten cakes. Kathryn washed her hands and hurriedly ate these, then went into her writing-office, where she opened Arderne's *Herbarium*. She took a quill, a scrap of parchment and hastily wrote down the symptoms she had seen.

'But what would cause that?' Kathryn stared at the wall. Both old ladies had followed her rules and regulations about keeping the chambers clean as well as washing their hands and faces regularly. But there was something familiar about this illness . . . Kathryn closed her eyes and gripped the table-top, trying to recall a patient her father had treated. She remembered the symptoms, the very same experienced by Maude and Eleanor, but how had her father treated them? She went back to the *Herbarium*. An entry caught her eye, *Digitalis purpurea*. 'Foxglove!' Kathryn whispered to herself. She went back into the kitchen and out into the garden, walking amongst the banks of raised herbs until she found what she was looking for. The foxglove growing there had long flowered, their dull pink and magenta colours were beginning to fade, but they still vigorously thrived, waiting to flower once more. Kathryn crouched and touched the hairy leaves and wondered how two old ladies would have anything to do with such a dangerous plant.

'Kathryn.' Thomasina came up quietly behind her.

'Foxglove,' Kathryn replied. She got up and turned.

'Thomasina, how on earth can two old ladies be eating fox-glove?'

'That would kill them,' Thomasina said.

'Oh, no! If given in small doses, however, it might bring about the same symptoms they are suffering from: giddiness, nausea, a bilious stomach. Are you sure the water was clear?'

'Of course, Mistress, the butt was well cleaned, the rain-water pure.'

Kathryn went back to the house, Thomasina following her.

'Unless,' Kathryn declared, 'someone else has been giving them something to eat? But they'd tell me that.' Kathryn stopped, an icy prickle going along her spine. 'Wuf!' she called.

A crashing on the stairs and the boy danced into the kitchen. Kathryn crouched down beside him.

'Wuf, run as fast as you can to the Guildhall, seek out the clerk, Master Simon Luberon.'

'Oh, yes, I know him, short and fat.'

'Yes, Wuf, short and fat. Tell him he is to bring some bailiffs down to the plague house in Old Jewry Lane.'

'And where will you be, Mistress?'

'I'll be there.'

Kathryn made Wuf repeat the message: The boy sped off as Thomasina collected their cloaks and left instructions with Agnes the housemaid. Then the two women walked out up Ottemelle Lane.

Rawnose hopped along to thank Kathryn for the medicine but Kathryn just hurried by. On the corner, Goldere the clerk, still scratching his codpiece, moved to block their way, but one look at Thomasina's face and he slunk back. Kathryn had already decided on what she should do. She ignored Thomasina's wail of protest and entered the musty darkness of the Traveller's Rest just round the corner from Old Jewry Lane.

'Faugh!' Thomasina muttered. 'The place smells of beer and onions. Mistress, what on earth are you doing here?'

Kathryn stood in the doorway. She stared round, then smiled

and waved as she saw the two corpse-collectors. She walked over, docile as a lamb.

'Sirs, I owe you an apology.'

The two corpse-collectors stared at her in amazement, mouths and chins dripping with the froth from their beer tankards.

'What are you talking about?' one of them spluttered.

'The two old ladies, Maude and Eleanor. You were correct: they have the plague! Either that or a tertian fever.'

'Are they dead?'

'No, but they soon will be.' Kathryn shrugged. 'I have just visited them. There is nothing more I can do except, as city regulations state, inform you.' Kathryn spun on her heel, walked to the door and hastened down Old Jewry Lane.

A haggard Eleanor answered her pounding on the door. She allowed Kathryn to push her gently inside whilst Thomasina grumbled about such unseemly haste.

'Come,' Kathryn urged, leading the old lady back into the solar. 'Soon we will have visitors. Thomasina, go to the water butt with a tray of four—no, six—cups, fill them to the brim but do not drink from any.'

Kathryn smiled as a knowing look replaced Thomasina's astonishment. The nurse did as she was asked and brought them back to the solar where Kathryn ordered everyone to remain silent. The old ladies, weak and sickly, obeyed. Kathryn sat on a stool rocking herself backwards and forwards.

'They'll come,' she whispered.

She thought of Wuf's journey, his searching out of Luberon, and remained confident that the clerk would only arrive after her visitors. Kathryn's patience was soon rewarded. There was a sharp rap on the door. She gestured with her hand for all to stay still. Another series of knocks, then the door opened and they heard footsteps slithering along the passageway. The two corpse-collectors walked into the solar. Kathryn did not know whether they were more surprised to see the two old ladies alive or her and Thomasina sitting there so quietly.

'What is this?' one of them growled. 'What nonsense?'

'Oh, Maude and Eleanor are ill.' Kathryn smiled, rose and picked up two of the cups from the tray. 'Please have a drink, fresh water from the butt.'

The corpse-collectors took the cups.

'I never drink water,' one of them replied instantly.

'Oh, you will this time. Indeed, we all will!' Kathryn shared out the other cups. 'You see,' she continued, 'even if you don't drink, I am going to.' She raised the cup to her lips, glimpsing panic in the man's face.

'No, don't!' he said.

Kathryn lowered the cup. 'Why shouldn't I?'

'Oh, shut up!' The elder one rounded in fury on his brother. 'Just shut up, you stupid poltroon!'

'Why should he?' Kathryn declared. 'He'll confess in the end. The ward court will meet, they'll assemble all the neighbours, everyone will swear how they avoided this house on your instructions.'

She looked at Eleanor, who was now nodding wisely.

'The only people to come into this house were you and myself. I came here as a physician. I had the water butt cleaned. I regularly checked its purity, but your persecution of these old ladies is well-known.'

'Piss off!' the corpse-collector sneered.

'It's true!' Maude screeched. 'You came into the house only yesterday. You said you were sorry for any harm caused, but you were only doing your duty. You asked for a ladle of water.'

The corpse-collector snatched the cup from his companion and slammed both cups down on the table.

'I don't have to listen to this!' he snarled.

'Oh, it won't take long,' Kathryn said. 'And don't threaten violence. You came into this house with a small pouch of foxglove, which you sprinkled into the water butt. The old ladies would become weak, sicken and die. You would then help yourself to whatever possessions you wanted.'

'It's not true,' the younger one muttered.

'Oh yes, it is,' Kathryn whispered. 'And you must make your mind up whether you stand before the King's Commissioner in Canterbury accused of attempted murder or accept the King's pardon and confess all.'

Whatever reply the corpse-collector was going to make was drowned by a deafening knock on the door. Thomasina went to answer it and returned with Luberon and a posse of bailiffs behind him.

'What's all this?' the clerk puffed, his face wreathed in a look of official concern.

Somewhere behind the bailiffs Wuf was shouting and jumping up and down, screeching for Mistress Swinbrooke. Kathryn picked up her cloak.

'Three things, Master Luberon. First, I'll leave Thomasina here and take Wuf home. Secondly'—she pointed at the corpse-collectors—'these are guilty of attempted murder.' She went to walk past them.

'You said there were three?' Luberon asked.

'Oh, yes! For God's sake, don't drink the water!'

'Why?' Luberon demanded.

'Ask them!' Kathryn stared accusingly at the two corpse-collectors. The two men now stood crestfallen, heads down, so Kathryn could hardly tell them apart. The same bodies yet different heads, she thought, and then remembered the decapitated corpse pulled from the river. 'What if . . . ?' she murmured to herself.

'Pardon?' Luberon asked.

Kathryn stared at the little clerk. 'The headless corpse,' she replied. 'The one we viewed. Tomorrow, can it be coffined and taken to the castle?'

Luberon shrugged. 'It's not to be buried till this evening. I could stop it.'

'Please do,' Kathryn said absent-mindedly. 'I may have made a dreadful mistake.'

Chapter 8

*T*he next morning Kathryn went down to Saint Mildred's Church, where she heard Mass in a chantry chapel. After the priest had sung the "Ite, Missa Est," Kathryn lit candles in front of the statue of the Virgin and went to pray beside her father's tomb. She looked down at the carved inscription she had composed for the repose of his soul. For a while Kathryn day-dreamed about her youth: trotting beside her father through the streets of Canterbury, she and Thomasina out in the fields looking for certain plants or herbs. Kathryn blinked back the tears, kissed the tips of her fingers and pressed them against the cold grey stone.

'I miss you,' she whispered.

Kathryn genuflected towards the high altar and left the church. She sat on a stone plinth outside the porch enjoying the sunshine and watching the carts and pack-horses make their way down to the Buttermarket. She thought about her visit to the castle and hoped she would be proved correct about the headless corpse fished from the Stour.

'Kathryn, are you day-dreaming about me?'

She shaded her eyes with her hand and stared up at Colum. He pointed back to the church gate.

'I have been out to Kingsmead and back to tease Thomasina. I have collected your horse from the stables.' He leaned down and touched her gently on the cheek with his glove. 'Were you really day-dreaming about me, Kathryn?'

Kathryn smiled back. 'And if I was, Irishman?'

'Ah,' he said. 'Well, that would be reward enough for a hard day's work.'

Kathryn narrowed her eyes. She was about to tease him further when Widow Gumple swept up the path, her face pursed tight as if she were sucking on a sour lemon. The widow's voluminous billowing gown and her ridiculous head-dress made her look like a fat-bellied cog in full sail.

'Good morning, Mistress Swinbrooke.' Gumple's voice was honey-sweet.

'Good morning, Widow Gumple. Are you well?'

Widow Gumple bowed her head patronisingly, looked nervously at Colum who glowered fiercely back, then swept on into the church to tend, as the good widow always declared, 'to the Lord's affairs.'

'Just an excuse for malicious gossip,' Thomasina had once observed. 'That fat cow's never said a proper prayer in her life!'

Colum watched the widow's retreating back. 'You were going to say, Mistress Swinbrooke, or daren't you now?' He helped her to her feet. 'Are you,' he continued, 'frightened of such clacking tongues?'

Kathryn brushed the dust from her dress.

'Frightened, Irishman?' she replied with mock curiosity. 'Frightened of what?'

'Of clacking tongues?'

'And what, pray,' Kathryn asked sweetly, 'could they clack about?'

Colum took a deep breath; he was being drawn into one of Kathryn's clever traps.

'About me,' he stammered.

'Irishman, what is your meaning?'

'Well,' he stammered, 'I stay at your house.'

'So does Wuf.'

'I am a man,' Colum said.

'Are you?' Kathryn asked innocently. 'And why should tongues clack about you being a man?'

Colum could stand it no longer and gripped her by the elbow.

'Now, now, my bonny, you know full well what I mean.'

Kathryn smiled at him. 'You are a friend, Colum,' she said. 'A dear, close friend. I trust you. If you left, not a day would pass without me thinking of you. But . . .'

'But what?' Colum demanded.

Kathryn gestured back towards the church. 'I've just prayed over my father's grave.' She clutched Colum's wrist. 'Years ago, Murtagh, a man like you would have swept me off my feet.' She grinned. 'In every sense of the word. But as we grow older, Colum, life becomes twisted. It's a struggle to make sure it doesn't twist us.'

Kathryn paused and stared as the bellman walked ponderously past the church gates down to the market-place. He was followed by a beadle leading a fishmonger down to the stocks, the rotten produce the trader had tried to sell slung round his neck.

'Alexander Wyville,' Kathryn went on. 'Not Widow Gumple's clacking tongue. He's the ghost who haunts my soul. He said he loved me but he was nothing more than a drunken bully.'

'And you think the same of me?' Colum retorted.

'No, no.' Kathryn slipped her arm through his and they walked towards the gate. 'Wyville was a drunkard and a bully boy. He could be alive, so, in God's eyes, I am still married. Yet,' she sighed, 'that's only the flotsam and jetsam on the river's surface, beneath it lies the hurt. The soul has wounds as well, Colum. The pity is,' she continued, 'they heal so slowly.'

Colum saw the tears brimming in her eyes.

'Well,' he said, squeezing her hand. 'As long as you daydream about me, it's more than any Irishman could ask.'

He began to tease her, knowing that it would be cruel to persist in his questioning. They collected their horses and walked quietly down Winchepe towards the castle.

'So Master Luberon will have the corpse ready? What do you hope to prove?'

Kathryn paused to loop the horse's reins round her wrist. The crowds were milling about them, so they had not bothered to ride. The stalls were busy and the air dinned with the curses of carters who were shouting loudly: 'Make way! Make way!'

Kathryn waited until they had threaded their way through.

'I asked Luberon to bring the corpse to the castle because I think it may be identified there. I may have made a mistake.' She went on to explain. 'The corpse belonged to a vigorous, well-fed man, so I immediately concluded it couldn't be a prisoner. However, Sparrow was a young, strong man. He must have been to overcome that turnkey.' She shrugged. 'Moreover, Webster seemed to be a kind-hearted gaoler. I doubt if any prisoner in Canterbury Castle was starved. The food may not be good but there'd be plenty of it.'

'Yet you said there were no manacle marks around the corpse's wrists or ankles.'

'You should have realised that mistake,' Kathryn replied tartly.

'What do you mean?' Colum taunted. 'Are you reproving me, Mistress Swinbrooke?'

'Tell me, Irishman,' Kathryn teased back. 'You once served as the King's marshal?'

Colum nodded.

'You put men in prison?'

Colum agreed.

'And how many of them were loaded down with chains and manacles?'

Colum smiled and touched Kathryn gently on the tip of her nose.

'Clever woman,' he said, leading his horse on. 'Of course! Just because Sparrow was wearing manacles when he escaped, that does not mean he wore them all the time. In his prison cell these would be taken off. They'd only be put on when he was taken out onto the castle green.'

'And that,' Kathryn said, 'does not make our task any easier.'

'In what way?' Colum asked.

'Well . . .' Kathryn replied slowly. 'Sparrow escaped by killing the turnkey and unlocking his manacles.' She winked at Colum. 'Oh, by the way, we never asked what happened to those. Anyway, Sparrow slips from the castle. Quite an easy task, it was dusk and the garrison was reduced to a skeleton force. Now, Irishman, what would you do if you were the escaped prisoner?'

Colum raised his eyebrows. 'I'd steal some food, a horse, a sword, a dagger, whatever. I'd certainly put as much distance between myself and Canterbury as possible.'

'Yet Sparrow doesn't do that,' Kathryn replied. 'Oh, I suppose warnings were issued in the city. However, once the prisoner's free, he'd be miles away before the good burgesses were acquainted with his new-found freedom.' Kathryn stared up at the castle's forbidding keep and thought of Webster falling to his death. 'Something kept Sparrow in Canterbury,' she observed. 'He apparently met a violent death, but at whose hands? Someone ruthless enough not only to kill him but to decapitate his corpse and throw the torso into the Stour.'

'If I follow your thinking,' Colum said, 'the person who murdered Sparrow was frightened of him? Blackmail?'

'Did Sparrow know something about Brandon's death?' Kathryn asked in turn. 'And then use that knowledge?'

'But what would the escaped prisoner know?' Colum asked. 'What, Kathryn, if Sparrow was blackmailing Webster? Did the Constable kill Sparrow, toss his body into the Stour, then suffer some sickness of the mind which led to his suicide from the top of the keep?'

Kathryn led her horse over the drawbridge. 'We are building our castles with straw,' she said. 'We still have to find out whether the corpse is really Sparrow's.'

They found Luberon hopping from one foot to another beside a huge four-wheeled cart standing in the bailey. He waved Colum and Kathryn across.

'I have been here some time,' he declared roundly. 'Mistress Kathryn, this corpse should be buried.' He gazed reprovingly round at the scrawny chickens pecking in the dust and the hounds lazing in the early-morning sun, impervious to his sharp words. 'No one,' he complained, puffing out his fat chest, 'no one here seems to know who I am. I approached that clerk Fitz-Steven but the caitiff just told me to piss off!'

Kathryn seized the little man's hand. 'I am grateful, Simon. And so is Colum. Now,' she added mischievously, 'watch our Irishman stir this nest.'

Colum was already walking towards an ostler sitting on the keep steps, sucking on a piece of straw. He rapped out his orders and the man skipped away, as agile as a rabbit. One by one the officers of the garrison assembled dourly in the yard. All, except Gabele and Fletcher, were scowling as they greeted Colum and Kathryn.

'What is it now?' Fitz-Steven wailed.

'We've brought your prisoner back,' Colum said. 'At least we think it is him. May I also introduce Master Simon Luberon, secretarius to the Archbishop of Canterbury, principal clerk of the city council. A man who, in a bad mood, could make life very difficult for anyone in this castle.'

Luberon was greeted with false smiles, the shuffling of feet and a mumbled apology from Fitz-Steven.

'What is it?' Gabele asked quietly. 'You have brought Sparrow back?'

Kathryn went to the cart and wrenched off the lid of the coffin.

'Well, most of him,' she said drily, wrinkling her nose at the sour smell which seeped from the battered casket.

Colum waved them all forward. 'One at a time, please.'

He jumped onto the cart and helped each of the garrison up. Fitz-Steven was the first and immediately vomited, making him leap from the cart, much to Luberon's satisfaction. The rest were more pragmatic. Peter the chaplain sketched a hasty benediction, bowed his head and left. Fletcher, however, stared hard at the headless corpse.

'Turn it over!' he rasped, gesturing at Colum. 'Just do as I say.'

Colum did so. Fletcher pointed to a faint pink scar which ran across the base of the spine.

'It's Sparrow,' he declared. 'I recognise that scar.' He pointed to the man's hands. 'And if you look on the palm of the right hand, you will see the skin is pitted. Sparrow once told me he burnt his hand when he threw burning charcoal at a law officer in a tavern brawl.'

Colum touched the spongy white flesh. 'They are there.' He turned. 'Gabele?'

The master-at-arms shook his head. 'If Fletcher recognises him, that's good enough for me,' he said, rubbing his stomach. 'I have just broken my fast. I don't want to disgrace myself.'

Colum placed the lid back on the coffin and jumped down from the cart. He gave Luberon a slightly mocking bow.

'Master Simon, I thank you.'

'Do you wish me to stay?' Luberon looked expectantly at Kathryn.

She shook her head. 'We have kept you long enough from important affairs.' She smiled. 'I'll let you know, in God's good time, what happens here.' She addressed the others. 'In the meantime, gentlemen, if you can spare us some of your time?'

Whilst Luberon started shouting for his carter, Colum and Kathryn led the protesting group up into the main hall of the keep. As they gathered round the weak fire burning in the great hearth, Kathryn drew Colum aside.

'On this occasion,' she whispered, 'let us question them individually.'

Colum nodded. Gabele strode across, a look of concern on his face.

'Irishman, we can guess what is coming next. However, this is one of the King's castles and we have business to do. Father

Peter still has to say Mass. The garrison needs its orders, stores have to be checked.'

Colum pointed to the hour-candle spluttering on its iron spigot at the corner of the hearth. The flame was half-way between the tenth and eleventh red circle.

'At eleven,' he said. 'But this time, Simon, we would like to meet you each individually. And yes, you are correct in your surmise: Sparrow escaped from this castle. We believe whoever murdered him resides here and has something to hide.'

Gabele raised his eyebrows in surprise.

'But keep that quiet,' Kathryn added.

Gabele nodded and strode away. He murmured a few words to his companions, which provoked fresh scowls and groans but then they left. Gabele offered Colum and Kathryn wine, which they refused. Once the hall was cleared, Colum arranged a chair and two stools in a far corner under a dusty, battered array of shields. Kathryn gazed around.

'Not too clean,' she muttered.

'Castles never are,' Colum replied.

'What is life like here?' she wondered. 'As a child I remember staring up at the walls and towers. I used to see the banners flying in the wind and thought a castle was a marvellous place. Fairy-tale buildings, full of brave knights and ladies in silks. Dark, mysterious buildings, grim dungeons and tourney grounds which echoed to the beat of pounding hooves and the clash of steel.'

'Lord, woman,' Colum said, gesturing at the chair. 'You spin dreams in your mind.' He looked up at the smoke-blackened rafters and along the wall to the battered hearth. 'For God's sake, Kathryn, look at the moth-eaten drapes.' He kicked the yellowing rushes. 'Castles are the most boring places on God's earth. Poor, rancid, salt-coated meat and wine which curdles the stomach.' He laughed sharply. 'And the garrisons are no better.' He sat down on a stool next to her. 'Every one of those officers,' he continued, 'has something to hide. Now they are all bitter.' He noticed the surprised look on Kathryn's face. 'Oh, yes. All of them are soldiers: Gabele and Fletcher fought on the blood-soaked fields of Towton and Wakefield. Fitz-Steven and Father Peter were camp clerks. Men who, because of their murky past, will receive no benefice from a bishop or preferment in some lord's household. For a while the war between York and Lancaster changed all that.' Colum's eyes gleamed. 'Exciting days, Kathryn! Fast marches against the enemy. Banners and pennants waving. Destriers pawing the ground. Line after line of mounted men. The sky darkening with arrows.' Colum smiled. 'Even I miss it.' He paused. 'Oh, death marches by your side, but it always does. If you're the loser you escape because you're a commoner. Even better, you can change sides. If you are victorious, however, rich pluckings are yours.' Colum waved round the sombre hall. 'Now it's all over. Boring garrison duty, and Canterbury is a *good* posting. Can you imagine what it's like at Alnwick on the Scottish march? Or in the wild wastes of the Welsh march?'

Kathryn leaned forward. 'So any of these men could kill?'

'Of course.' Colum half-laughed. 'We are all killers, Kathryn. Mercenaries, it's the only thing we know. I wager Father Peter has cut a man's throat after he has heard his confession.'

'Even a man like Gabele?'

'Oh, he's got his honour. A good comrade. He'd keep his word but, Kathryn, we are talking about riches. A sapphire which would dazzle these men's souls. An escape from all the boredom of this tawdry life.' Colum paused as a servant walked through the hall and placed another log on the spluttering fire. 'And that makes our task all the more difficult,' he continued as the servant closed the door behind him. 'Prisoners are rarely ill-treated in castles. They are seen as a welcome relief to the boredom. Remember what we were told about Brandon? Everybody went down to the dungeons, even the Righteous Man. Boredom also explains why such a creature found good lodgings here.' Colum played with his leather wrist-guard.

'And,' he continued, 'whatever is said, Brandon told one or all of these officers about the Eye of God.'

Kathryn started as the door was flung open and Gabele came in.

'Well.' The master-at-arms pointed to the candle. 'Come on, Irishman, ask your questions.' He slumped down on the stool and wiped the sweat from his brow with the back of his sleeve. 'Lord, I wish I was free of here.' He smiled at Kathryn. 'I'd do a week's march rather than spend a day sifting through castle stores.'

Kathryn stared at the soldier's hard face and recalled Colum's words. Could this man have met Sparrow in some lonely copse near the Stour, killed him and chopped off his head?

Gabele scratched his unshaven cheek with dirty finger-nails.

'Well, Mistress?'

'You talked to Brandon?'

'Aye, everyone did. And why not? He was a likeable young squire. He had many a droll story.'

'And your daughter took his food to him?'

'Sometimes she did. Sometimes I did, sometimes Father Peter or Fitz-Steven.' He grinned at Colum. 'Fletcher liked him too.'

'And Sparrow?' Kathryn asked.

'Oh, he was a mean bastard. He'd talk, but he was more determined on escaping the hangman's noose.'

'Did the two prisoners ever talk to each other?'

'As I have shown you,' Gabele explained, 'there is a loose brick between the cells. Of course they could talk.'

'And Sparrow's escape?' Colum intervened. 'He was loaded with chains and manacles when he was taken out.'

'Oh, yes, they were put on then.'

'And who was responsible for these?'

'I was,' Gabele replied with a grin. 'Go down to the dungeons; outside each cell hangs a set of manacles, chains and gyves. However, when the prisoner puts these on, it is the turnkey who locks them.'

'What happened to them?' Colum asked.

Gabele pulled a face. 'Sparrow took them with him. For God's sake, Irishman, you have seen the castle. There's more pigeons than soldiers. I suspect Sparrow killed the turnkey, knocked him unconscious and garrotted him. Remember, it was evening. Sparrow took his clothes, the dagger and the manacles with him. A set of loose chains is as deadly as a flailing mace.'

'Did you,' Kathryn asked, 'know Sparrow before his imprisonment?'

Gabele shook his head.

'Or Brandon?'

Again the denial.

'And Sparrow's murder?'

The master-at-arms spread his hands. 'For God's sake, Mistress, why should I kill Sparrow?'

Kathryn could not answer this question. She thanked him. Gabele left and Fletcher came in. He gave virtually the same answers to the same list of questions, except when Colum asked about Brandon.

'Did you often talk to the prisoner?'

Kathryn was sure Fletcher was about to deny this.

'Well, did you?' Kathryn persisted.

Fletcher rubbed his sweat-soaked palms down his dirty jerkin.

'Yes, yes, I did,' he mumbled. 'I captured the man. I rather liked him.'

Kathryn glimpsed the sadness in the man's eyes and began to wonder.

'You are a bachelor, Master Fletcher?'

The fellow positively blushed with embarrassment.

'I greatly liked Brandon,' he stuttered. 'He was witty. He made me laugh.'

'And Sparrow? Did he make you laugh?' Colum asked sharply.

'Sparrow was a ruthless, cunning bastard,' Fletcher retorted. 'That turnkey was clumsy. A man like Sparrow would seize any opportunity.'

'And Webster's death? His strange conduct on the green?'

'I don't think Sir William was murdered,' Fletcher replied in

121

a rush. 'His wits were turned. He had lost two prisoners and the King was angry.' Fletcher played with the pommel of his dagger. 'And if you have no more questions, Master Murtagh, I'd best be about my business.'

Colum agreed, watched him go, then winked at Kathryn.

'And that's another aspect of garrison life,' he said. 'Not every man is what he appears to be.'

Fitz-Steven was next. He was as graceless as ever. Despite Colum's glowering looks and Kathryn's persistent questions, he said as little as possible. Mostly they received grunts for answers or a shake of his head. Kathryn caught a gleam of hate in the man's eyes. You don't like me, she thought to herself, you are wicked enough to kill and hard enough to conceal it.

Colum curtly dismissed him and Father Peter came down, muttering about candle grease on his gown. Kathryn asked him the same questions about Brandon's death, only to receive the same answers.

'He became sick,' the priest said quietly. 'Very sick, very quickly. I gave him the last rites.' He shrugged. 'The rest you know.'

'And Webster?' Kathryn asked. 'Did the Constable talk to you the day before he died?'

'No,' Father Peter replied. 'But he had been drinking. All that stupid mummery on the castle green. He wanted to retrace Sparrow's steps, so I humoured him. It made no sense to me.'

'And did you talk to both prisoners?' Colum asked.

'Well, everyone talked to Brandon: Fitz-Steven, Webster, Gabele.' The priest smirked. 'Certainly Fletcher spent hours with him.'

'And you had never met Brandon or Sparrow before?' Kathryn asked.

The priest blinked and licked his lips nervously.

'You'd met Sparrow before, hadn't you?' she insisted.

The priest nodded. 'Ten years ago,' he admitted, 'I was with the Earl of Pembroke when he battled against the King at

Mortimer's Cross. Sparrow was a young archer then, but just as nasty.'

'So,' Colum smiled. 'You followed the Lancastrians?'

The chaplain laughed. 'Every man in this castle has. We are not all like you, Irishman, enjoying the favour of princes,' he added spitefully. 'Even Gabele fought with Warwick for a while.'

'Did you know Sparrow well?' Kathryn asked.

'No, he didn't recognise me but I recognised him. I saw him kill a man on the eve before Mortimer's Cross. Sparrow choked him to death in a latrine pit.' The priest looked away. 'I was going to enjoy watching him hang.' He picked at a piece of candle grease on his dirty gown. 'I know nothing more.'

He left. Colum and Kathryn collected their horses from the castle stables and left the castle, bidding farewell to no one. They rode in silence for a while. Colum grumbled about the weather, as it had begun to cloud over and a slight rain was beginning to fall. At Saint Mildred's Church he reined in and nodded back to the castle.

'Enough of that for one day,' he said.

'We missed two people,' Kathryn replied. 'Margotta and the Righteous Man.'

'Well, Margotta could not have killed Sparrow,' Colum said. 'If she's involved, she's only an accomplice.'

'And the Righteous Man?'

Colum shook his head. 'The pardoner is probably busily selling his tawdry trinkets in the city. Remember, Kathryn, the pardoner is an outsider. If he did anything untoward in that castle, anything at all, the others would have told us. Now . . .' Colum looked up at the sky. 'I am off to Kingsmead to see what those idle buggers are doing!'

Colum leaned over and kissed Kathryn on the cheek. She absent-mindedly touched her cheek where Colum had kissed her and watched him ride off towards Westgate. She dismounted and led her horse down Ottemelle Lane. Colum was right, she reflected, young Margotta could not kill a man like

Sparrow. But Kathryn was not too sure about the Righteous Man. Couldn't he have slipped something into Brandon's food? A knife into Sparrow? Moreover, dressed in black, the pardoner could flit like a ghost round that dark castle.

Kathryn stabled her horse and walked back to the house. She found the kitchen deserted. Thomasina was at the market, so Kathryn went into her chancery office where she tried to make sense of her jumbled thoughts. She opened the ink-horn, picked up the quill and wrote down the names of all those who lived in the castle. She crossed a line through Margotta's name but concluded that the rest had the means and the strength to kill Brandon as well as throw Webster off the top of the keep.

'What if,' she whispered, 'what if the murders were quite independent of each other?'

She tapped her fingers on the parchment: Fletcher had been as smitten by Brandon as any lovesick swain over a girl. Peter the chaplain may have had a grudge against Sparrow. And Webster's death? Kathryn sighed and threw her quill down in exasperation.

'I wish Colum had come back with me,' she grumbled.

Kathryn heard a sound from the garden and went to the back door. Agnes was kneeling by one of the far flower-beds; she was dressed in her brown cowled gown because of the rain.

'Agnes, how long has Thomasina been gone?'

'I am not Agnes.'

The figure turned and Wuf's cheeky face peered from the hood. He ran down the garden towards Kathryn.

'Thomasina's gone shopping. Agnes is with her. I am hunting for more slugs, so I took Agnes's gown.'

Kathryn kissed him on the head. 'Then you'd better take it off,' she said gently. 'Before Thomasina returns.'

Kathryn walked back to the chancery and stared down at the list of names. She shivered as she drew a circle round all of them.

'What if it was a conspiracy?' she murmured. 'What if they are all involved in the murders of Brandon, Sparrow and Webster?'

Chapter 9

Kathryn and the household had just finished their evening meal. She was about to prepare some medicines for her patients when she was interrupted by a loud knock on the door. Wuf was already in bed, Thomasina was busy in the buttery whilst Colum, strangely silent, sat in front of the fire armed with a large needle and thread, carefully replacing the stitching in one of his bridles. Thomasina had offered to do this but Colum had growled that he was capable enough. He was now stabbing furiously at the piece of leather, reflecting about what he should do with the two corpse-collectors, who had confessed all. Thomasina answered the rap on the door and brought the two visitors, Gabele and Fletcher, into the kitchen. Both of them were armed, booted and spurred, their faces bright with excitement.

'What's happened?' Colum threw the bridle down. 'More trouble at the castle?'

'No, Irishman.' Gabele stood with one foot slightly forward, gently beating the riding crop against his leg. 'I bring orders from his Grace the Duke of Gloucester.'

Kathryn came out of the writing-office. 'He's here,' she exclaimed, 'in Canterbury!'

'Yes, he stopped at the castle to snatch a mouthful of food and a cup of wine. He's with his henchmen—Lovell, Ratcliffe, Catesby and the rest. They have come direct from the King with orders to levy men both from the castle and Kingsmead. Tomorrow morning we go hunting Faunte. Gloucester is determined to capture, try and hang him within the day.'

Colum whistled under his breath.

'Why now?' Kathryn asked.

'His Grace didn't say much,' Fletcher spoke up. 'But the King's spies have reported that tomorrow Faunte may well leave the security of the forest to reach one of the Kentish ports and a ship abroad.'

Colum grabbed his boots, which had been drying in the ingle-nook, and started to pull them on.

'Oh, yes,' he declared. 'Our noble king never forgets a traitor. Just before he advanced against Warwick at Barnet, he cursed Faunte for rousing Canterbury against him and closing the road to Dover.'

Kathryn stared out of the window. 'But it's dark!' she cried. 'It's bad enough to travel the streets of Canterbury in the dead of night, never mind trying to hunt someone across the weald of Kent.'

Colum got to his feet, the spurs on his boots jingling. He took his leather war-belt from a hook on the wall.

'No, no, we'll probably go to Kingsmead where Gloucester will devise his plans. He'll want the hunt to be in progress by daylight. If Faunte breaks cover he'll do so early, when the roads are deserted and the countryside's asleep.'

Colum graciously refused Kathryn's offer of food and wine. He collected his cloak and saddle-bag, smiled good-humouredly at Kathryn, and followed Gabele and Fletcher out.

'Oh, by the way,' Kathryn called.

Gabele and Fletcher stopped.

'Webster's death,' Kathryn continued, 'have you discovered anything?'

Gabele blew his lips out. 'We told Gloucester everything. But no, Mistress, Webster's cold in his grave and it's still a mystery whether he jumped, slipped or was pushed.'

Kathryn thanked them, closed the door and leaned against it, eyes closed. Thank God, she thought, at least Colum will be safe surrounded by Gloucester and his men.

She went back into the kitchen where a sleepy-eyed Agnes was clearing the table, bringing out the dough, bowls, jugs and platters to prepare the bread for the early-morning baking. Thomasina helped her and then, gently scolding the girl, ordered her off to bed. Kathryn studied the little maid closely. Agnes was tired but she kept fingering the small purse she had taken to wearing round her neck. Kathryn sat down on the table bench.

'Agnes,' she called. 'Come here!'

The housemaid scurried across, expectant, eager to please. Kathryn smiled.

'Sit down.'

The housemaid did, her eyes watching her mistress closely.

'Agnes, how long have you been with us?'

The housemaid screwed her face up. 'I think I'm thirteen. Your father took me seven years ago.' Agnes opened her eyes. 'From the Foundling Hospital.'

Kathryn smiled. She rememberd the day well. Her father was always caring for waifs and strays. He'd gone to treat one of the sisters and had simply brought the girl home. No one had ever asked Agnes to be a housemaid, and when Kathryn tried to stop her, the shy little girl had cried for days.

'Agnes, what's in your purse?'

'Oh, Mistress, the coins you give me. They are going to be my dowry.'

'And have you chosen the lucky man?' Kathryn chewed her lip.

'No, but . . .' The girl blushed.

'Are you sure?' Kathryn teased.

'I like Wormhair.'

'Who?'

'Wormhair, the altar boy at Saint Mildred's.'

Kathryn recalled a young boy with the face of an angel and hair so greasy it stood up in spikes. Kathryn had to laugh and she covered her mouth with her hand.

'Agnes, are you happy here? Is there anything I can do?'

The girl just stared at her owlishly.

'Why, Mistress? Aren't you happy with me?'

Kathryn waved her hands as the tears began to well in Agnes's eyes.

'No! No! I am! Thomasina and Wuf treat you well?'

'Wuf's a scamp,' Agnes said. 'Thomasina and I find him a handful.'

Kathryn nodded. 'You had better go to bed,' she said.

The housemaid scurried away.

'Oh, Agnes.'

'Yes, Mistress?'

'Never worry about your dowry. What is mine is yours.'

The girl gazed unblinkingly back.

Kathryn smiled. 'And who knows, perhaps Wormhair could join us one night at supper?'

Agness nodded and ran down the passageway. Thomasina busied herself round the kitchen, singing and humming like some large bumble-bee. Now and again she chattered about the local gossip; how she intended to give Goldere a clip round the ear for his impudence and would Rawnose ever stop talking? Kathryn grinned secretly at that.

'Is the Irishman going to stay here forever?' Thomasina asked abruptly.

'Why?'

'He has his boots well and firmly under the table,' Thomasina declared, looking fiercely at Kathryn.

'I like him,' Kathryn replied. 'I really do, Thomasina.'

'He's not like Chaddedon.'

'Yes, he is,' Kathryn said crossly. 'True, he's also different, yet he's honest and straight.'

'He's bloody moody!'

Kathryn sighed. 'He's worried. He seems to be hapless in this matter entrusted to him by the King and he lives in dread of an assassin.'

Thomasina's face softened. She went to crouch beside her mistress, stroking her gently on the back of the hand.

'Kathryn, he's a soldier, a courtier well-favoured by the princes. If you dance to their measure you'll always live in danger. Now come on, Torquil the carpenter's arriving tomorrow. We have to fix his arm and you know what a baby he is.'

Kathryn grinned and got to her feet. 'Bring me bryony,' she said. 'And, Thomasina, a small potion of nightshade. And wear gloves!'

'I know all that!' Thomasina snapped, bustling down the corridor.

A few minutes later she returned carrying two linen cloths containing the bryony with its thick tuberous root stock, which still bore some shrunken dry berries. Kathryn, also putting on a pair of gloves, removed these and the rough leaves, then, with mortar and pestle, began to crush the juice out of the stem. She stopped and stared down at it, her nose wrinkling at the bitter-sweet smell as she remembered her father's advice.

'Many natural things, Kathryn,' he had often repeated, 'contain the deadliest poisons. I have seen more people die from eating the wrong plant than from wounds in battle. Remember, bryony and nightshade are the most dangerous!'

Kathryn continued her pressing. Her father never knew why or how, but he had warned her how such juice could still be dangerous even if you thoroughly washed your hands afterwards.

'Somehow,' he had declared, 'the skin can breathe it in. I once heard an Arab at Salerno explain how and why, but I found it difficult to understand.'

Kathryn held the small wooden bowl up and carefully

poured the juice into a small phial. A little of it she would add to water and use for chilblains; mixed with a tincture of wine, it would also ease coughs, especially in children. Then she picked up the nightshade and studied the dark dull-green oval leaves, the drooping purple bell-shaped flowers. These were already dead and rotting. She placed the herb on the board and began to crush the juice from the root as well as the leaves. The smell became even more unpleasant. Kathryn walked into the garden for a while, wondering when the stock she had ordered from London would arrive. She went back and continued, taking great care, for the nightshade was costly. It flourished only in chalky limestone and was one of those herbs that spicers and apothecaries paid dearly for. At last she had finished. She mixed some of the bryony with the nightshade in a small cup; she would give this to Torquil the carpenter the following morning to ease his pain. Once this was done, she and Thomasina scrubbed all the implements as well as the table-top with scalding hot water.

Leaving Thomasina in the buttery, Kathryn walked to her writing-office. She heard an owl hoot from the garden and shivered. Didn't Thomasina say the call of a night-bird was a portent of ill omen?

'Oh, for God's sake, Kathryn!' she whispered to herself. 'You are a woman, not Thomasina's child.'

She unlocked a small coffer and took out the piece of parchment she had been writing on. Pulling the flickering candles closer, she carefully read what she had written there. Brandon's death was a mystery, she concluded, and Colum was right: the exhumation of his corpse was the only loose thread they could tug at. She leaned back in the chair, closed her eyes and reflected on Webster's fall from the lofty keep of Canterbury Castle. She pictured the Constable walking on the tower, the brazier spluttering and flickering in the early-morning breeze.

Why should a man who is going to commit suicide light a fire to warm himself? she thought. Why walk about? And that bruise behind his right ear. How did that happen? How did the murderer get onto the tower top unnoticed by Webster or the guards, strike the Constable and toss his unconscious body over the parapet? How did the assassin leave the tower in such a way that the trapdoor was still locked on the other side? In her mind's eye Kathryn visualised the sentry walking up and down the parapet-walk. They had seen a flash of colour as Webster fell and heard his death cry. Death cry! Kathryn opened her eyes.

How could a man who was unconscious cry out?

She felt a flutter of excitement in her stomach. She had been certain of this all day: the cry must have come from someone else. The murderer!

'But how?' she exclaimed aloud. 'How could it be done? And why?'

Kathryn chewed her lip. No one had reported anything untoward about Webster's behaviour except that business with the priest: Webster's attempt to replicate the circumstances which led to Sparrow's escape.

'It's there,' she muttered. 'Someone must have seen Webster do this and became worried. But what was it Webster had discovered?'

Kathryn jumped at the loud knocking on the door. Thomasina's footsteps pattered along the corridor outside, then she hurried back.

'Mistress, there's a poor man outside, his arm's all a-bleeding.'

'Bring him into the kitchen,' Kathryn called.

She took her box of implements and went into the kitchen where Thomasina was helping the man down onto the stool. The stranger seemed in great pain, his body huddled over, favouring his right arm. Kathryn could see the blood specks on the newly scrubbed kitchen floor.

'Who are you?' she said.

The man's head was bowed, his hood pulled forward. Kathryn went to take his arm and the man moved quickly, straightening up. He pulled a small arbalest from beneath his

131

cloak, the crossbow bolt ready in its groove. Kathryn exclaimed and stood back. Thomasina, preparing water over the fire, heard her cry of surprise and turned. She recognised the danger in one quick glance and advanced threateningly; the stranger pulled back his head, revealing a mass of blood-red hair framing his face and falling down to his shoulders. The patch over his right eye gave his thin white face an even more vicious look. Kathryn caught a glimpse of those bloodless lips and guessed who this man was.

'You are Fitzroy?'

The man cocked his head on one side. 'Now there's an intelligent woman,' he exclaimed. 'Bright as a button, sharp as a needle.' He turned, moving the crossbow slightly, aiming it fully at Thomasina's stomach. 'And you must be the nurse? Now don't be a silly girl. Don't do anything rash or old Padraig will have to kill you!'

'Sit down, Thomasina,' Kathryn ordered. 'I don't think Master Fitzroy means us any harm.'

The fellow's good eye studied Kathryn coldly. 'You are toothsome enough,' he declared. 'Trust old Colum to find a pleasant port.'

'Shut your filthy mouth!' Thomasina snarled. 'Mistress Swinbrooke is your better!'

Padraig shifted the crossbow in his hand and glared at Thomasina.

'Listen, you old bitch, I have killed everything that moves, men, women, even the occasional old crone.'

'I suppose that was easy,' Thomasina retorted. 'Especially if their backs were turned!'

Fitzroy laughed. 'You'll come to no harm from me,' he assured them. He took a pace back and gestured with one hand. 'Please, Mistress Swinbrooke, don't do anything rash or stupid.'

'You have come to kill Colum?'

'Aye, dark-eyed Colum. Judged by our council to be a traitor.'

'He's no traitor,' Kathryn said, just wishing she could stop

132

her legs from trembling, and why must she appear so breathless? 'He's no traitor,' she repeated firmly. 'He was a mere boy when York took him. What would you do? Accept a pardon or be hanged?'

'My brother had no choice. He died kicking at the end of an English rope.' Fitzroy touched the patch over his eye. 'And when they took me, they squeezed this eye out of its socket.'

For a few seconds Kathryn caught a look of sadness in the man's hard face.

'That's the way of the world, Kathryn. I can call you Kathryn?' He didn't wait for her reply. 'Once we were golden boys, Colum and I, fast as the deer. Swift as the plummeting hawk. Blood-brothers.'

'And now you have come to kill him?'

'Yes, it should come as no surprise. Surely he's been expecting me?'

'And the Eye of God?' Kathryn asked suddenly.

Fitzroy's grin widened. 'Aye, we'd like it back. If Colum can promise to deliver it, we'd consider a pardon.'

Kathryn stared at the muscle twitching high in Fitzroy's cheek.

'You are lying,' she said softly. 'You'll kill him whatever he does. Don't lie to me!'

Fitzroy nodded.

'Look!' Kathryn pointed to the blood dripping from the man's arm. 'You are wounded!'

'Oh, no.' Fitzroy moved the crossbow. He put his hand up his sleeve and took out a small blood-soaked sponge. 'I dipped this in the gutter outside the Shambles.' He threw it on the floor, the blood spattering in scarlet drops. 'Do you know, it always works.'

'Colum's not here,' Kathryn said defiantly.

'Oh, I know that, but we have to do everything according to the ritual. Bring me a cup of wine, put it on the table, add a little vinegar, next to it place a small piece of bread covered in salt.'

'Why?'

'Do it, woman, and remember I have my eyes on Thomasina!'

Kathryn obeyed. She put the wine in a cup, added a drop of vinegar and placed the salted bread beside it.

'Would you like some wine?' she asked hopefully.

Fitzroy walked over and touched her gently on the cheek.

'You are a brave lass, Kathryn, but I'm not stupid. A cup of wine with something to make me sleep?'

Kathryn wiped her sweat-soaked hands on her dress as she held the Irishman's gaze.

'Why?' she asked.

'He should never have taken the English King's pardon.'

'And why so long?'

Fitzroy stepped back. 'Hasn't he told you, Kathryn? I am the fourth they have sent. The other three never returned. Now, Kathryn—'Fitzroy gestured at Thomasina to stand. 'Turn round and stare at the fire.'

Kathryn pointed at the wine and bread.

'Oh, don't worry about that,' Fitzroy smiled. 'Colum will know. Now please, turn around.'

Kathryn and Thomasina had no choice. They heard the shuffle of Fitzroy's footsteps and the sounds of the door closing behind him as he disappeared into the darkened street. Kathryn slumped down on the stool.

'Well, that's the last time we do that, Thomasina.'

Her nurse came over and put her arm round her shoulders. She could feel Kathryn tremble.

'No, it won't, Mistress.' She gently stroked Kathryn's tumbling black hair. 'If someone was really hurt, you'd help.' She went to the buttery and brought back a big-bowled cup of claret. 'Come on,' she coaxed. 'Drink it slowly. It's that bloody Irishman! Why had he to bring his sack of troubles here?'

Kathryn sipped from the wine.

'If he was killed, Thomasina, if he died . . .' Kathryn grasped Thomasina's hand and looked over her shoulder. 'I think something in me might die.'

'Fiddlesticks!' Thomasina blurted out.

She flounced round the kitchen, cleaning up the blood from the floor, keeping ever so busy so that Kathryn would not see the tears brimming in her eyes.

'Bloody Irishman! Bloody, bloody men!'

At last Thomasina was exhausted by her stream of curses. She and Kathryn doused the fire and candles and retired to bed, the wine easing Kathryn into a dream-ridden sleep.

She was woken early the next morning by Wuf, running up the stairs pretending to be a knight, rattling the wooden sword Colum had made along the rails of the stairs. Kathryn washed, dressed and broke her fast in the kitchen. Agnes, cheerful as ever, built up the fire, oblivious to the silent, sombre faces of Kathryn and Thomasina. It was good the patients arrived early, Torquil the carpenter amongst them. Kathryn dealt swiftly and coolly with their complaints, keeping her mind on the business in hand, trying not to glance at the cup of wine and piece of salted bread. Thomasina offered to throw them away.

'No,' Kathryn declared. 'It's a message for Colum, he will decide.

She continued to deal with her patients' complaints. Little Edith came last, still gripping her stomach. Kathryn, feeling sorry for her, dispensed a rather costly herbal potion made from the herb of grace or rue whose blue-green leaves provided a juice which seemed to ease menstruation pains. After the girl had left, Kathryn washed her hands and walked down to a deserted Saint Mildred's Church to light a candle and kneel before the Lady Altar as her father had taught her. She said a prayer for his soul and for her own peace of mind. She was still confused by the events at the castle and frightened of what the future held for Colum. She found it difficult to concentrate and wondered if she should go and see Father Cuthbert at the Poor Priests' Hospital. She lit another candle and left. On the corner of Ottemelle Lane Rawnose stood, a small crowd gathering around him. This self-proclaimed herald of the ward was dispensing his usual stream of gossip. Only this time Kathryn stopped and listened.

'Oh, yes.' Rawnose's voice strengthened. 'Nicholas Faunte the rebel has been captured trying to cross the weald of Kent. He and five others are at the Guildhall where they will be tried and hanged. His Grace the Duke of Gloucester is most pleased. He has issued a proclamation saying once Faunte is dead, the King will restore the privileges of the city.'

Rawnose's statement was greeted by gasps and sighs. Kathryn fairly sped up Ottemelle Lane, throwing the door of the house open so violently she almost knocked over Agnes, who was laying fresh rushes. Colum was in the kitchen, his face drawn and tired and covered from head to toe with flecks of caked mud. He hardly lifted his head as she entered but stared at the cup and piece of bread placed in the middle of the table. Thomasina and a strangely silent Wuf stood by the hearth, both of them watching the Irishman, their eyes round as owls' eyes as they awaited his reaction.

'You've heard the news, Mistress Swinbrooke!'

Colum's eyes did not move. He just scratched his straggling black hair, then undid his sword-belt, which he threw on the floor beside him.

'Yes, I have heard the news,' Kathryn said, sitting opposite him. 'And Thomasina has told you about our visitor?' She started as Colum leaned forward and dashed both the wine-cup and the bread onto the floor.

'God damn him!' he shouted. 'God damn his black soul!'

Wuf began to cry and pushed closer to Thomasina. Kathryn turned and indicated with her head that they should both leave. Thomasina needed no second bidding, whilst Agnes continued to sift the rushes time and again, as if frightened to re-enter the kitchen.

'What does it all mean, Colum?' Kathryn asked.

The Irishman glanced up at her, his eyes red-rimmed with dark circles beneath. He scratched his chin.

'What does it mean?' Kathryn repeated. 'Fitzroy said he was the fourth to come after you.'

'Aye, he's right.' Colum sighed. 'I sent the other three packing. This'—he waved his hand at the fallen cup—'this is how they always warn you. The cup of bitterness and the bread of sorrows.' The Irishman smiled bleakly. 'Fitzroy is saying my death is very close.'

'And you are afraid?' Kathryn could have kicked herself as soon as the words were out of her mouth.

Colum straightened up, resting his elbows on the table, his hands up to his mouth, looking strangely at her.

'Afraid?' he said. 'Afraid of Fitzroy? No, I am not frightened, Kathryn. I am angry that he came here to leave his filthy message. I would have had more respect for him if he had gone to Kingsmead. But that's the way of Fitzroy, he always did have a bully-boy streak in him. Believe me, for that I'm going to kill him. I don't know how or when, but I am going to kill him!'

Colum refused to say any more. Thomasina came back and, without being invited, served him bread, cheese and a jug of beer. After that, Colum went upstairs to shave, wash and change. He came down a different man, almost happy. Kathryn knew that Fitzroy's visit was now a closed book and Colum was eager to tell her about Faunte's capture.

'He was betrayed,' the Irishman declared, sitting by the hearth to put his boots on. 'His following was reduced to six. One of these sent a message to a powerful burgess in London, offering to betray Faunte in return for a pardon. We captured him as he left the wood, like a hawk would a pigeon. Making for a port they were. They surrendered without a fight.'

'And where are they now?' Kathryn asked.

'At the Guildhall, Faunte and five others. They are going to be tried at noon and hanged at one o'clock. Or at least Faunte will. The traitor has already received his pardon and been released.' Colum glanced at Kathryn and winked. 'I want you to come with me. In fact, the Duke is most insistent on that.'

'Why?' Kathryn asked. 'Colum, did Faunte have any news about Wyville?'

'You'd best come,' Colum repeated.

Kathryn left instructions with Thomasina and hurriedly prepared herself. Colum went to collect their horses from the tavern at the far end of the street. They were not even half-way up Hethenman Lane before Kathryn realised that the news of Faunte's capture had swept through the city. When they turned into the High Street the crowds were already massing. Colum had to force their way through to the Guildhall steps, which were thronged by soldiers wearing Gloucester's livery; men-at-arms in their steel conical hats and chain-mail hauberks; archers in their leather jackets and green hoods whilst, at the top of the steps, stood three heralds each carrying a flag bearing the arms of England, York and Gloucester. At the entrance to the Guildhall one of Gloucester's henchmen, a heavy-lidded, handsome-faced man who introduced himself as Lord Francis Lovell, allowed them into the passageway thronged by servitors, chamberlains and more soldiers.

They found Gloucester in the upper council chamber, seated behind a long, polished oak table which the aldermen of the city used. He was talking softly to Gabele and Fletcher whilst, at one end of the table, a busy-looking Luberon was preparing parchments, ink and wax for the coming trial. As soon as Gloucester glimpsed Colum, he waved the two soldiers away and beckoned both Kathryn and the Irishman forward. Rising in that lopsided way of his, he firmly clasped Colum's hand and, with a swift jerking movement, raised Kathryn's fingers to his lips.

'Mistress Swinbrooke,' he said. 'Once again I have the pleasure.'

Kathryn smiled but she was apprehensive; in his half-armour and chain-mail coif, Gloucester, unshaven and tired, looked even more dangerous than the smooth courtier she had met in London. The Duke sat down, beating a tattoo on the table with his fingers.

'We are most pleased,' he declared. 'Most pleased with you, Colum.' His green, cat-like eyes studied the Irishman. 'You knew the roads well, or Faunte could have slipped through our fingers. Oh yes, oh yes, he could have done. Now he will stand trial for his life. You, Mistress Swinbrooke, will be a witness at the trial. Our loyal servant Luberon the clerk, and I, under letters patent issued by my good brother the King, will be Faunte's judge. Master Murtagh, you will assist me, as will my henchmen, Lovell, Catesby and Ratcliffe.' He caught the look of disbelief in Kathryn's eyes. 'I know what you are thinking, Mistress,' he snapped. 'No trial by jury, but this is war. Faunte was a rebel and a traitor. When I rode against him this morning I carried the unfurled banner of the King of England. Faunte fled from that, which is treason. He will be tried by the rules of war and condemned. Now——' He got to his feet, his fingers resting on the table as he leaned over. 'This business of the Eye of God, Irishman.' Gloucester's eyes were cold and hard. 'No success! No success! But time will tell. You have our permission to exhume Brandon's body.'

'But whom do we have who can recognize him?' Colum enquired.

Gloucester's lips crooked into a smile, his eyes slid to Kathryn.

'Have a word with Faunte,' he said. 'And his companions. We are inclined to be merciful. Faunte must die, but there's no need for the rest. Oh, and Mistress Swinbrooke, ask Faunte and his followers about Alexander Wyville.' He watched Kathryn's face pale. 'No,' he continued softly, 'don't be afraid, let them tell you what they know.'

He sat down, shouting for the captain of his guard to take Kathryn and Colum down to the cells beneath the Guildhall.

A few minutes later Colum and Kathryn were ushered into Faunte's sour-smelling cell. A small, narrow chamber with no grille or window, only a torch spluttered in its rusty holder high in the mildewed wall. Nicholas Faunte, once the proud mayor of Canterbury, crouched on a tattered sack which served as a bed. Kathryn remembered the mayor in better days. She could hardly believe her eyes as she and Colum sat on stools provided by the guard. Faunte's face was almost hidden by straggling hair and beard, all she could see were dirty cheeks and the man's sad eyes. He was dressed in rags, bound hand and foot with chains and gyves. Every time he moved, the heavy manacles clinked. Kathryn felt a pang of compassion at the tight chain which linked the iron clasps about his ankles to those round his wrists: it pulled his shoulders forward, making Faunte look hunchbacked and misshapen. He stared at Colum, who looked away.

'What's the matter, Irishman?' Faunte mumbled. 'Have you come to gloat or to torture me?' He lifted his clasped hand and gingerly felt the purpling bruise over his left eye. 'There was no need for that,' he whispered.

'I am sorry,' Colum replied.

'It's when they brought me down here,' Faunte retorted.

Kathryn noticed the blood bubbling at his lips. Colum turned and called for the guard.

'A skin of wine,' he ordered.

The man was about to refuse.

'Do it!' Colum snarled. 'Or I'll have you digging latrines for a month!'

The man shrugged and hurried away. He came back with a wineskin. Colum gently raised the man's head and put it to his lips. Faunte drank greedily until he spluttered and coughed.

'Leave it,' he begged as Colum took the wineskin away. 'When you leave, please leave it. No man should die sober.'

Colum placed the wineskin by his stool. Faunte nodded at Kathryn.

'Who is she and why is she here?'

'My name is Kathryn Swinbrooke, my father was a physician in Ottemelle Lane.'

'Swinbrooke?' Faunte's head went back. 'Ah yes, I remember him. A good physician.' He leaned forward, the chain tugging

140

at his neck and hands. 'So you are his daughter?' He coughed. 'I did you no injury.'

'No, sir, you did not,' Kathryn replied. 'But you may have known my husband, Alexander Wyville, an apothecary. He joined your master early in the year.'

'Glorious days,' Faunte said wistfully. 'Do you know I really did think Warwick would be victorious at Barnet. What did your husband look like?'

'Tall, blond-haired, his nose slight, a small birth mark on his cheek, smooth-shaven.'

Faunte just shook his head. 'So many,' he murmured. 'And so many died. But wait, an apothecary? Yes, I remember him.' Faunte rubbed his face in a rattle of chains. 'Two men in one; sober he was good, clean and effective, but when drunk, an ugly character. I had to warn such a man, just after we left Canterbury, about an alleged attack on a woman.' Faunte shook his head. 'Secretive and sly he seemed. Yet he didn't call himself Wyville but Robert . . . yes, Robert Lessinger.'

Kathryn's stomach churned. 'Lessinger, you are sure?'

'Yes, why?'

'It was his mother's name.'

'Well, that's what he called himself, and before you ask, Mistress, I don't know whether he lived or died. He was in my troop at Barnet, but after that . . .' Faunte sneered. 'Most of them ran like rabbits. Lessinger, or whatever he called himself, amongst them.'

'Did you know Brandon?' Colum asked abruptly.

'Warwick's squire?'

'The same. You saw him at Barnet?'

Faunte shrugged. 'From afar. Why? Have he and the other poor bastards been caught?'

'The others?' Kathryn asked.

'Yes. When York attacked and Warwick fell, the cry went up, "Sauve Qui Peut!" Every man was left to his own. I and my companions fled into the woods. Some days after the battle we were alarmed by news of a troop of horsemen, so we planned an ambush. We thought they were pursuers but they still wore Warwick's colours—Moresby, Brandon, and four other companions from the battle.'

'Four?' Colum interrupted.

'Oh yes, I had nothing to do with them. Ask one of my comrades. Yes, Philip Sturry.' Faunte laughed. 'I think he's close by and not very busy. I left them alone but Sturry, Moresby and Squire Brandon exchanged gossip. The squire confirmed Warwick was dead and said he hoped to reach Canterbury. They were going to break out of the woods and go to Harbledown.' Faunte shrugged. 'That's all.'

Colum nodded and helped Kathryn to her feet.

'I am sorry,' he said, picking up the wineskin and handing it to Faunte. 'Is there anything I can do?'

'How about a pardon?'

Colum shook his head. Faunte cradled the wineskin.

'Then give my love to the sunlight.' The ex-mayor grinned. 'Drink a cup of claret for me on a soft summer's evening. Oh, and ask Gloucester for a priest.'

Chapter 10

*S*turry and the rest of Faunte's companions were huddled in the next cell. They were convivial, relieved their trials were over as well as confident that, unlike their master, they would not pay the supreme penalty for their opposition to the King. Sturry was a talkative little man, merry-eyed; his hair should have been blond but it was covered with dirt and mud. Like Faunte's, Sturry's beard and moustache had grown straggling like a bush. Neither he nor his companions were Canterbury men but hailed from the villages and towns around, so none of them recognised Kathryn nor she them. At first Colum reassured them all would be well and that Richard of Gloucester would not exact full retribution for their treason.

'Indeed,' Colum declared, 'if you can help us in our present enquiries, God knows what our good Duke might decide.'

Sturry scratched his beard, pulling out the straggly ends.

'We'll take no oath against Faunte,' he said. 'Nor provide any testimony. We may be beaten men, Master Murtagh, but we don't betray good friends.'

'No, no,' Colum replied. 'We are more interested in your

meeting with Moresby and his party after Warwick's defeat at Barnet.'

'Ah!' Sturry grinned. 'Why not be honest, Irishman. You are really interested in what they were carrying.'

'Then tell me,' Colum ordered.

Sturry shook his head. 'I don't know what it was but both Brandon and Reginald Moresby, the captain of Warwick's bodyguard, were most secretive about what they were guarding.'

Sturry moved to ease the chafing of the chains biting into his wrist. 'You don't have to be a scholar from Oxford, Irishman, to put two and two together. Brandon and Moresby never let that wallet out of their sight. Moreover, they had just avoided Yorkist patrols and were eager to slip quietly into Canterbury.' Sturry glanced slyly at Colum. 'What was in the pouch?' he asked. 'Some precious item belonging to the dead Earl?'

Colum shrugged.

'Did Brandon or Moresby say anything else?' Kathryn asked.

'They cursed their fortune and that of Warwick's. They said they would reach Canterbury, do what they had to do, then either go into hiding or take a ship abroad.'

'What was Brandon like?'

'Cultured, diplomatic.' Sturry sniffed. 'In appearance a sturdy, pliant fellow with sandy hair. The real leader was Moresby. He exercised great discipline over the rest.'

'Who were they?'

'Squires from Warwick's household.'

'Listen.' Kathryn crouched down, hiding her distaste at the sour, foul smells of the cell. 'Did Moresby and Brandon describe what route they'd take into the city?'

'No, except they were going to break out of the woods, hide by day and ride by night. They had already decided to conceal themselves at Sellingham. You know the place, Mistress?'

Kathryn nodded. 'A deserted village ten miles north of Canterbury. There's an old church and some ruins. One of those places devastated by the plague.'

Sturry agreed, his eyes bright with excitement. 'The same. Brandon said he would lead his group there. Moresby invited us to join them but Faunte ruled against it. After that, we parted.'

Colum and Kathryn thanked the man and prepared to leave.

'Irishman!' Sturry called out. 'You'll speak to Gloucester for us?'

'Aye.'

'And, for the love of God, some water, a little food?'

Colum promised he would do what he could. When they left the cells, he did ask the captain of the guard, as a personal favour, to ensure the prisoners were fed.

They returned to the Guildhall chamber where Gloucester was putting final touches to the tribunal. He waved Colum to an empty seat and introduced his henchmen. Kathryn quickly glanced at these. Warriors all, she thought, with their hard faces and hooded eyes. A group of falcons come to mete out judgement: Faunte would find little mercy with them.

'We should begin,' one of Richard's henchmen declared. 'Your Grace said Faunte would hang within the hour.'

'If it pleases your Grace.' Colum got up, tapping the table-top. 'Your Grace, if it pleases, may I make a request?'

Gloucester nodded.

'Faunte is a traitor,' Colum said. 'But, your Grace, I beg you to show mercy to his followers, especially Sturry, who may be of help to us in another matter.'

Gloucester half-turned and studied Colum's face.

'If your Grace remembers,' Colum persisted, 'it is your brother's policy to execute the leaders but show great compassion to their followers.'

Gloucester raised one green-gloved hand, the jewelled ring winking in the weak sunlight, and beckoned Colum forward. The Irishman went and leaned over the high-backed chair. Gloucester whispered and Colum replied. The Prince nodded and whispered again before dismissing Colum with a flicker of his fingers.

'Faunte will stand trial,' Gloucester pronounced, straightening in his chair. 'The rest can cool their heels in the cells for another month. They will be freed on a pardon after their families have each paid a fine of one hundred marks. Sturry is an exception, he will be released into your custody, Irishman. If he provides assistance, he shall go free.'

After that Faunte's trial began. The prisoner, still loaded with chains, was hustled up into the chamber. Luberon, in a strong voice, read out the charges and Kathryn had to admire the ex-mayor's courage. He refused to deny anything.

'I fought,' he declared, 'for the Lord's Anointed, Henry the Sixth, God rest him, by divine favour, King of England. If I have to die,' he said, smiling, 'then I die in his service. No king had a better servant than I.'

Kathryn watched the formalities being observed as the trial swung to its inevitable conclusion. It lasted, at the very most, half an hour, before Luberon took a black silk cloth and placed it carefully on top of Gloucester's head.

'Nicholas Faunte,' Gloucester declared, 'you stand convicted as an attainted traitor, of bearing arms against your rightful sovereign, Edward the Fourth, King of England, Ireland, Scotland and France. Now hear the sentence of this court!' Gloucester's voice became sombre. 'You are to be taken from this place on a hurdle and carried to a legal place of execution where you will be hanged, drawn and quartered; your bowels removed; your head struck off and the parts of your corpse sent to different areas of the kingdom as the King's will directs! May the Lord have mercy on your soul!'

Faunte paled a little at each terrible word Gloucester uttered.

'I ask the court for mercy.'

'No mercy!' one of Gloucester's henchmen shouted.

The Duke raised a hand.

'My family?' Faunte asked.

'We do not make war against women and children,' Gloucester replied.

'A priest, I wish to be shriven.' The prisoner lifted manacled hands.

'I am of noble blood!' Faunte exclaimed. 'I beg my poor body be spared the indignities of the sentence. Death is enough!'

'Denied!' The henchmen shouted in unison.

Colum looked at Kathryn who gazed unblinkingly back, her eyes said everything. Colum raised a hand to speak and Gloucester nodded his consent.

'Your Grace, Faunte was most co-operative in answering certain questions.'

Gloucester stared stonily back.

'He was well liked in this area,' Colum continued rather stumblingly. 'Great mercy befits a great prince.'

Gloucester pushed away the papers in front of him.

'The sentence will be death alone!' he declared and beckoned to the captain of his guard. 'Let the traitor have a priest. Once that's done, take him out and hang him!'

The tribunal broke up. Gloucester and his henchmen huddled in consultation. Colum came over to Kathryn, pale and tense. Kathryn pinched him on the arm.

'You did a noble thing.'

The Irishman gazed bleakly at her.

'Why do you say that? Because I had the sentence commuted?' Colum stared around and lowered his voice. 'I wish to God I could claim merit for that but Gloucester ordered me to plead for Faunte. The protracted agonies of a popular man might have excited sympathy.' Colum looked away. 'None of the rest would do it. Come, let's get out of here!'

Colum quickly escorted Kathryn out of the chamber. Outside, the corridors and stairs were thronged with soldiers watching Faunte being taken down for the last time to his cell, a brown-garbed Franciscan monk following.

'Why does the smell of death make people so excited?' Colum whispered. Linking his arm through Kathryn's, he steered her half-way down the corridor. He opened the door of a small, dusty writing-office, now deserted, as the clerks joined the throng in the streets below waiting for Faunte to be taken out.

'What do you think?' Colum asked.

'Gloucester would make a bad enemy.'

Colum grinned. 'No, about what we learnt.'

Kathryn stared at the dusty window frames, noticing the huge cobwebs in the corner and the ink-splattered tables.

'Colum, we must exhume Brandon's corpse, though there seems little contradiction between the Brandon Sturry described and the prisoner kept in Canterbury Castle.'

'And what else?'

Kathryn pursed her lips, feeling slightly embarrassed; she and Colum were rarely in the same room alone. Kathryn recalled those hard-eyed men who had just sentenced Faunte to death and realised how different she and the Irishman were. They came from separate worlds. Perhaps Thomasina was right; Chaddedon belonged to hers, but Colum was a warrior dealing in death, harsh measures and brutal judgement. She heard a roar from outside: Faunte must have been shriven and was now being taken out to the makeshift scaffold hurriedly set up in the Buttermarket.

'What else did you learn?' Colum repeated.

'There's no doubt Gloucester wanted Faunte's death, but the Eye of God must be something special. What secret can it hold?'

Colum looked sharply at her. 'And what about Lessinger?' he asked.

'To me,' Kathryn replied, 'he'll always be Alexander Wyville.' She chewed the corner of her lip. 'I couldn't care,' she continued, 'what he calls himself or where he is; if he returns here, I shall confront him.' Kathryn played with the ring on her finger. ' "Sufficient for the day is the evil thereof," ' she murmured and stared at the dust-motes dancing in the sunlight which poured through the mullioned glass window.

Colum got up from the table he was resting against and opened the door.

'Then let's leave. Sturry will be released, given a shave, a rough wash and a change of clothing, whilst we shall both go to the castle and pluck poor Brandon from his grave.'

They went downstairs and were almost out of the Guildhall when Kathryn caught a flash of red hair as Megan hurried towards them, shouting Colum's name at the top of her voice.

'What's the matter, woman?'

'It's Pul——' Megan tried to pronounce the horse's name.

'Pulcher!' Colum said.

'Yes, he's broken loose. There's no one about. I followed him down to the gibbet near the crossroads, but . . .' Megan fluttered her hands, her green eyes seemed even bigger in her pale white face.

'Of course,' Colum grumbled. 'All the men are here in Canterbury, only the women and children remain at Kingsmead. Come on, Kathryn!'

They walked into Burghgate, Megan trotting beside them, chattering about how the horse was so skittish. They went up some steps. Kathryn looked quickly in the direction of the Buttermarket, over the heads of the crowds massed there. She glimpsed the black-garbed executioner, the great two-armed gibbet soaring above him. Faunte leaned against the scaffold rail, talking to the crowd, but she couldn't hear what he was saying. Colum hurried her on. They collected their horses from a nearby stable and, with Megan perched up behind him, Colum bade Kathryn a hasty farewell.

'I'll deal with this matter,' he said. 'Collect Sturry from the Guildhall cell, then we shall go to the castle.' He gathered the reins in his hands. 'Oh, Kathryn, you be careful; open the door to no one!'

Kathryn agreed, ignoring the malicious grin on Megan's face as she grasped Colum round his waist. Kathryn watched them ride away and, turning her horse's head, ambled down a narrow alley-way which would lead into Whitehorse Lane. Behind her the clamour of the crowd was stilled just for a few seconds. She was sure she heard the clatter of the scaffold ladder being pushed away, followed by a wild roar of approval. She wondered why people became so excited at the sight of violent death and recalled her father's words: "Always remember, Kathryn, we are half angel and half beast. Unfortunately, the latter half often prevails." Kathryn sighed. She hoped Colum would be safe and tried to dismiss her pang of disapproval at the way Megan had sat so perkily behind the Irishman, her red hair trailing in the breeze. They would go to the crossroads near the old gibbet . . . Kathryn stopped, clutching at her stomach as it lurched in fear.

'Oh, Lord,' she breathed, 'Oh, my God! What did Rawnose say about disembodied voices at the crossroads? A witch with flaming hair? And now Colum is being taken there!'

She turned her horse's head round, digging her heels in to urge it faster, and headed back towards the High Street. The crowds would still be there, so she lost precious time threading her way through alley-ways which debouched into Hethenman Lane, turning left at All Saints. She went up Kingsbury, to Saint Peter's Street, towards Westgate and the bridge across the Stour. Kathryn was not the best of horsewomen and the crowds impeded her progress. Time and again abuse was hurled at her, even handfuls of mud, but at last she went under the great yawning mouth of Westgate into Dunstan Street, following the road north along the country lanes to Kingsmead. Kathryn passed the manor basking quietly under the late-afternoon sun. She quickly dismissed any thought of going there for help and desperately wished Wuf and Thomasina were with her. Of Colum and Megan she couldn't catch a glimpse; the Irishman, being a master horseman, would have travelled much faster. However, a peasant digging ditches just beyond the manor said he had seen the soldier and a red-haired woman riding towards the crossroads. He loudly assured Kathryn that she was on the right track.

'Everyone's going there,' he called. 'Well,' the fellow said in answer to Kathryn's puzzled look, 'an hour before the soldier and his redhead, another man passed by, strange he looked, with a black patch over his eye.'

Kathryn hurried on. Just before the bend in the trackway Kathryn dismounted, hobbled her horse and quietly edged round, keeping close to the wild bushes in the overgrown hedgerow. From the corner of the lane, she could see the top of the old three-branched scaffold. Kathryn moved closer. Colum was only a few paces from where Fitzroy stood holding a loaded arbalest. Megan lay sprawled on the grass beside Fitzroy, moaning as she held her face. Fitzroy, holding the heavy Brabantine crossbow, apparently was taunting Colum, and shouting at him to keep his distance every time the Irishman edged forward. Kathryn stared in panic.

'He's going to kill him,' she whispered. 'If I run, both of us might die. What can I do? What can I do?' Kathryn closed her eyes and muttered a prayer, then jumped to her feet and shouted, 'Fitzroy, stop!'

The ruse worked. Fitzroy, startled, looked up the track as Colum threw himself at his enemy, knocking the crossbow flying. They both grappled to the ground. Fitzroy kicked Colum away, stood up, retreated and picked up the great two-handed sword resting against the scaffold. Colum drew his and, as Kathryn ran towards them, both men began their deadly dance, swords up, level with their chest, legs slightly apart.

Fitzroy steadied his breathing. 'So, Colum, ma fiach, just like boys again, eh? Do you remember wooden swords, two ragged-arsed boys pretending to be knights in a world of chivalry?'

Colum didn't flinch. 'God forgive me, Padraig!' he whispered. 'But I am going to kill you!'

'You are forgiven!'

Fitzroy attacked, sword jabbing forward, then coming back in a wide sweeping arc aimed at Colum's neck. Murtagh feinted. The silence of the forest was broken by the rasp and hiss of steel. Kathryn could only stand and watch. She wished she had a dagger; rules of chivalry or not, this was a fight to the death. Fitzroy meant to kill Colum and he was ruthless enough to leave no witnesses. At first she could see Murtagh was clumsy, out of sorts, but as the deadly dance continued, his skill and confidence grew. Never once did he leave his chosen place, constantly inviting Fitzroy on. Sometimes the sword blades would simply flicker at each other like the tongues of snakes, followed by sweeping arcs, sudden parries and cuts. Both men became drenched in sweat. Megan sat up, holding her swollen face where Fitzroy had punched her.

'I am hurt!' she wailed. 'I am hurt!'

'Shut your mouth, you stupid bitch!' Kathryn hissed. 'Or it will be nothing to what I'll give you!'

Megan lapsed into silence, head forward on her knees as the two swordsmen clashed and drew apart, their arms growing heavy, sweat coursing in great fat drops down their faces. Both men paused and gasped for air. The swords came up again. Colum turned sideways, arms up, the sword blade level with his eyes. Fitzroy moved. Kathryn only glimpsed what happened next. Colum's sword snaked forward, beat Fitzroy's down and then, in a great shimmering swish, took Fitzroy clean through the neck. The head bounced like a ball on the grass, a great arc of blood bubbling from the severed head. Kathryn turned away, crouching in the grass to control the terror seething inside her. She felt fingers clutch her hair and looked up to see Colum resting on the great hilt of his sword, gasping for breath.

'If I have said it once,' he panted, 'I'll say it again. You're a bonny lass, Mistress Swinbrooke, and if anyone gainsays it, he is a liar!'

Kathryn looked past him at the fallen headless torso, the blood forming a blackened, congealing pool around it.

'God rest him!' Colum breathed. 'He was a good man until hate took his heart.' He flung his sword down and crouched beside Kathryn. 'That's the demon in all our souls. We begin killing to defend ourselves, but in the end some of us begin to like it, an insatiable appetite for death.' He wiped his face on the sleeve of his jerkin. 'Or, as Chaucer says, 'Oh treacherous homicide, oh wickedness.'' '

Kathryn leaned forward and dabbed his cheeks with a kerchief.

'If you quote from Chaucer once more, I'll take your head myself, Irishman!'

She struggled to her feet, drawing deep breaths. Colum, still panting, got up to join her.

'Leave Fitzroy,' he grunted. 'I'll send others to bury him.'

'Oh, Master Murtagh.' Megan came crawling on her hands and knees towards him. She looked up, her face a picture of grieving terror. 'I had to do it!' she wailed. 'He summoned me here to the crossroads! He said if he didn't take your head he'd take mine!'

'And if I told Holbech,' Colum muttered, 'he'd take yours, red hair or not!' He turned away. 'Oh, for God's sake, woman, get to your feet. If you don't say anything, neither will I!' He grinned. 'Perhaps I'll tell Holbech he abducted you.' Colum's grin widened. 'Yes, I like that, the chivalrous knight aiding a damsel in distress. As Chaucer says . . .'

Kathryn looked warningly at him.

'Never mind,' Colum said. 'Let's get our horses.'

'Where's Pulcher?' Kathryn asked.

She roughly helped Megan to her feet and dabbed at the bruise on the woman's cheek.

'Bathe that in witch hazel,' she declared matter-of-factly. 'And hold some raw meat against it. In a few days you'll look as pretty and treacherous as ever.'

Colum walked to the edge of the forest, put his fingers in his mouth, gave a long whistle, and Pulcher and Colum's horse appeared, as calm and docile as if they had been on a pleasant day's jaunt. The Irishman carefully examined his favourite horse.

'I didn't do anything,' Megan wailed.

'If you had, I'd have cut your hair off! Come on, let's go.'

Colum put Megan on his own horse, mounted the dead Fitzroy's, collected Kathryn's for her, and they rode back to Kingsmead, Pulcher trotting behind them.

At the manor Colum pressed Kathryn to stay but she felt unwell, eager to return home. Colum said he would ensure all was well at Kingsmead, arrange Sturry's release and join her at Ottemelle Lane.

Kathryn continued into Canterbury, quiet and subdued after the hasty execution earlier in the day. Faunte's battered corpse now swung from the battlements above Westgate.

'It will then be dismembered,' a garrulous sentry informed her. 'The parts sent to adorn the gateways of other towns.'

Kathryn nodded and rode on. Suddenly she began to shake and tremble, feeling rather faint after the bloody fight she had witnessed, Colum's dispassionate ruthlessness, and now seeing the tattered remains of poor Faunte. The noise of the crowd around her sounded strange. She felt nauseous and slightly light-headed. She passed the Righteous Man; his lips were moving, gibbering nonsense, but his eyes seemed large, intent on watching her. Kathryn urged her horse on with a prayer; 'Oh, Lord, don't let me faint!' She was trembling with cold, yet her hands were so clammy the reins began to slip. She turned corners, riding as if in a dream, then her horse abruptly stopped.

'Go on!' she urged. 'Go on!'

'Mistress, what is the matter?'

Thomasina was staring up at her.

'I must go home,' Kathryn said weakly.

She looked round. She was home, the horse had stopped before the house in Ottemelle Lane. She had apparently leaned down and knocked on the door and Thomasina, Agnes and Wuf were standing anxiously in the doorway. Kathryn mustered her dignity. She slipped from the horse, tossing the reins at Wuf.

'Please,' she said, 'take it to the stable. There's a good lad!'

Thomasina clutched at her arm, fearful at Kathryn's white, drawn face and staring, dark-rimmed eyes.

'I'll be fine,' Kathryn muttered but she allowed Thomasina to help her gently up the stairs into her chamber. Kathryn lay on the bed. She took a small bolster, one she had used as a child, and pressed it against her stomach, trying to concentrate on her breathing to ease the fluttering inside her.

'Colum killed a man,' she explained, staring up at the bed canopy above her. 'He killed the man who was here yesterday, took his head off, Thomasina, like you'd cut a flower, and he didn't seem to care.'

Thomasina sat on the bed and gently stroked the back of Kathryn's icy hand.

'They have to be like that,' Thomasina whispered. 'That's the world of soldiers. If they stop to think, to reflect, they'd do what you are doing now, grip yourself in terror. My second husband was like that,' she continued. 'He was a soldier, thighs like tree trunks he had, and was forever bouncing me in bed. But at night he had dreadful dreams. Ah, here's Agnes with some wine and bread.'

She made Kathryn sit up, nibble at the freshly baked man-chet loaf and helped her gulp the herb-infused wine, whilst whispering to Agnes to make up the fire as well as light and wheel in one of the charcoal braziers which stood in the gallery outside. Kathryn began to relax, her body felt warm, lulled by Thomasina's deliberately aimless chatter. She handed the cup back and slipped into a deep sleep.

Thomasina woke her two hours later. Kathryn's eyes flew open, her mouth tasted sweet after the wine and she felt stronger. She dismissed the nightmares which had haunted her and bathed her hands and face in a bowl of rose-water, then combed her hair, put on a new veil and went down to the kitchen, where Colum and a now smartly groomed, well-fed Sturry sat before the hearth. Colum had shaved and washed, showing little sign of his deadly fight earlier that day except for his eyes, tired and heavy from lack of sleep. Sturry, however, was as cheery as a cricket in spring and wouldn't let anyone get a word in edgeways as Thomasina served hot broth and cups of watered wine. Kathryn asked if he'd met anyone called

Wyville or Lessinger but Sturry shook his head and continued with his chatter.

After the meal Kathryn, Colum and Sturry left for the castle. Darkness was falling, the market-stalls had been put away, and citizens were either hurrying home or answering the bells of the churches calling them to evening prayer. Kathryn rode behind Colum and a still chattering Sturry until they entered Winchepe, where Colum pulled his horse back to ride alongside her.

'Thomasina said you were unwell, Kathryn?'

'Oh, not really,' Kathryn tartly replied. 'I'm used to seeing one man hang and another lose his head all in one day.' She glared across at Colum. 'Doesn't it bother you?'

'Yes, it does.' Colum tapped the side of his head. 'But I don't think about it, Kathryn . . .' His voice faltered. He wanted to thank her but now was not the time.

They entered the castle. Grooms took their horses whilst a steward led them up into the main hall. For a while they kicked their heels just inside the doorway as the household finished their meal. Kathryn sat silently, now revelling in the relief at Colum's escape. She also tried to recall something she had seen whilst visiting Faunte's cell at the Guildhall. She shook her head, her brain was too tired for anything elusive. She gestured at the high table.

'Are they expecting us?'

'Yes,' Colum said. 'But they don't know what we want.'

The meal ended, Fletcher, Gabele, Margotta, Fitz-Steven the clerk, Peter the chaplain, as well as the Righteous Man, looking garish as ever, joined them around the great hearth.

'The hour's late, Irishman,' Gabele began. He nodded at Sturry. 'What's he doing here?'

'He has a King's pardon,' Colum replied. 'He's here to assist me.'

'How?'

'He's probably one of the last people who saw Brandon alive before his capture.'

The group fell silent.

'I have got His Grace the Duke of Gloucester's permission,' Colum continued, 'to exhume Brandon's corpse. I want it done now!'

'For God's sake!' Peter the chaplain retorted. 'That's blasphemy. The castle's cemetery is God's own acre.'

'And I am the King's loyal servant,' Colum said. 'In pursuit of his justice as well as God's. Brandon's corpse is to be exhumed.'

'But the body will be decomposing!' Fitz-Steven the clerk cried. 'Stinking, rotten with corruption.'

'Have the body brought up!' Colum ordered Gabele. 'The coffin lid removed, then send for us.'

'Where is it to be taken?'

'Nowhere. Justice can be seen by torch glow as well as in the full light of day.'

Fletcher was about to protest.

'I speak for the King,' Colum repeated. 'I want Brandon's body exhumed now, and until it is done, no man is to leave the castle!'

'But my trade!' the Righteous Man wailed. 'The work of God! The city taverns are full of resting pilgrims.'

'It can wait awhile!' Colum snapped. 'Until I look on Brandon's face—or at least, what remains of it!'

Chapter 11

$\mathcal{T}$hey all left the hall, but Kathryn and Colum remained. Sturry went up to the high table to collect any remaining scraps of food. Colum grinned as he watched him.

'He wants to catch up on everything he has missed,' he observed.

'And what will happen to him then?'

Colum shrugged. 'I'll let him go. He'll return to his family and wait for better days.'

'What do you mean?' Kathryn asked archly.

Colum leaned forward, hands on his knees. 'Do you think it's over, Kathryn, the civil war? Oh, York's star's in the ascendant, but in Brittany, Henry Tudor plans rebellion and invasion. The rallying port for all rebels and all those who escaped Barnet. No, no.' Colum shook his head. 'The dance is not over yet. The King's children are only babes, and if something should happen to Edward, Gloucester and Clarence are waiting like wolves in the shadows.'

Kathryn pulled her cloak closer about her. She gazed round the hall, noting how the weak fire made the shadows jump and dance against the wall. I should be at home, she thought, back in Ottemelle Lane, mixing my potions and elixirs; healing a wound, giving comfort to a patient, chattering to Thomasina or allowing Wuf to tease her.

'I do not like these affairs,' she breathed. 'If Fortune's wheel turns again, Colum, you might have to play the part of Faunte.'

Colum stretched out his hand to the blaze, then looked squarely at her. 'I don't think so, Kathryn. My warring days are over.'

At the top of the hall Sturry exclaimed in pleasure and came back gnawing on a chicken leg, a cup of claret in the other hand. For a while the former Lancastrian sat and regaled them with his adventures in the wilds of Kent before Fitz-Steven the clerk came bustling back, his face wreathed in concern.

'The coffin's been raised,' he declared. 'And the lid removed . . .'

'Well?' Colum snapped.

'Sir, you had best see for yourself.'

They followed him out of the castle, across the inner and outer baileys to the small cemetery. A blighted place with overgrown weeds, sombre yew trees, the darkness all the more eerie by the ring of torchlight in the distance. A night-bird chattered from a tree, long-winged bats circled and swooped against the starlit skies. Kathryn coughed and Sturry cursed, throwing away the chicken leg at the stench of corruption wafting on the cool night breeze. The group standing round the open coffin looked macabre in the glaring light of the flaming torches. Colum and Kathryn stared down into the makeshift coffin. The corpse's head was slightly twisted, the decomposing face turned to one side.

'Oh, my God!' Colum breathed. He snatched a torch, looked into the coffin, at the inside of the lid, then at the corpse's fingers, black with encrusted blood.

Kathryn followed his gaze. 'Oh, Lord, save us!' she whispered. 'He was buried alive!'

'Impossible!' Peter the chaplain tremulously wailed. 'I gave him the last rites of Holy Mother Church! He was dead! He was dead!'

'Look at the way he's twisted,' Colum snarled. 'Look at his finger-nails and the coffin lid. He revived whilst under the earth; he tried to claw himself out but died for lack of air.'

Kathryn grabbed a torch, pinched her nostrils and looked at the corpse.

'Such cases are common,' she observed. 'Sometimes it's hard to certify death. Some people ask for a stake or a knife to be driven through their heart, or their wrists cut, lest they revive.'

'But is it Brandon?' Colum asked.

'It's Brandon all right!' Sturry declared abruptly, his face white and pasty as he clutched his stomach, probably regretting the chicken he had gulped. He covered his mouth and nose with his hand and bent down to examine the corpse. Then he got up, brushing the dirt from his knees.

'I swear by all that is holy,' he declared, 'this man is Brandon!'

'How can you say that?' Colum said sharply. 'The body is beginning to decompose.'

'But not enough to hide his features,' Sturry retorted. 'Master Murtagh, go, if you wish, to the Guildhall, talk to my companions. They, too, met Brandon; they, too, will declare the truth. If you brought the sacrament,' he added defiantly, 'I'd take any oath the Church required and declare the same.' He waved a hand at Colum, gulped and walked back, almost stumbling into a headstone.

Colum tugged at Kathryn's sleeve and they walked away from the rest.

'God help us!' Kathryn murmured. 'Brandon is dead, so's Moresby, and the rest of the party has disappeared.' She seized Colum's wrist. 'They could have killed Moresby and now be across the seas with the Eye of God!'

The Irishman kicked at the grass. 'Hell's teeth!' he cursed. 'I did wonder if the real Brandon was still alive, hiding somewhere.' He sighed. 'Now we find that Brandon was captured only to be buried alive. A pretty mess, Kathryn. Perhaps Webster did commit suicide.' Colum grinned wolfishly. 'When Gloucester hears of this . . .' He let the threat hang in the air and walked back to the rest, clapping his hands noisily to still the clamour which had broken out.

'Enough!' he ordered. 'We have seen enough. Master Fletcher, have this coffin re-interred. The rest of you, we need to discuss certain matters in the hall.'

It was a very cowed group which sat down at the high table on the dais. All of them, even Gabele and the Righteous Man, were subdued and pale-faced. Colum allowed wine to be served before addressing them.

'Let us first reflect on what we know. Last Easter Sunday morning,' he continued, 'Richard Neville, Earl of Warwick, was killed at Barnet. He entrusted a precious gold pendant with a sapphire called the Eye of God to his body squire Brandon, possibly with the knowledge of Moresby, the captain of his guard. Warwick was killed and we now know that Brandon, Moresby, and at least four others fled into hiding. They probably intended to take the pendant to Christchurch Priory in Canterbury, but something happened. Moresby was mysteriously killed; the rest have disappeared; and Fletcher here captured Brandon, whose corpse we have just viewed. Mistress Swinbrooke, what else do we know?'

Kathryn was staring at the white-faced priest. 'According to what people here told us,' she began slowly, 'Brandon was put in a cell next to that of a murderer called Sparrow. He may have talked to this man, who later escaped. We do not know, as Sparrow's death and murder remain a mystery.'

The Irishman shrugged.

'Brandon,' Kathryn continued, 'said little to anyone. He fell ill and, according to all the evidence, died. Our good chaplain here treated him and finally anointed him.'

'But it's true,' the priest wailed, springing to his feet. 'God be my witness, Mistress, it's true! He had a fever and died!'

'How did you know he was dead?' Kathryn asked.

'There was no life-beat in his neck or wrist,' the priest exclaimed. 'No sign of breath.'

'Did you use a mirror?' Kathryn asked. 'Or a piece of glass held up against his mouth and nose?'

'Of course not,' the priest declared, sitting down again. 'Christ be my witness, Mistress, I thought he was dead!'

'He died in the afternoon,' Fletcher added. 'He was put in a box and buried the same evening. God, how the poor bastard must have suffered!'

'Which brings us finally,' Colum interrupted, 'to Webster's mysterious fall from the tower.' Colum looked round, studying each of their faces. 'On your allegiance to the King,' he added quietly, 'can anyone here throw a light on these mysteries?'

They all shook their heads, chorusing their denials, so Colum drew the meeting to an end. He rose, stretching until his joints cracked.

'No one,' he declared, 'no one from this castle is to leave without my permission, except you, Master Sturry.' Colum opened his wallet and drew out a small red-ribboned scroll. He pushed this and a silver piece into the man's hand. 'You may go where you wish. For the rest, anyone who leaves Canterbury, and this includes you, Master Pardoner, will be proclaimed as a murderer, a thief and a traitor!'

Colum and Kathryn left the hall. They collected their horses and rode quietly back into the city and the warmth and security of the house in Ottemelle Lane. Kathryn and Colum hardly spoke; even when they had doffed their cloaks and were sitting round the kitchen table, both remained lost in their own thoughts and the implications of what they had learnt that evening.

'A stirring day,' Kathryn observed as Thomasina served them ale, slices of smoked ham, bread and cheese on a platter.

'I discovered that Alexander Wyville is now calling himself Robert Lessinger. Mayor Faunte was hanged. You killed a childhood friend who was hunting your life. We learnt that Brandon escaped from Barnet with the Eye of God but the

162

sapphire has disappeared. Moresby was killed. Brandon was captured, only to be buried alive.' Kathryn pushed the platter away and leaned her elbows on the table. 'Moreover, we haven't a clue about how Webster was killed, where Brandon's former companions are, or, more importantly, of the whereabouts of the Eye of God.'

Colum gulped from his wine-cup. 'It's enough to drive a man to drink.' He smiled sourly. 'Do you have any thoughts on the matter?'

'I told a lie at the castle,' Kathryn replied. 'There was no mistake. Brandon was deliberately buried alive. I suspect he was given hemlock. Do you know anything about its properties?'

Colum shook his head.

'It's a common wild plant,' Kathryn explained. 'Its Latin tag is *Conium maculatum,* and it is very poisonous. The Greeks gave it to Socrates to drink, and according to a story my father told me, the god Prometheus brought fire to mortals on a hemlock stalk. Hemlock is dangerous, not only because it is poisonous but also because it is very similar in appearance to parsley and fennel. Failure to distinguish it can prove fatal. Moreover, there are many varieties of the herb; hemlock and water hemlock are particularly dangerous. They can be found growing along hedgerows, in ditches or open woodland. Hemlock has an unpleasant bitter taste as well as a disagreeable stench, though this could be disguised in wine.'

'So Brandon was given hemlock?'

'All the symptoms indicate that,' Kathryn said. 'High temperature, lassitude, increased heartbeat; the victim will then lapse into a very deep sleep or coma which results in death.'

Kathryn played with her wine-cup. Colum looked under his eyebrows at her, trying to control his own fear. She's dangerous, he thought; I kill with dagger or sword, but she can use a harmless-looking plant for murder.

'I remember a Greek proverb,' Colum muttered, ' "I was a

healthy man before I met physicians." I am wary of you, Mistress Swinbrooke.'

Kathryn shrugged. 'Most people are of physicians. The knowledge of herbs is most dangerous, particularly of a plant like hemlock. I once treated a child who'd eaten some. The symptoms were very similar to what happened to Brandon: to all intents and purposes the child seemed dead.'

'So you are saying someone in the castle garrison gave Brandon this? He falls into this deep swoon. The priest gives him the last rites, he is hurriedly buried and then revives in the grave?'

'Yes, I am,' Kathryn answered. 'The poor man would be trapped, weak and nauseous, fighting for air. He may have been conscious for about an hour before swooning again.'

Colum rapped on the table-top. 'But who and why?'

'Wait.' Kathryn got up and went to her writing-office and brought back a battered, greasy scroll. 'Let's follow Brandon's path from Barnet.' Kathryn cleared the table and unrolled her father's crude map of Kent, pointing to Canterbury and the roads north. 'Now we know,' she said, 'after Warwick's defeat at Barnet, Brandon fled in the direction of Canterbury. For a while he and his companions lurked in Blean Wood, where they met Faunte and his party. Later they broke out into open country and went to Sellingham, a deserted village.' Kathryn shrugged. 'After that, nothing! Moresby is killed, supposedly by outlaws; Brandon is captured; and the rest disappear.'

'So what do you propose?' Colum asked.

'Well, not to return to Canterbury Castle but visit and search this deserted village. Perhaps Brandon hid the Eye of God there?' Kathryn rolled the map up. 'God knows, it's better than doing nothing.'

'If *he* goes'—Thomasina stood at the entrance to the buttery, pointing at Colum—'then *I* go!'

'What about Wuf?'

'Agnes is here, she can look after him. But you, Mistress Kathryn, are not wandering the countryside with some wild Irish soldier.'

'Yes, I think you'd better come,' Colum said softly. 'Both your mistress and I will need protection.'

Thomasina glared at him and stomped off. Colum rubbed his face in his hands.

'We should leave at first light. Your patients?'

'Nothing which can't wait. Colum, we need to resolve this matter.' Kathryn rubbed her own eyes. 'One way or the other it should be finished. Either we dig out the truth or tell His Grace the Duke of Gloucester that it's all a great mystery and neither the King nor anyone else will have the Eye of God.'

'Are you tired, Kathryn?'

'Well, yes.' She stared dully at him.

'No, I don't mean that,' he continued hastily. 'But before I came to Canterbury, your life was . . . well, in the main, serene. You had your practice, your ambitions.'

Kathryn got to her feet. 'Yes, Colum, everything was quiet.' She smiled as she picked up her cloak. 'But, there again, the same thing could be said of a graveyard.' Kathryn's smile widened and she was out in the kitchen before Colum could think of a suitable reply.

Once she was in her own chamber, Kathryn wondered about Colum's question as she sat on the bed and loosened the laced ribbons on her bodice.

What if there were no Colum? she thought. There'd be no Eye of God, no Hounds of Ulster, no murders. But what would I have? Alexander Wyville would still haunt me and I would be floating aimlessly like some leaf on a stream. She chewed her lip as she reflected further: violence was part of her life. Alexander Wyville had begun the dance and now she had to see it through. She closed her eyes and thought of her husband—his face on their wedding day and then those same features flushed with drink and anger. 'I don't want you!' Kathryn whispered. 'God forgive me, I don't care if you live or die! And if you return, I shall use every influence, yes, even Colum himself, to petition the Church courts for an annullment.'

Kathryn finished undressing, washed herself with a sponge

and a small piece of Castilian soap, carefully dried her body and put on her night-gown. Thomasina came in, slipped a warming pan between the sheets and handed her a cup of hot milk spiced with nutmeg. Kathryn allowed Thomasina to fuss over her, solemnly promising that Thomasina would accompany them the following morning. After that she finished the milk, doused the candles and slipped between the sheets, pulling the blankets over her head as she used to do when she was a girl. She stretched, warm and sleepy, allowing her mind to drift—if only she could remember what she had seen in Faunte's cell. Kathryn suddenly thought of the Righteous Man and recalled the lines from Chaucer's "Pardoner's Tale":

> Is it such danger then this death to meet?
> I'll seek him in the road and in the street.

'When will I meet him again?' Kathryn murmured. 'Or is death always with me?' She closed her eyes and drifted into a dreamless sleep.

They left early the next morning. Thomasina packed panniers with bread, cheese, and dried meat, and a flash of wine. She left detailed instructions to a heavy-eyed Agnes, and swore the most terrible oaths to Wuf about what would happen to him if he didn't behave. Kathryn told Agnes that any serious case should be sent to Physician Chaddedon whilst the others must wait until her return.

'Oh, and tell Wuf,' Kathryn added, 'to visit the old sisters in Jewry Lane; they should be well but it would be prudent to check.'

Colum, refreshed after a good night's sleep, prepared and saddled the horses. He was fully armed, with his great war-belt packed about his waist and an arbalest looped over the horn of his saddle.

'What about Kingsmead?' Kathryn asked.

'Oh, Holbech's a sturdy man. He expects me when he sees

me. Anyway, the manor's still ringing with the aftermath of Gloucester's visit.' He grinned. 'Megan's glad of the distractions.'

'Has the Duke left?' Kathryn asked.

'Yes, that's Gloucester, ruthless as ever. He came to kill Faunte and now he's completed that task for his beloved brother. Before I left the Guildhall, the Duke ordered me to report to him in London within the week about what progress was made in recovering the Eye of God.' Colum grinned bleakly. 'If we discover nothing today, then a week will be too long.'

They mounted and, shouting farewells to Agnes and Wuf, left Ottemelle Lane, going up Steward Street towards Westgate. The city was quiet. It was too early even for the church bells to be ringing for morning Mass. Now and again the occasional garishly dressed whore would slip across the street, eager to escape the clutches of the watch who patrolled the thoroughfares, staves in hand, faces heavy with sleep. The dung-collectors were busy in Hethenman Lane, their huge four-wheeled carts stacked high with the ordure and filth raked from the sewers. The stench was so great that Colum, Kathryn and Thomasina had to wrap their cloaks round their mouths and noses whilst they ignored the cheerful catcalls of the dung-collectors, who revelled in the chaos they were causing. Two debtors from the city gaol, manacled together at hand and foot, mournfully patrolled the streets, begging for alms. In the stocks outside the Black Friars near Saint Peter's Gate, a group of drunken roisterers were already arrayed to spend the day being abused by the same citizens whose sleep they had so roughly disturbed the night before.

Westgate was open, and carts full of farm produce were being driven through, down to the Buttermarket in preparation for the day's business. Kathryn closed her eyes as they went under the arch and breathed a prayer for the repose of poor Faunte's soul. They continued up by Saint Dunstan's Church, past the crossroads, taking the road to Whitstable, where the taverns and the farms which straggled the highway gave way to open countryside. The fields were thick and lush, already dotted with peasants preparing for the harvest whilst their children danced through the corn armed with slings to frighten away the marauding crows and ravens. The sky brightened, the grey-white clouds breaking up under the strengthening sun. Kathryn and Colum stopped at a small alehouse, musty and warm, to break their fast on watered wine and oatcakes. Kathryn had brought her father's map and she and Thomasina advised Colum on what route to take.

In the main, they found the roads and trackways empty, except for the occasional pedlar, tinker or wandering hedge-priest who pushed his paltry possessions before him in a small handcart. Now and again, especially at alehouses and taverns, they met groups of pilgrims on their way to Canterbury, all chattering excitedly, agog to see the greatest shrine in Christendom. On one occasion Kathryn and Colum became lost, but a bleary-eyed farmer with red chapped cheeks put them back on the right track. About an hour after noon, they turned into a narrow overgrown pathway which led to the deserted village. Their horses found it heavy going so they dismounted, trying to avoid overhanging branches, quietly grumbling at the way the brambles caught at their clothes. The air had a heavy stillness, broken only by the chatter of a bird or the buzzing of bees hunting above the wide-faced, sweet-smelling wild-flowers. At last they had fought their way through, and there, before them, in a small hollow in the hillside, sprawled the ruins of a deserted village.

'Sweet Lord above!' Colum breathed, patting his horse.

They stared across at the ruined houses, some built of stone, their roofs either fallen in or stripped of their tiles. Others, fashioned out of wattle and daub, were little more than piles of refuse. Kathryn pointed to the disused mill standing on the bank of a small stream; the roofless tavern, the post which held its sign now crooked and lopsided; and the overgrown village green. Beyond this lay the simple village church, really a small chapel. Its nave was now roofless, the square tower on its western end weather-beaten, the home of rooks and crows which cawed raucously above them, angry at being disturbed.

'Why?' Colum asked. 'Why this desolation?'

'My grandfather told me.' Thomasina spoke up, wiping the sweat from her face. 'My grandfather said the great death came. Much worse than the sweating sickness. Whole towns disappeared. They say two out of every three people died.'

'Thomasina's right,' Kathryn agreed, leading her horse forward. 'There are villages and towns like this the length and breadth of the kingdom.' She shivered. 'The haunts of ghosts and spectres.'

'Someone was here,' Colum asserted. He crouched and sifted with his dagger amongst the thin sparse grass. 'Horses were hobbled here, the dung is dry and beginning to crumble.'

They wandered round the village. Kathryn tried to ignore the prickling between her shoulder-blades, a feeling that she was being watched, as if the ghosts of the people who lived and died here resented such abrupt intrusion. The very silence of the place was oppressive. Sometimes she thought she could hear footsteps or a low throbbing behind the walls; whispers of doors creaking open. She tried to dismiss these as the work of a fevered imagination and the eerie, silent atmosphere of the place.

Colum and Thomasina were no different. Now and again they broke their watchful silence as they found traces of horsemen, certainly Brandon's party, in the village.

'Why did they come here?' Colum asked.

'It stands to reason,' Kathryn answered, standing outside the disused mill. 'Don't you feel it, Colum? This place is haunted, forgotten, the ideal hiding-place.' She bit her lip and glanced at the crows circling the old church tower. 'I suspect someone in Brandon's party knew of this place, though God knows,' she murmured, 'what happened here.'

They continued their search, now and again going into one of the disused houses. Suddenly Colum shouted in excitement.

169

'Come, Kathryn, here!'

She left her horse and stepped through the battered door-way. Colum pointed to a pile of black ashes in one far corner, a small mound of horse droppings nearby.

'Brandon certainly came here, but apparently so did some-one else, and quite recently.' Colum walked over and kicked the pile of manure. 'This is fresher, more recent.'

They continued searching and found similar indications of a recent visit.

'Two horsemen,' Colum concluded. 'On different occasions. Two horsemen came here, searching for what?'

'The only place left,' Kathryn replied, 'is the church.'

She looked over where Thomasina was sitting, rather deject-edly, on a low, crumbling wall.

'Perhaps it's time we stopped for something to eat.'

They hobbled their horses in what used to be the church graveyard and went through an open gap of the tower which led them into the small sanctuary where they stood looking down the nave. The church was gaunt and empty, the roof long gone. The greying walls were covered with lichen and moss whilst the pillars on either side, dividing the nave from the narrow transepts, were beginning to flake and crumble under the wind and rain. Kathryn gazed round the sanctuary. The old altar was there, built against the apse of the church. She glimpsed a small enclave in the wall for the offertory cruets, a painting, now faded, and the great gaps on either side of the sanctuary where the rood-screen had once stood.

'So sad,' she murmured, 'to think people worshipped and prayed here.'

Thomasina suddenly squealed as a bird, nesting high in the wall of the church, broke free in a flutter of wings.

'Come on!' Kathryn put the panniers on the floor, and for a while they sat eating and drinking in silence. When finished, all three wandered off down the church.

'If you see anything,' Colum called, 'shout!'

'There's nothing here,' Thomasina grumbled, kicking at the moss-covered floor.

Kathryn wandered down one of the transepts, running her fingers against the lichen growing on the wall.

'How old do you think this church is?' Colum asked. 'It reminds me of chapels in Ireland.'

'Very old,' Kathryn replied absent-mindedly. 'Perhaps built before the Conquest, simple and stark.'

She wandered back into the sanctuary and leaned against the altar. She pushed at this but there was no movement, and looked down at her feet. There was more moss here, but then she noticed the twigs and packed soil. She recalled her father's advice, which she was always quoting to herself when treating patients.

'Discover what is strange, out of the ordinary.'

Kathryn looked down.

'Colum!' she exclaimed.

'What's wrong?' he asked, coming back to join her.

'Well, there are twigs, parts of bark and packed soil, but there's no overhanging tree, nor has a fire been lit here.'

Kathryn knelt down, brushing the twigs aside. Colum went outside and took a rushlight from his saddle-bag. He came back and lit it, the flame's shadow dancing against the stone.

'There's a letter here,' Kathryn said. She crushed aside more of the twigs and dirt. 'The moss has been cleared. Look, there are more letters!'

Thomasina hastened over to join them as Colum pushed the rushlight forward, handing Kathryn his dagger so she could clear away the dirt.

' "Levate!" ' Kathryn exclaimed excitedly. ' "Levate Oculos ad Montes"! "Lift your eyes to the hills," ' she translated, smiling at Colum. 'The same prayer Brandon had scrawled in his cell at Canterbury Castle.'

'Why is it there?'

'Some sort of tombstone,' Kathryn answered. 'There's probably a burial pit beneath here belonging to some local long-forgotten lord.' Kathryn smiled. 'There's a tradition that when the soul leaves the body, devils and angels fight over it, so people like to be buried in a sacred place.'

Colum was now moving the rushlight away and was digging with his dagger.

'There's a gap,' he said. 'It can be raised.'

Once the large flagstone was cleared of debris, Colum, using pieces of wood, his sword, scabbard and dagger, was able to prise the massive stone up.

'There's probably an easier way,' he grunted, 'but I don't know it.'

Kathryn and Thomasina helped him. The heavy flagstone was raised and forced back, a musty smell made them cough and sneeze. When the dust cleared, they glimpsed a yawning pit and a narrow set of steps leading down. Armed with the rushlight, Colum carefully entered the pit. Kathryn was following when the Irishman's exclamation of horror set her teeth on edge, curling the hair on the nape of her neck.

'Colum, what is it?'

'Oh, my God!' Colum shouted. 'Oh, the poor bastards!'

Kathryn hastened on. The steps were flaking and crumbling. She almost screamed as she reached the bottom, put her hand out and touched the cold, white arm of a skeleton jutting out from its decaying coffin. She turned and looked. Colum was standing in a pool of light. Kathryn could glimpse shapes about him.

'Colum, it's only a mausoleum.'

Colum waved her forward.

'No, no,' he whispered hoarsely. 'It's a murder pit.' He held the rushlight up. 'Look, Kathryn!'

Kathryn moved forward and stared in horror at the decaying corpses of the four men sprawled there, the flesh on their faces and hands shrunken and dry. They lay sprawled, eye-sockets empty, mouths gaping. Kathryn, taking the rushlight, went over and knelt beside them. She pulled aside a tattered, mildewed cloak and made out the faint impression on the linen of the man's jerkin: a bear, chained and muzzled, holding a ragged staff.

'Warwick's arms,' Colum said. 'We have found the rest of Brandon's party, Kathryn. But how did they die?'

Kathryn overcame her distaste and carefully examined each of the cadavers, particularly the skulls and the front of their jerkins.

'No sign of violence,' she murmured. 'No mark on the skull or blood on the cloaks. I am only guessing, Colum, but I think these men starved to death.'

Colum, however, had caught sight of a small leather saddle-bag pushed into a niche in the wall. He pulled this out, cut the rotting clasps and brought out a golden pendant; even in the darkness the sapphire caught the weak flame of the rushlight and shimmered as brilliantly as a star.

'The Eye of God!' Colum pushed it into Kathryn's hand. 'We've found the Eye of God!'

Kathryn stood up, taking care not to knock her head against the low ceiling, and stared down at the golden lozenge-shaped pendant. The workmanship was beautiful: pure filigree gold sculpted and carved in the Celtic fashion, yet it paled to insignificance against the fiery sapphire set in the top corner above Christ's head.

'It's beautiful!' she exclaimed.

Kathryn was so immersed in admiration she almost ignored Thomasina, who now bustled down and screamed at the horrid sight. This abruptly turned into a gasp of delight as Thomasina saw the pendant.

'A King's fortune,' Thomasina whispered. 'No wonder the Duke of Gloucester wants it back. Men would kill for that!'

Kathryn glanced up. 'Men have,' she whispered. She glimpsed one of the decaying faces. 'Let's get out of here.'

Colum moved the torch; as he did, Kathryn saw the fresh scratchings on the wall. She grabbed the torch and pushed it against these. In the flickering light she made out the crudely etched names: "Appleby, Claver, Durston and Farnol." She read, "Jesu have mercy." Kathryn glanced at Colum.

'A last, terrible prayer,' she whispered.

'Aye,' he replied. 'And it proves both Moresby and Brandon were not with them.'

They climbed the steps and re-positioned the stone.

'What do you think happened?' Thomasina asked.

'I don't know,' Colum said. 'But we'll have to think upon it. I don't know why or how, but some demon incarnate murdered those four men, left them there to die!'

Chapter 12

They left the deserted village, Colum vowing he would send men to arrange honourable burial for the corpses. The day was drawing on. They rode silently and swiftly, though it was night-fall by the time they reached Canterbury.

Kathryn, as a physician, had a key to a postern gate of the city near Westgate. They went through and made their way down to Ottemelle Lane. The house was quiet. Wuf was al-ready asleep, so was Agnes, her head resting on the table. She awoke, yawned and stretched, assuring her mistress that noth-ing untoward had happened. Thomasina bustled her off to bed whilst Kathryn and Colum sat down at the kitchen table. Thomasina returned and said she would serve something to eat and drink.

Kathryn was saddle-sore and wished she could just bathe, change and have a good night's sleep, but the scene in the burial vault still haunted her—that shadowy recess with those corpses, grotesque in death, and the beautiful Eye of God, which Colum had already locked away in a coffer in his own chamber.

'Why?' Kathryn wondered. 'Why had they to die like that?'

'What worries me,' Colum replied bluntly, 'is that all of them are dead: those four in the burial chamber, Moresby in a ditch, whilst Brandon was murdered in Canterbury Castle.'

'They were murdered,' Kathryn continued. 'Four able-bodied men wouldn't stay in a burial vault and accept their fate as a matter of fact.'

'I think they were put there,' Colum replied, 'perhaps to hide them from pursuers, perhaps to ensure they would not flee with the jewel. 'Promised that someone would come back, and the tomb was sealed. You saw how difficult it was to enter from above. With the stone re-laid, those unfortunates would have found it impossible to push it up from the inside.'

Kathryn shrugged. 'It's happened before. There have been similar deaths involving children in deserted ruins around Canterbury.'

She paused as Thomasina served them wine, manchet loaves, sliced cheese and pieces of dried ham. Kathryn sipped the watered wine carefully. She felt so heavy-eyed she was sure that if she drank too much she would copy Agnes, rest her head on the table and fall fast asleep. She absent-mindedly pulled at the cord round her waist.

'All we can surmise,' she said, 'is that Brandon escaped. Those left in the burial vault kept the Eye of God as some form of surety that he would return.'

'But why didn't he?' Colum asked. 'Or was Moresby the one who was supposed to return?'

Kathryn chewed her lip. 'No,' she replied. 'It was Brandon. He knew the phrase, "Levate Oculos ad Montes," the clue to where the Eye of God and his companions were. But then he was captured and was unable to go back. He was probably planning to do so, once he'd received a pardon and been released, but he is then mysteriously murdered.'

'In which case,' Colum said despairingly, 'what do we do now?'

Kathryn stared at Thomasina, who was bustling around the

kitchen, happy to be away from macabre burial vaults, deserted villages, and jobbing about on the back of some hack.

'Something is very wrong,' Kathryn said. 'First, what was Moresby doing?' She licked her lips. 'Did Moresby and Brandon leave those men in the vault? Did Brandon also kill Moresby and then allow himself to be captured, hoping he would receive a pardon, be released and return to collect the Eye of God? In which case,' Kathryn concluded, 'Brandon was a cold-blooded killer and deserves to burn in Hell!'

But would Moresby give his life up so easily?' Colum asked. 'We are also forgetting something. First, whose was that corpse found in a ditch? How do we know it was Moresby? Secondly, we discovered traces of Brandon's party at that deserted village but also signs that two different horsemen had visited the place. So who were they, eh?' Colum sighed and shook his head. 'Is it possible, Kathryn, someone else followed Moresby, Brandon and their companions after the Battle of Barnet?'

'Possibly,' Kathryn replied, popping a piece of cheese into her mouth. She stared down at the table, and when she looked up, Colum was half-asleep, his hand round his wine-cup. 'Come on,' Kathryn said gently. 'It's time we all slept. There's nothing that won't wait.'

Colum blinked, rubbing his face. 'At least we have the Eye of God,' he mumbled.

He staggered to his feet and touched Kathryn gently on the head. Colum blew a kiss at Thomasina and staggered up the stairs, shouting that, God willing, tomorrow morning he would be refreshed and able to think more clearly.

Kathryn helped Thomasina for a while and then went into her writing-office. She smoothed out a piece of vellum and, picking up the quill, quickly wrote down what they had discovered. She leaned back in the chair, dozed for a while, then got up to return to the kitchen for a stoup of water. She was still absent-mindedly pulling at the cord round her waist, nibbling at the gold tassel on the end. The cord jerked and she recalled

Faunte in the cell, loaded down with chains, the manacles round his wrists. Kathryn paused.

'Lord, save us!' she murmured, 'Of course, that's what Webster realised.'

She hastened back into the kitchen, splashing cold water over her face, telling Thomasina to build up the fire, for she intended to stay there.

'Oh, how long?' Thomasina wailed.

'For as long as I need to.'

Kathryn brought her writing-tray into the kitchen. She went out to refresh herself in the cold night air and looked up at the starry sky.

'At last,' she whispered, 'God be thanked, the mystery unravels!'

Kathryn went back and began to work, writing quickly and easily as if telling herself a story. Thomasina fussed around her, clucking like an angry chicken. She then resignedly sat down beside Kathryn, watching the bold strokes of her mistress's quill.

'You were always stubborn,' Thomasina muttered. 'Even when you were a little girl, you were stubborn.'

'I think I know the murderer,' Kathryn said. She gripped Thomasina's wrist. 'I know what happened, Thomasina. I know who murdered the prisoner in the castle. Even, perhaps, how Webster died.'

'How do you know?'

Kathryn grinned and tapped the side of her head. 'A piece of cord told me.'

After that Kathryn refused to be drawn. She finished writing, rolled the vellum into a neat scroll, tied it with a piece of scarlet cord and retired to her bed. She only slept for a few hours and woke before dawn. She washed and dressed quickly, shouting at Colum not to be such a lazy-bones for they had business to attend to. Colum was always heavy-eyed in the mornings. Only after he had washed and shaved did Kathryn sit down with him in the kitchen. She let him break his fast, then called Thomasina to bring Wuf and Agnes in.

They all sat in the kitchen rather heavy-eyed. Wuf said he was thirsty, so Thomasina brought him a cup of buttermilk and another for Agnes. Colum sat on a stool near the hearth, secretly admiring Kathryn; she had had little sleep yet he could see how the excitement had coloured her cheeks whilst her eyes danced with life.

'Thomasina, sit down,' Kathryn began. 'We are going to play a game.'

Wuf immediately leapt to his feet, clapping his hands.

'Can I play?'

'Yes. Colum, I want you to tie Wuf's hands and feet together, like we saw poor Faunte at the Guildhall.'

Wuf crowed with excitement but stayed still as Colum fetched the rope and did what Kathryn asked. The little fellow stood, his hands and feet tied together, a rope connecting the bonds round his ankles with those about his wrists.

'Wuf, stop giggling,' Kathryn said. 'Agnes, go and stand beside him.'

Agnes, round-eyed, obeyed.

'Now, Wuf, remember,' Kathryn warned. 'It's only play. Try and grab Agnes round the neck.'

Utter confusion followed. Agnes stepped hurriedly back. Wuf leapt up and down before he fell, laughing, onto the rushes. Colum stared across at Kathryn.

'Sparrow and the turnkey?' he asked.

'Of course,' Kathryn replied. 'No, Wuf, don't ask me about those. Colum, cut his bonds.'

Colum released the still laughing Wuf, who ran to stand beside Kathryn and gave her a hug.

'What's this all about?' Thomasina demanded.

'We are trying to catch a killer,' Kathryn replied. 'Do you remember the old sisters, Eleanor and Maude? Everyone thought they had the plague, but we knew it really was pellagra. Our killer in the castle is like that. He has presented us with facts, but these really distort the truth.' She smiled at Colum. 'We thought Sparrow killed the turnkey and took the key to release his manacles. He escaped, later tried to blackmail Brandon's murderer in the castle and was killed himself.' She shook her head. 'I was tugging on the cord of my dress when I suddenly realised that a rope or a chain tied tightly greatly hinders movement.'

'So,' Colum intervened. 'Sparrow's manacles must have been unlocked before he killed the turnkey! He was allowed to escape by his accomplice, who later murdered him to keep him quiet.'

'Exactly,' Kathryn replied. 'I applied the same logic to all the other murders, refusing to accept what we had been told. Now, Wuf—' Kathryn pointed at the door. 'If I told you that door was bolted on the outside and you wanted to get out, what would you do?'

'Go through the window,' Wuf replied.

'No, no,' Kathryn laughed. 'Let us say the room had no windows.'

'I'd get a hammer or a log and smash it down,' Wuf said stoutly, enjoying Kathryn's attention.

'And if you were in a hurry?' Kathryn continued. 'Let us say there was a fire raging. Once you were out in the garden, you would not really check if you had made a mistake, that all along the door had been locked from the inside, not the other way around.'

Colum slapped his hand against his thigh. 'The trapdoor in the castle!'

'My suspicions began,' Kathryn added, 'when I wondered how Webster could cry out if he was unconscious.'

'But,' Colum continued, 'Webster was seen at the top of the tower.'

'Was he?' Kathryn asked. 'A few days ago, I came back to this house and thought I saw Agnes in the garden because I glimpsed her brown robe, but it was Wuf. No, no!' She held a hand up at Agnes. 'Now is not the time to start quarreling about that. Can't you see, Colum? The murders were so simple. We saw distorted images. Brandon died, but in fact he was poisoned. Did Sparrow escape? No, he was allowed to. Webster was seen on the tower and the trapdoor was locked from his side. But was he there? Was the trapdoor locked?'

'Then who's the murderer?' Colum asked.

Kathryn rubbed her eyes. 'Well, we come to another distorted image. Brandon, Moresby and four others left Barnet carrying the Eye of God. Now, after our visit to Sellingham, we have seen the corpses of all of them except?'

'Except Moresby,' Colum replied.

'Yes,' Kathryn breathed. 'Except Moresby. Is he really dead? Did someone take his place? Now, let's clarify this image.' She got to her feet and stood by the fire. 'Who at the castle might not be what he pretends to be?'

'The pardoner.'

'And who at the castle can wander round to his heart's delight?'

'The pardoner,' Colum repeated, this time Wuf, Thomasina and Agnes chorusing it with him.

'Then, Irishman, it's to the castle we should go. Before anyone leaves.'

'Can I come?' Wuf cried.

Kathryn kissed him on the top of his head. 'No, you and Agnes have already been a great help.'

She and Colum collected their cloaks, made their farewells and went out to the stables.

'Do you think,' he said, 'you know the murderer?'

'One thing still bothers me,' she answered. 'Two riders visited that deserted village, on different occasions, quite recently, yes?'

Colum nodded, dabbing at a nick on his cheek inflicted by a rather hasty shave. 'I know horse tracks,' he said. 'I cannot be fooled.'

'In which case,' Kathryn continued, 'we might have to reconsider who had access to Brandon, Sparrow, and that trapdoor.'

Having collected their horses, Kathryn and Colum proceeded to the castle. On the Winchepe, just before the gates of the castle, Kathryn paused. 'While I occupy the others, you must examine the lock on the door,' she said. And, with an apt quotation from Chaucer's "Wife of Bath," Kathryn gave him a pithy lecture on what, she called, the very obvious. At last Colum conceded, moving his horse gently to one side to allow two large carts to rumble into the castle.

'But what proof do we have?'

'None,' Kathryn lightly replied. 'At least, not yet. But, as soon as we are in that castle, you are to go and search out what I asked you to do.'

Colum caught her pointed finger and squeezed it gently.

'Do you know,' he said, edging his horse forward, 'I always thought Thomasina would make an excellent Wife of Bath. However, after hearing you speak, I am not too sure.'

Kathryn stuck her tongue out at his retreating back before moving her horse alongside his.

'Colum, aren't you concerned? You seem . . .'

'Resigned?'

'Yes, resigned.'

Colum shook his head. 'I have lived with death all my life, Kathryn. I've fought in battles, ambuscades, hacking and hewing in villages, fields, or along some river bank. I have hunted and been hunted.' He gathered the reins more tightly. 'When you live like that, you become hardened. Do you think the King or Gloucester cares about Brandon? It's that pendant they are after.'

They had entered the castle grounds, so he wouldn't speak any further. A sleepy-eyed groom took their horses whilst another was sent to summon the household to the great hall.

They all gathered, one by one. Fitz-Steven the clerk was tousle-haired and unshaven. Pulled straight from his bed, he looked angry. Peter the chaplain seemed nervous. Gabele was stony-faced. The Righteous Man looked as strange as ever. And finally came an irate Fletcher, who spoke for them all.

'I am tired of this,' he shouted, glaring at Kathryn. 'Sick to death of being summoned hither and thither! Where's the Irishman?'

'He'll be with us soon,' Kathryn replied. 'He has to see something.'

'What?' Fitz-Steven growled.

'Never you mind,' Colum retorted, striding into the hall and sitting down at the end of the high table opposite Kathryn.

'I can see you are all impatient, so let me summarise very briefly.'

Colum ignored their grumbles of disapproval and gave a succinct description of what had happened in the castle over the last few days.

'What's new about that?' Peter the chaplain snapped.

'Nothing really,' Colum admitted, smiling. 'Oh, by the way, Mistress Swinbrooke, I did look where you asked me to and you are correct.'

'So,' Gabele asked. 'Why are you here?'

'Well, first,' Kathryn declared, 'we have found the Eye of God.'

She looked quickly at their faces, searching for a reaction.

'One thing, however, I still don't understand,' Kathryn continued, 'is Webster's death. Master Gabele, you reported him as walking along the tower?'

'Yes, I did.'

'And the guards heard him scream before his death?'

'Yes.'

'And you went up there?'

'I've told you that,' Gabele retorted. 'I couldn't lift the trapdoor because Webster had bolted it from the other side. I told everyone to stay away until the Irishman arrived.'

'The trapdoor was locked on the tower side but unbolted from the stair side.'

Gabele licked his lips.

'Well, was it?' Kathryn persisted.

'Of course.'

'In which case,' Colum interrupted, 'I have just examined the trapdoor. The locks on both sides have been replaced.'

'Well, of course. They would have been damaged when we forced our way through,' Fletcher explained.

'Yes, but when I looked at them again, very closely, the bolt on the tower side had simply been replaced; there's very little sign of forced entry, such as wood splintering, which should have occurred when the soldiers forced their way through.' Colum tapped the table-top gently with his fingers. 'What is even more curious is that the bolt on the stair side has been replaced. But why? If it was drawn back, it shouldn't have been broken.'

'What are you implying?' Gabele snapped.

'Well . . .' Colum held his hand up. 'You have a trapdoor with a bolt on either side. On the tower side Webster is supposed to have drawn the bolt closed and we later forced it. However, there's no real sign of force. On the stair side'—Colum pointed to the other side of his hand—'which was supposed to have been unlocked, there are definite signs of force being used.'

'In other words,' Kathryn continued, 'that trapdoor was only bolted on the stair, not the tower side.' Kathryn looked down the table at a pale-faced Gabele. 'So I shall tell you what happened. The Constable went to the tower and climbed the steps for his usual morning walk. You, Master Gabele, lurking in the shadows, struck him a blow on the back of the head, took his cloak and beaver hat and pretended to be the Constable walking backwards and forwards. The guards only saw what they expected to see, and from where they were standing in the gray light of dawn, they could hardly be expected to make out your features. You did everything Webster would do: walk around, light the brazier, even call down to the guards. From such a height, one man's voice can sound very similar to another. You then left the tower, locking and bolting it from the inside.'

'This is nonsense!' Gabele shouted.

Colum, sitting beside him, gripped the master-at-arms by the wrist.

'You then put Webster's cloak and hat back on him,' Kathryn continued, 'and peered through the slats of the sally-port, that great wooden window just under the trapdoor to the tower. You may remember, the one built in the wall?'

Gabele refused to look at her.

'You watched the sentries, tired and cold after a long night's duty. You undid the latch, waited till their backs were turned, and pushed poor Webster's body through. As the sally-port door closed, you cried out, the guards turned, they glimpsed a flash of colour, heard the shout and reached the logical conclusion that Webster had either fallen or jumped from the top of the tower.' Kathryn paused. 'I would never have guessed,' she continued, 'if you had struck Webster on the same side of the head which hit the ground.'

Gabele got slowly to his feet. 'You're a lying bitch!' he snarled.

Colum leaned forward: the Irishman's dagger pricked the side of Gabele's neck whilst, with his other hand, Colum plucked Gabele's knife from his sheath.

'Sit down, please!'

Gabele did so; if looks could kill, Kathryn's head would have bounced off her shoulders.

'But,' Peter the chaplain spoke up, 'I thought the bolt on the tower side of the trapdoor was broken? Surely you saw that, Master Murtagh?'

Colum shrugged. 'On reflection, what I saw was that the clasp which held the bolt was loosened to make it look forced. Gabele probably did that before he left the tower.'

Fletcher sprang to his feet and pointed accusingly at Gabele.

'You bastard!' he hissed. 'You bloody bastard! The Irishman's right. You came back and said the trapdoor was locked. We believed you. No one checked. On your orders, we stayed away.'

'He's lying!' Gabele screamed. 'The Irishman can't prove what he says. I replaced . . .' His voice faded as he realised the enormity of what he was admitting.

'You did what?' Kathryn quietly asked.

Gabele looked away.

'Oh, I know what you did,' Kathryn continued. 'You replaced both bolts. Colum saw that they had been changed when he visited the tower this morning.' She placed her elbows on the table and leaned forward. 'Now why should you do that, Master Gabele? Why replace both bolts? The one on the side of the stairs should not have been broken. So why replace it? And why you? Hasn't the castle got a carpenter?'

'Look.' Fitz-Steven beat his hand on the table-top. 'You are saying, Mistress, that Gabele waited for Webster on these darkened stairs, struck him on the head, borrowed his cloak and hat, then pretended to be the Constable?'

Kathryn nodded.

'After which,' the clerk continued, 'he loosened the bolt clasps of the trapdoor on the tower side, locked it from the stairs, put the cloak and hat back on Webster and tossed the poor bastard's corpse through the sally-port?'

'Yes, you have it, Master Clerk. Remember it was dawn. The guards were tired and looking the other way.'

Fitz-Steven scratched his chin.

'I accept that, Mistress, but why, when we forced the trapdoor, didn't you notice the bolt on the inside was undrawn?'

'Simple,' Colum interrupted. 'Gabele had ordered that no one approach the tower until I arrived. Secondly, the stairway is very dark. Thirdly, even if we had noticed the bolt, would it have mattered? Gabele could always claim he had done it for security purposes. Finally, and most importantly, remember how we approached the tower? Gabele went first and ordered the soldiers up before us to force the trapdoor, just in case we might observe something wrong.'

'But why?' the chaplain asked.

'Oh, I think Webster was killed,' Kathryn explained, 'because he realised Sparrow's escape was no accident; that's why Webster engaged in that little mummery on the castle green with Peter the chaplain the night before he died. You see, according to the story, the turnkey was strangled. But how could Sparrow do that, if the manacles on his hands were tied all the more securely by a chain linking them to the gyves on his ankles? How could you, in such a situation, raise your hands to strangle a man? No.' Kathryn shook her head. 'I suspect those manacles were rendered faulty, so they never locked properly.'

'Of course,' Peter the chaplain breathed. 'The Constable was acting strangely, he took me into the recess. He had his hands clasped against his chest as if in prayer. He then looked at me, muttered something about talking to the Irishman, spun on his heel and walked away. Webster must have realised Sparrow's manacles had been loosened, though,' the priest added, 'Sparrow could have first struck the turnkey and taken his keys.'

'True,' Colum replied. 'But that would have led to a scuffle, some form of struggle. According to what we were told, Sparrow went into a darkened recess, the turnkey followed, and Sparrow killed him by throttling him. The turnkey must have been taken completely by surprise. Sparrow then changed clothes and disappeared.' Colum shrugged. 'As his manacles were damaged, Sparrow must have had an accomplice in the castle. This is what Webster suspected.'

'And Sparrow?' Peter the chaplain asked.

'Oh, under the pretence of continuing their association, Gabele later met him in the deserted meadows along the Stour: he killed Sparrow, decapitated his corpse and flung it into the Stour.'

'When we brought Sparrow's corpse here,' Kathryn intervened, 'we established that he had escaped, probably through his own cunning. Webster knew different. We concentrated on the possibility that Sparrow may have then tried to blackmail someone here in the castle and been murdered.' She shrugged. 'In truth it was the other way around: Sparrow was allowed to escape so he could be silenced about what he knew.'

'Why should I do all this?' Gabele muttered.

'Ah!' Kathryn pushed her chair back. 'Now we come to the heart of the matter. Brandon was imprisoned in Canterbury

Castle. He keeps his mouth shut but begins to intimate to Gabele that he is a possessor of a great secret; he knows where a precious treasure is hidden. He gives no clues except a quotation from the psalms: "Levate Oculos ad Montes," "Lift your eyes to the hills." '

'Why should Brandon tell Gabele?' Fletcher asked.

'Oh,' Colum answered, 'better treatment, a swift pardon. Brandon was a killer. Once he was free, Gabele would be just another obstacle to be overcome or removed. Until then'— Colum spread his hands—'Gabele would be fed tidbits such as the treasure was hidden in a church. Gabele, keeping his own greed under control, entered into a pact with Brandon, but Sparrow, in the gap between the cells, overheard what was going on.'

'So Sparrow,' Kathryn continued, 'blackmailed Gabele: either he escaped or he would tell everything to Webster. Gabele agreed. Sparrow's manacles were unlocked and, seizing his opportunity, Sparrow killed the turnkey and escaped. Gabele, in his turn, kills Sparrow, and then, when our master-at-arms realises Webster is becoming suspicious, arranges the Constable's death as well.'

'But why?' the Righteous Man spoke up.

Kathryn noticed how all the pardoner's pretended gestures had now disappeared; the man was cold, hard, watchful.

'But why did Gabele kill the prisoner?' The Righteous Man leaned forward and stared at Kathryn. 'You did say he killed the prisoner?'

'Oh, yes,' Kathryn replied. 'Gabele realised that if the treasure was hidden in a church, it must be a place not used. Gabele would know the area around about Canterbury and the deserted village at Sellingham, so he decided to take his chance. After all, he would have all the time in the world, and once Brandon was dead, he wouldn't have to share the booty. Moreover, if both Brandon and Sparrow were sent to their Maker, Gabele's reputation was also protected.'

Kathryn sat down. 'Brandon's death was easy to arrange,'

she continued. 'Hemlock is as common as the grass in the fields. Margotta, his daughter, brought Brandon his meals, so Gabele simply mixed the poison into the food. A sudden sickness, high fever and unconsciousness would ensue, and the prisoner's gone before he can protest or realise he has been tricked.'

'Surely,' Fletcher whispered, 'Brandon would have suspected?'

'What happens if he did?' Colum replied. 'What could he say? Confess to Father Peter or Webster that he was being poisoned because he knew where a great treasure lay? Killer though he may be, I doubt if Gabele even bothered to think that the prisoner was in a deep coma and might revive in the grave only to meet an even more terrible death.'

'Why didn't Gabele find the treasure?' Fletcher asked.

Kathryn stared down at the master-at-arms who sat, both hands on the table, lost in his own thoughts. By the man's drawn white face and slumped shoulders, Kathryn knew she was speaking the truth.

'Oh,' she murmured, 'he was looking, but he overlooked Brandon's prayer, as did the other person searching for the Eye of God.'

The Righteous Man rapped the table-top. 'Who else was there? And how did he know about the pendant?'

Kathryn smiled at the pardoner. 'Oh, I think you know the answer to that,' she whispered. 'You are no pardoner; your name is Reginald Moresby, captain of the guard to the late Earl of Warwick, recently slain at the battle of Barnet.'

The pardoner stared coolly back.

'I am right, am I not?' Kathryn could have sworn the man's eyes smiled at her. 'It's the only logical explanation.'

'You have nothing to fear,' Colum added. 'Master Moresby, I swear, by all that is holy, if you tell the truth, I will personally guarantee a King's pardon is issued to you.'

The pardoner was about to protest, then he sighed and,

wrenching the garish necklace of relics from his neck, threw it on the table.

'When all is said and done,' he whispered, 'all is said and done. Let me tell you a tale, Mistress Swinbrooke, to chill the marrow of your soul. I am Reginald Moresby of Newport in Shropshire, captain of the guard to the late, and well-beloved, Earl of Warwick. God forgive us, both I and Brandon fled from Barnet carrying the Eye of God. For a few weeks we skulked in woods, remote parts, away from the thoroughfares and crossroads. My main aim was to reach Christchurch Priory in Canterbury and then ride south to Dover to take ship to France. However, the countryside was crawling with Yorkist soldiers. There were, including myself, six of us: Warwick's most trusted men, or so I thought. It was Brandon who was carrying the Eye of God. He claimed to know of a deserted village and church where we might hide. We gave this information to Nicholas Faunte when we met him whilst hiding in Blean Wood.' Moresby wetted his lips. 'After we met Faunte we split up. I left Brandon and the other four whilst I tried to discover what had happened to Warwick's body as well as plot the safest route into Canterbury and on to Dover. Now the rest of the party trusted me and I left the Eye of God with them.' He shrugged. 'It was also a guarantee that I would return. I was weeks on the road and lost more time hiding from a party of Yorkist moss troopers. Now, we had agreed to meet at Sellingham. I reached the village. The rest of my companions had been there, but I could see no sign of them. I began to search, yet it was still so dangerous I kept in hiding, thinking my companions had moved on.

'Why did you disguise yourself as a pardoner?' Kathryn asked.

Moresby smiled bleakly. 'I thought it was appropriate. Do you know your Chaucer, Mistress Swinbrooke?'

'More than you think!' Kathryn retorted.

Colum coughed drily.

Moresby ran his fingers through his strangely dyed hair.

'In the "Pardoner's Tale," ' he continued, 'a group of young men end up killing each other over a precious hoard. Now, when I first visited the deserted village and found no one, I thought Brandon and the rest had been forced to flee. I then heard of Brandon's capture and imprisonment in Canterbury Castle. I could discover no sign of the rest and began to wonder if some terrible crime had been committed. Chaucer's "Pardoner's Tale" occurred to me and, strangely enough, in a tavern outside Maidstone, I met one of these creatures. I noticed how he could wander the length and breadth of the kingdom without being troubled, so I spent every penny in my wallet buying his relics, clothes and licenses. I found a corpse beaten and disfigured in a ditch; I gave it my clothes and possessions. I became the Righteous Man and travelled directly to Canterbury.' Moresby spread his hands. 'You know the rest. I approached Sir William Webster, saying the hostels and taverns were full, and could I buy a bed in the castle? Webster, of course, agreed. I bided my time and visited Brandon.' He paused to collect his thoughts. 'It was after Sparrow had escaped. Brandon was full of himself. He knew who I was but couldn't betray me without betraying himself. He claimed he didn't know where the rest of his party was or the Eye of God.' Moresby shook his head. 'I knew he was lying.' He looked in puzzlement at Colum. 'I returned to that deserted village a number of times but could find nothing. So how did you?'

Colum told him. The rest of the company sat in shocked silence at the Irishman's stark description of what they had discovered in the burial vault beneath the derelict church. Moresby's face grew even paler. He sat open-mouthed, not even attempting to brush away the tears which rolled down his cheeks.

'You found them?' he whispered. 'Like that?'

'Aye,' Colum murmured.

Moresby put his face in his hands. 'Oh, God, have mercy on them!' he cried softly. 'Oh, Christ, have mercy on them!' He pulled his head back. 'And God damn Brandon! He murdered them, didn't he?'

'I think so,' Colum replied. 'Brandon knew about the burial vault. He wanted the Eye of God and laid his plans. He plotted to take you all to that church and bury you alive in that vault. The stone is fashioned so it can be opened from the outside but not from within. He must have suggested the vault as a hiding place, invented a reason to leave the four others, and left the Eye of God to ensure his return. As the vault-lid closed, they must never have dreamt that it would not open again.' Colum looked sideways at Gabele, who seemed now to be a shadow of his former self. 'Gabele may be a murderer, but Brandon was a demon in human form. He knew those men would die. He could always tell some fairy-tale if you ever returned. He might have waited for years before coming back for that treasure.'

'But why did he let me capture him so easily?' Fletcher spoke up. 'I mean, I caught this killer in the open fields sleeping by his horse?'

'I've answered that,' Kathryn said. 'Brandon wanted to be captured. He'd spend a short time in prison, receive a pardon, slip back into a normal life and bide his time.'

'In which case,' Peter the chaplain spoke up, 'why didn't Brandon use a false name?'

'I asked him that,' Moresby said. 'But the bastard just smiled sweetly.' He laughed sourly. 'Afterwards I realised how clever he was. First, as Warwick's body squire, he could, if forced, claim he had no knowledge of the Eye of God and sow the seed that the Earl might have given it to someone else. Secondly, it was a way of silencing me. Don't you see, if I came forward claiming to be Moresby, I would have to answer some very embarrassing questions.'

'Father.' Margotta stepped out of the shadows where she had been hiding. She looked as white as a ghost, her pretty face now haggard. 'Father,' she repeated hoarsely, 'what is this?'

'Oh, my God!' Gabele groaned.

Kathryn glanced quickly at Colum and steeled herself.

'Stay where you are!' she ordered.

'What do you mean?' Margotta moved hesitantly towards her father.

'Were you his accomplice?' Kathryn accused. 'After all, you took the prisoner's food down to him.'

'Shut up, you clever bitch!' Gabele snarled from the bottom of the table. 'My daughter knew nothing of this, though I did it for her.' He glared at Colum. 'That jewel was my reward for the years of hard service and cruel knocks!'

Colum seized him by the arm. Gabele shrugged him off and got to his feet.

'What you say is true, but my daughter's innocent.' He pointed a finger at Fitz-Steven. 'Get this fat turd to write out my confession and I'll sign it.' He shoved his wrists out towards Fletcher. 'Come on, you lazy bastard, put the chains on, don't you know your job?'

Colum nodded. 'Take him away,' he ordered quietly. 'Look after the girl.'

Fletcher drew his sword and hurried out of the hall shouting for soldiers. A few minutes later Gabele, his sobbing daughter behind, were hustled out of the hall. Colum picked up his cloak.

'We've finished,' he said. 'What is to be done here will be at the orders of the King, but thank God, I have finished!'

Kathryn picked up her own cloak. They were near the door of the hall when Moresby caught up with them.

'How did you know?' he asked.

Kathryn pulled at the cord of her dress. 'A piece of rope.' She smiled at Moresby's puzzlement. 'Once we realised Sparrow's manacles were unlocked, then he must have had an accomplice. Gabele could arrange that and he was the one who guarded the trapdoor to the tower.' Kathryn shrugged. 'The rest followed.'

'And me?' Moresby asked.

'A matter of logic: we knew Brandon and the rest were dead. We knew Gabele had visited Sellingham, but who else? The only death which could be suspicious was yours.' Kathryn smiled again. 'Your presence here was a coincidence, but your resemblance to Chaucer's Pardoner was uncanny.' She sighed. 'And, thanks to the Irishman, there's very little about Chaucer I don't know!'

'Will you keep your word, Irishman?' Moresby asked abruptly.

Colum nodded. 'Aye. I suggest you take sanctuary at Christchurch. The King is merciful. What you did I would have done.' Colum looked him up and down. 'But first, I suggest you have a bath and wash your hair. If you only knew how frightening you appear.'

'I'll take the pardon,' Moresby replied. 'But, within the month, I'll have joined Henry Tudor in Brittany.'

Colum scowled. 'That's your business.'

'No, no,' Moresby replied softly. 'One day Fortune's fickle wheel will turn again. I'll not forget your kindness, Irishman.'

And Moresby spun on his heel and walked down the hall.

Colum and Kathryn collected their horses from the stables and rode out of the castle into Winchepe.

'What will you do now?' Kathryn asked.

'I'll take the Eye of God to London,' Colum replied.

He reined in his horse and patted its neck gently and gazed up between the dark overhanging houses. He then leaned over.

'I know why Gloucester wanted it,' he whispered. 'The Eye of God. The pendant can be snapped open. Inside I found a small scroll, a thin strip of parchment, a promissory letter signed by George, Duke of Clarence.'

Kathryn went cold.

'It's dated six months before Barnet,' Colum continued. 'In it Clarence swears he will remove his own brothers and any children they may have from the inheritance of England. In return Warwick would make him King and he would make

Warwick his First Minister. A pretty mess, eh, Mistress Swinbrooke?'

'Will you remove it?' Kathryn asked curiously.

'No, nor will I say I have ever seen it. I will put it back as I found it.'

'What will happen?'

Colum gathered the reins into his hands. 'Clarence will die. Mark my words, Mistress Swinbrooke. The "Pardoner's Tale" applies not only to Brandon and his friends but to those three great princes in London. They have found the treasure, the Crown of England, and I think they'll kill each other for it.'

Kathryn leaned over and squeezed his hand.

'What is it the "Knight's Tale" says:

> 'I did see madness scoffing in its rage,
> Armed risings and outcries and fierce outrage.'

Colum looked at her. 'Which means?'

'Put not your trust in princes, Irishman. Moresby is right. Fortune's wheel will turn again. Keep your distance from Gloucester and his ilk.'

' "Oh, mirror of wifely patience," ' Colum quipped back, grinning from ear to ear.

Kathryn nipped him on the leg and, urging her horse forward, looked over her shoulder in mock severity at the laughing Irishman.

Conclusion

There are a number of themes in this novel. First, the pendant known as the 'Eye of God' does exist, although it is now known as the Middleham Jewel. This fifteenth-century pendant with a large sapphire on the front shows the Trinity with the inscription "Ecce agnus dei qui tollis peccata mundi miserere nobis: tetragrammaton ananizapta." The reverse side is engraved with a scene of the Nativity, with the child lying on the ground bathed in light. The border contains the figures of the saints. The pendant was found near Middleham Castle in North Yorkshire, home of the Nevilles and King Richard III.

The Battle of Barnet, the confusion over Oxford's attack and Warwick's death are accurately described by the chroniclers of the time. Richard Neville, Earl of Warwick, had once been a powerful supporter of the House of York and he retained close links with one of the Yorkist princes, George Duke of Clarence. Clarence's treachery was never forgotten by his kingly brother, Edward IV, or the latter's beautiful and ambitious wife, Elizabeth Woodville, who vowed that, whilst Clarence lived, he would pose a threat both to herself and her two baby sons. Indeed, there was a prophecy that, after Edward IV died, someone whose name began with 'G' would seize the throne. Everyone thought this prophecy referred to George, Duke of Clarence. Shortly after the events described in this novel, Clarence is supposed to have been murdered by being drowned in a vat of malmsey in the Tower of London. According to tradition, Richard, Duke of Gloucester (about whom the above prophecy was more accurate), is supposed to have carried out the murder. Twelve years later, in 1483, Gloucester, who loved his brother but hated his sister-in-law, seized the crown of England and imprisoned both his nephews in the Tower.

Medieval Canterbury and the fall of its mayor Faunte are accurately described here. The same is true of the potions Mistress Swinbrooke used; they are all culled from a medieval book of herbs and have regained new fame in the twentieth century as alternative medicine.

Mistress Swinbrooke's profession as an apothecary and physician is also accurate. In the first novel of the series I pointed out that women physicians were even hired by the royal family whilst, during the same period that Kathryn lived, the nuns at Syon on the Thames were establishing themselves as the finest surgeons and physicians in Europe. As N. V. Lyons wrote in his *Medicine in the Medieval World* (McMillan Education, 1984): "As early as the 11th century, women are known to have practised medicine." It was only when the practice of medicine was regulated by Act of Parliament in 1521 that women were deprived of this important role.

P. C. Doherty
(C. L. GRACE)